Y0-DNL-918

QUMRAN

Heralds of Imminent Redemption

COPYRIGHT 2013, LIGHT OF THE WAY, LLC

Qumran: Heralds of Imminent Redemption

Copyright © 2013 Light of the Way, LLC.

All rights reserved. No part of this book may be reproduced in any for by an means without the prior written permission of the Publisher, excepting brief quotations used in conjunction with reviews written specifically for inclusion in a magazine, newspaper or other electronic media.

Published by The Storyline Group, Inc.
Atlanta, Georgia

Cover design: Mabry-Green Studios

Contributing Editor: Karen Hutto

ISBN: 978-0-9791115-4-9

Dedication

This book is dedicated to my family, who encouraged me and allowed me the freedom to pursue this work. To my wife, Emily, who I love dearly and have for almost fifty years. To my son, Scott, and his wife, Cindy, who worked tirelessly to continue our family business. To my son, Mark, whose advice and input were invaluable. To my daughter, Ginny, and her husband, Dan, whose recommendations always proved helpful. I am a most blessed man because of them all.

This book is also dedicated to everyone who hungers and thirsts to know how Jesus saves his followers while his enemies are destroyed.

Foreword

BY ROBERT EISENMAN

Professor of Middle East Religions, Archaeology, and Islamic Law; Director, Institute for the Study of Judaeo-Christian Origins, California State University Long Beach.

With every new archaeological discovery, historians are confronted with new evidence that compels them to revise the history books. Nowhere is that more true than the discoveries made at Qumran. The archaeological clues in and around the Qumran compound and the revelations found in the texts of the Dead Sea Scrolls demand that history – especially that of the Christian Church – includes the characters and events recorded in those ancient documents. After years of study and teaching on the subject, as well as my on-site research and discovery in Israel, I have joined with other colleagues to overlay these new findings on Church history, with high hopes that those who are interested will gain new insight and clarity to some of the mysteries that seemed for so long to be unsolvable.

One of my more recent colleagues is Ed Whitesides, author of this remarkable story. For some time now, Ed and I have deliberated about the interpretive details surrounding Qumran and the events that occurred there 2,000 years ago. I have to say that while we both stubbornly cling to our own conclusions, the ongoing discussion (on his boat or over exquisite meals at his home in Atlanta) has been enlightening for both of us – and a whole lot of fun!

Ed's passion for "getting to the truth" is infectious, and this book is a reflection of his resolve to tell a new story about Christian origins that will indeed stir controversy among some quarters while it brings entertaining enlightenment to most. The beauty of historical fiction is that it affords the reader a way to learn while he or she enjoys a good story. For sure, *Qumran*, Heralds of Imminent Redemption is a good story and an enjoyable read no matter what your convictions or religious affiliations are. If nothing else, this book will provide the open-minded reader with fresh perspectives regarding who the earliest Christians were and what happened to them.

If, however, you happen to be one who refuses to budge from your traditional religious tenets, no matter what the latest evidence suggests, then I must warn you. This book is probably not for you. On second thought, maybe it is.

Preface

I grew up in the church, but not without questions about my faith. As a youngster, I attended Sunday school at a rather sophisticated Presbyterian church, and by the time I was a teenager I already had a good understanding of their Bible interpretations and basic theology. After graduating from college with a Civil Engineering degree and then getting married, my wife and I joined a small Baptist church in Georgia. During those years as we raised our children, I began to notice that although these Baptists had similar teachings from what I had learned earlier, some of their biblical interpretations and conclusions were very different. I felt a gnawing desire to discover the truth for myself and began a regimented program of intense Bible reading and study. I discovered so much in the Bible that I did not understand, and I struggled to equate what I was learning in my studies and what was being taught in church.

Because of a career move, we relocated and joined a very small Baptist church – so small that I could easily engage the Pastor and ask all the questions that haunted me. To his credit, he did not limit himself to the Baptist point of view and offered his own unique approach to the Scriptures. He was an ordained preacher, but he had invested twenty years or more studying in the libraries of local synagogues. His understanding of Judaism – the history and tenets of the faith, and the language of the Scriptures -- was deep and profound. He reminded me often that the Bible was written by and about the Hebrews and their predecessors, and in their vernacular. As he explained it, one has to understand that world as it was then to grasp the true meaning of the biblical texts. However, he always added that though it was written to and about the Jews, and tells the story of how God dealt with them, the Bible also speaks to us Westerners today – and powerfully so.

As time passed, the preacher and I became fast friends, but I remained the student, ever learning and gaining from his vast knowledge in order to fast-forward my own. Finally, after years of study, my depth of understanding rivaled his, and we both took great delight in sparring over our interpretations and theories. We were both driven by our passion for getting to the truth about the mysteries and secrets that have been brought to light in recent years, most notably the Dead Sea Scrolls found near Qumran.

I often relied on my background in physics to solve questions about the plausibility of many biblical events that seem impossible in a natural world. I searched for explanations of prophecies and their relevance (or irrelevance) for today. I came to some startling conclusions and developed a host of theories that – given the light of day and more confirmation – could radically change everyone's view of early Christianity.

In 2005, we embarked on a journey to confirm our basis for those theories by getting a first-hand look at where it all started. We flew to Israel. It was there in Jerusalem, Qumran and other sites in Israel that the light came on. When we visited the sites where Jesus once stood and spoke to the multitudes about God's message to the world, we realized the monumental impact of those words. Each day, the light of understanding we gained from our research and discovery raised the hair on our necks; and it was hard to contain our excitement.

Most of this new enlightenment happened at the Israel Museum in Jerusalem and later in Qumran. At one point, stopping to rest on a bench at Qumran, my head swirling with one new revelation after another, I reflected on the significance of being at this very spot where Jesus, his brother James, and their cousin John most likely spent their days during those formative years when the Bible is silent about Jesus' whereabouts. This, I realized, is where the church should trace its roots, because this is where Jesus prepared the way for the great salvation of His first century Jewish followers. It was at Qumran that many mysteries would be revealed and secrets explained; and one of those secrets led us north to the most mysterious of all mysteries and the strongest confirmation yet of our theories. Then, with our eyes opened, we knew it was time to return home and tell the story.

By 2006, the Dead Sea Scrolls had been published in English. We obtained copies and dived in, comparing their content to the content in the Scriptures. The likenesses are amazing and further evidence of the Qumran connection with the first Christians. Then, for personal reasons, the preacher friend was compelled to slow down, so we worked separately but remained in contact. I browsed the internet to find all I could of the Qumran library. It was there that I discovered Dr. Robert Eisenman, Professor of Middle Eastern Religions, California State University, Long Beach. He had published a number of books on the subject. I bought them all and read them cover-to-cover, and I was again blessed by the work of a person passionate about the subject. It occurred to me that I may be able to approach Dr. Eisenman for a private interview, and to my great surprise, he agreed; not only that, but he would fly to Georgia.

After hours of discussion with Dr Eisenman in my home, I was able to accelerate the piecing of the puzzle. It was time now to tell the story. Again a blessing: I was introduced to Phil Bellury who is probably the only writer who could have helped me get this story and its message out of my head and into the right words.

So why tell this story? It became obvious that the Lord Jesus had a purpose; He has clearly led us here and blessed our efforts with those who could and did make so much come together. No matter where you are in your life, no matter how you were raised, you can find comfort and peace in this story. Yes, this is a novel, and we spiced it up with a dual storyline, but it is based on historical accounts and postulates a truth that I am convinced will shed new light on the past while it lights up the future.

Enjoy!

Introduction

In 70 AD, under the command of General Titus, the Roman army advanced on Jerusalem and annihilated the city, leaving behind total devastation and the slaughtered bodies of close to a million Jews. As prophesied years earlier, Herod's Temple was leveled and every stone was cast down. Its treasures were stolen away to Rome and used to fund construction of the famous Roman Coliseum. In fact, the triumphant arch of Titus is still there today celebrating his victory over Israel.

No one I know disputes the recorded history of Jerusalem's destruction, even if most of them do not know the details or the political and religious significance of it. Yet there is much more to the story than what we have learned in Sunday Schools, or through countless sermons, or even in most of our seminaries and universities. This book is the rest of the story, the little-known and often mysterious story that has far greater meaning for us today than we could ever have imagined before the mid-20th century discoveries at Qumran.

Qumran, Heralds of Imminent Redemption is the result of more than 20 years of research into what was happening behind the scenes in Israel two thousand years ago. My focus has been primarily on Qumran, a remote community just 14 miles east of Jerusalem and the site where the Dead Sea Scrolls were discovered. The compound at Qumran was constructed on a plateau above the Dead Sea, and the community was in operation from about 150 BC to 68 AD. The Jews who lived there referred to themselves as the Yahad, meaning unity. The Dead Sea Scrolls that were produced in the compound's Scriptorium contain statements of their mission; and at the most fundamental level, they considered themselves "heralds of imminent redemption."

Most people who know of Qumran's existence are not aware of its role in the history of Israel, although recent study and analyses of the scrolls has shed dramatic light on the subject. Many scholars and archaeologists concur that it is very possible – if not likely – that Jesus studied for the priesthood at Qumran during his biblically "silent years" between the age of 12 and 30. And if he was there, it is a certainty that his brother James and his cousin John were also there.

For sure, Jesus, James and John fit the profile of the inhabitants at Qumran. For example, the Dead Sea Scrolls express their disdain for the leaders of the Temple in Jerusalem. Jesus and John openly opposed the leaders of the Temple in Jerusalem, calling them serpents and a generation of vipers, and exposing their hypocrisies. The Maccabean Jews at Qumran believed the priests and the Sanhedrin had perverted the Law of Moses, and they were sure that God's judgment was imminent. Just days after Jesus made his triumphal entry into Jerusalem, he spoke sadly to his disciples of the looming destruction: "Seest thou these great buildings? There shall not be left one stone upon another that shall not be thrown down."

In 70 AD, that is what happened. However, the Qumran story was not only about imminent destruction; it was also about imminent redemption. The rest of the story, so to speak, is about how Jesus made good on his promise to save his Jewish followers from the hell that was about to befall Jerusalem. Repeatedly in the gospel accounts, Jesus warns them and implores them to follow him to a new place of salvation. I, along with a growing number of interested parties, now believe Jesus was referring not just to a spiritual place but a literal place of salvation. "Watch ye therefore," he says in the gospel account, "and pray always, that ye may be accounted worthy to escape all these things that shall come to pass…"

History records that over a hundred thousand members from the Jerusalem Church escaped the Roman destruction and made their way to unknown destinations. The speculation as to where they escaped to continues to run the gamut, but my heart (along with my research and personal visitations) tells me they were not simply scattered in the desert. There was a plan and an escape route that led to a pre-ordained location.

This is that story. Through the characters of this book, heroes who lived 2,000 years apart from each other, you will experience the political tension in Jerusalem just before it fell, and you will be part of a modern-day discovery that solves the most important mystery of the ages. It is my hope that this story will encourage you and leave you with no doubt that Jesus is still in charge and even today offers an escape for me and for you in these perilous times.

-- Ed Whitesides

Qumran: Heralds of Imminent Redemption

JERUSALEM, 30 CE

The rumbling noise that woke Daniel that night sounded at first like distant thunder, but steady and growing louder by the second. For a moment his sleepy, ten-year-old mind wrestled with the sound, unable to make sense of it. Then the rumble became the unmistakable sound of horses' hooves clattering through the tight, dusty streets of one of Jerusalem's poor districts, where the lower tradesmen lived. And now he heard them turning onto his street and coming fast. He sat up in his bed and remembered his father's stern warning two days earlier to the men at the Temple, just before he disappeared. And then Daniel knew, and he whispered the word that his father, Abram, often said was synonymous with evil: "Romans."

His mother Azara heard the noise too and rushed to his bed, wrapping herself in a tunic and gathering him into her arms, as if to escape. But it was too late; the horses had arrived already, and through the window curtain, they could see fluttering light from the torches, and they could hear the snorting horses that carried twenty armored Roman soldiers. Azara held Daniel tightly and instinctively backed against the clay wall of their small house.

"Be strong," she said as they crouched together on the floor. Daniel thought she was speaking to him, but when he saw the terror etched across her face, he realized she was talking to herself. Shivers of fear traced up and down his spine as they listened to soldiers reining in their mounts and a Roman captain barking orders.

"Break down the door!" he shouted, and Daniel felt Azara's arms tighten around him. But the door that was smashed open was not theirs; instead it belonged to the house across the street where Daniel's best friend Baram lived. Too terrified to move, they listened to the shouts from Roman soldiers charging into Baram's house, then

1

the rattling of swords, and then the screams from Baram's mother and sister as the soldiers dragged all three out into the street and shackled them to chains.

"We are next," Azara whispered. Daniel buried his face in his mother's chest and began to cry. For a moment that seemed an eternity, they waited, until they heard the deep commanding voice of the Captain.

"Which one is the blacksmith's house?" he asked, and the answer came from a soldier standing just outside their door.

"This one, Captain!"

Azara held Daniel so tightly he thought she would crush him. He could feel her trembling body and knew that she was expecting the worst. He could hear the wailing of Baram's mother and sister outside, and then the Roman soldiers shouting at them to be quiet or be flogged with the whip. And then there was a brief silence, broken only by the horses still snorting and prancing outside, and then a murmured conversation just outside their door. Finally, the click of the door handle, and the door swung open, revealing the large frame of the Roman captain. The light from the torches flooded the room, and Daniel raised his head from his mother's bosom just enough to see him in the doorway, a giant of a man made larger by his helmet and cape and silhouetted against the torches outside. Daniel watched the dark and sinister form slowly walking toward them with his sword drawn, poised to strike.

The fear that welled up inside Daniel made his frail little body quiver uncontrollably. Azara clutched him and turned her back to the sword to shield her son.

"Turn around, woman!" he said.

With head bowed fearfully, Azara turned to him and immediately felt the tip of his sword under her chin.

"Look at me," he demanded, forcing her face upward with his sword. Daniel looked up too, but he could barely see the captain's unflinching eyes peering at them from the shadows of his helmet. The huge man reeked of sweat, and his breathing was nearly as heavy as the snorting horses outside. With his free hand, the captain grabbed Azara's hair and pulled her face to within a few inches of his. He grinned wickedly, and then spit on her.

"Your husband spits on the ground when he sees us," he growled. "Now I spit on his wife!"

Suddenly, in an instant, Daniel's fear gave way to anger and a vicious hatred for this man. This was one of the Roman soldiers that his father had described as henchmen for an evil emperor. Enraged and screaming uncontrollably, he freed himself from his mother's arms and with the vengeance of a wildcat lunged at the captain. Instinctively, the captain swatted Daniel with his free hand and sent him reeling backwards against the wall. The impact knocked the wind out of Daniel's tiny chest. His legs buckled under him, and he fell, landing hard on his hip on the clay floor. He felt a sharp pain shoot down his leg just as his head hit the clay. He lay crumpled on the floor in a heap, still conscious but unable to move. His mother tried to go to him, but the captain pinned her against the wall with the sharp tip of his sword at her chest.

"Azara, is it?"

Azara made no attempt to answer, her fear having turned to anger as well.

"I'm not going to take you tonight, but I want you to get a message to the blacksmith. We will find him and his friend across the street, and when we do, we will nail him to a tree until he spits blood. Do you understand me?"

Again, Azara remained silent, but the captain wanted an answer. He turned his sword away from her and pointed it at Daniel's chest.

"Do you understand me?!" he yelled through clenched teeth. From his position on the floor, Daniel could now see the captain's face clearly, his eyes bloodshot and his face red and dripping with sweat. Though he still could not move, Daniel felt his rage welling up inside, and he screamed at the cruel man who had brought so much violence and fear into their lives. The captain inched the tip of his sword up Daniel's chest to his neck, the cold blade sending painful shivers through his little body.

"Tell me now, woman, or I will pierce him with this sword."

Azara closed her eyes, as if praying, and whispered, "I understand."

The captain steadied his breathing and then pulled his sword away from Daniel. He stared at Azara for a moment, as if he were deciding whether he had brought enough terror into her life; and deciding that he had, he turned and walked out the door.

Azara rushed to Daniel and together they listened as the captain ordered his men to mount their horses. Daniel tried to sit up but his twisted leg was numb and he felt dizzy from his head wound. Through the open door he could see the soldiers trotting away, the last of them pulling their chained prisoners on foot behind them. Just as he was growing faint, through eyes growing dim, Daniel saw his friend, Baram, looking back fearfully in his direction. Then he passed out in his mother's arms.

When he awoke early the next morning, Daniel found himself lying on a heap of clothes and blankets in his father's old hand cart as Azara guided it along the road that led north out of Jerusalem. Before dawn, Azara had gathered up as much as she could load onto the cart, made a bed for Daniel and fled the city under the cover of darkness. Fearing that the Roman soldiers might change their mind and come back for her, she had decided to find refuge with her cousin, Raisa, in the countryside near Tiberias. The journey would be long, three or four days, but Azara knew that they would be safe there, as Raisa and her husband Simeon led quiet lives as fruit growers and farmers.

"Mother, where are we?" Daniel asked just as the morning

sun peaked over the distant hills. Azara pushed the cart to the side of the road and stood beside Daniel, who lay on his back, trying to raise himself to his elbow. Azara held him down and wiped his brow with a damp cloth.

"Lay still on your back a while longer. We're going to visit Raisa. We'll be safe there."

Lifting Daniel's shirt, she could see that his ribs were badly bruised and his right leg dangled from his hip, but there was no time to tend to that now.

"My leg hurts," he said. "Is it broken?"

"I don't know, but drink this wine."

She handed him a wineskin, and he turned it up and sipped. She grabbed the bottom and raised it higher.

"Drink it all, Daniel, and try to sleep."

After he had gulped down the contents, Azara returned to her spot and continued to wheel the cart with its heavy but precious load. The trip was long and arduous, but a sympathetic young Jew, who had caught up with them on his way to Tiberias, volunteered to help Azara push the cart.

"God delivered one of his angels to us," she told Raisa when they reached her farm, which was located between Tiberias and the town of Magdala. After accepting food from Raisa in return for his kindness, the young Jew set out for his own destination, and Raisa and Simeon helped a tired and famished Azara tend to Daniel's wounds. Still weak and groggy from the wine and soothed by balms and herbs, Daniel fell fast asleep. As she looked sadly at Daniel's frail little body lying on a makeshift bed, Azara knew that if healing were to come, it would be a long process.

"You are both fortunate to be alive," Raisa said, reaching for Azara's hand across the table. "You are safe now, but you must be careful to not be seen in public for a while. If they return to your house and see that you no longer live there, they will ask your neighbors."

"The only neighbors who know about you, Raisa, were taken away. And if the Romans asked them, they would never tell."

Raisa squeezed her hand. "So, then it's settled. You will stay with us as long as you want, and Simeon and I will help you take care of Daniel."

TIBERIAS, 32 CE

Early one morning two years later, Daniel sat on a rock overlooking the Sea of Galilee and stared at the sun's golden reflection on the water. He had just completed his morning prayers, a discipline his father had taught him as far back as he could remember. Life had been pleasant enough in the countryside near Tiberias, the city that only twelve years earlier had been made the capital of Herod Antipas' realm in Galilee. Antipas built his palace on an acropolis there, and because he was a Roman-Jewish client king, he gathered families – mostly non-Jewish – from rural Galilee to populate his city. Born and raised in Tiberias, both Raisa and Simeon had witnessed the city's transformation, and though they publicly remained silent on the subject, they did not like what had taken place.

"Herod Antipas is a Roman at heart," Simeon had explained to Daniel and Azara, "and he has defiled the city even more than before by bringing in settlers who are not Children of God. We can no longer worship there because of their cemetery, which according to the Law makes it unclean. So now we worship at the synagogue in Magdala, which is not far from us."

As the sun rose higher in the eastern sky, Daniel rubbed his eyes and took one last look at the glimmering sea and the distant mountains beyond its far shores. Azara would have breakfast waiting, and as he began his walk down the slope to the house, his thoughts turned to Jesus of Nazareth. Like everyone who lived in the region near the western shores of the Sea of Galilee, Daniel had heard about the man who was miraculously healing people who were sick, lame or blind. So many people had witnessed it now for themselves that few were denying it anymore, even if they thought it was some sort of trickery or sorcery. Simeon said that he had heard him teaching in the synagogue at Magdala once, that his message was powerful, and that he had walked the village streets afterward with growing numbers of people following after him, clinging to his words, marveling at his knowledge and seeking him out to be healed of all manner of afflictions.

Whatever his methods were, Daniel wondered if the Teacher could heal his mangled leg. Although it was no longer painful, he still walked with a severe limp, a lingering result of that terrifying night when the Roman captain nearly killed him. Since then he and his mother had remained with Raisa and Simeon, with Azara working on the farm and cooking and cleaning to help out while Daniel recovered. Over time, his cracked bones had healed, and he had learned to live with frequent pain. But the sight of his noticeable limp still made Azara ache inside.

Although life in the country had been rejuvenating for her, Azara still grieved over the loss of her husband, Abram. At every opportunity, she asked Jews visiting from Jerusalem about him, but no one had heard anything. No one could say they had seen him on the Roman crucifixes, however, and that gave Daniel and Azara hope that somehow Abram had managed to escape the Romans who were searching for him. But they couldn't be sure, and they still lived in fear that the Romans would find them again and send them to prison – or worse. Azara had returned once to Jerusalem, concealing her face as she rode in on Raisa's vegetable cart, but she learned nothing of her husband's whereabouts. She did find out from a woman who lived in her old neighborhood that Baram's family had been separated in prison and then made slaves to Roman families, though no one knew where. The woman also said that the Roman captain and his men had come back once to ask families on their street about her and Daniel.

"It was a week after that night when they took your neighbors away," she recalled. "None of us knew where you had gone, of course, and when they threatened me, I told them you had probably fled to the wilderness, or maybe to the coast to find a ship to another country. They never came back. To be honest, Azara, I don't think they are looking for you anymore because I heard that the captain who came that night has returned to Rome."

Azara was pleased to hear the news, but still she mourned the fact that her husband was gone and probably dead. And she knew that Daniel missed him as well; she would often hear him weeping in his bed and calling to his father through the tears. His sleep was often interrupted by night terrors, and he would scream and fight the air and break into a sweat, until his mother would find him and hold him until he settled down. When he allowed himself to remember that awful night when the Romans came, he would always picture the captain's menacing face – and his heart would fill with hate. And if he were outside when the remembrance came, he would spit on the ground as a sign of his hatred for all things Roman, something he had learned from his father.

Over time, however, even some of Daniel's recollection of that night began to fade. Although he dearly missed his best friend Baram, life in the country had proved to be a peaceful change from the tension-filled environment his family had experienced in Jerusalem. Other than visits to the Temple, he had been confined to the narrow street outside his house or on the rooftops of his or Baram's house. But here in the countryside between Magdala and Tiberias he had room to run through the barley fields and olive orchards, and every morning he would rise before daybreak and hike up a foothill at the edge of the farm and watch the sun rise over Lake Galilee. And just as his father had taught him and others at the Temple, he prayed that Yahweh would rain down justice on the Romans and deliver his father back into their presence. And he always ended his prayer with a vow that he would boldly take up the sword and fulfill his duty in battle if it came to that.

One night, after waking from a horrible nightmare, Daniel got out of bed and walked outside to breathe in the night air. He noticed the flickering of candlelight through a window of the small tool shed that was attached to the back of the farmhouse. Curious, he peered inside and saw Simeon sitting at a table with parchments and pens spread out before him. Daniel tapped on the window, and Simeon smiled and motioned to him to come in.

"What are you doing?" Daniel asked.

Though he had been a farmer all of his life, Simeon also served as a scribe, often working late into the night copying sacred texts from the Torah for other Jews in the surrounding area.

"During the day, I raise crops that bring physical nourishment," Simeon replied, "but at night I copy sacred texts that bring nourishment to souls. Come closer and I'll show you."

Daniel watched as Simeon consulted his Torah before dipping his pen into his inkwell and writing text on the thin sheet of animal skin. As he wrote, he spoke the words out loud.

"To be a scribe," Simeon explained, "one must first be sure to write only on clean animal skin. The same skin must be used to bind the manuscript when it is completed. The ink must be black and prepared in a certain way, and each word must be written carefully."

"What do you do if you make a mistake?"

"Good question, Daniel. The priest will review my work, and if there are mistakes on three pages, I will have to rewrite the entire manuscript."

Simeon wrote another word, again verbalizing aloud as he wrote. Daniel stood by his side for nearly an hour, fascinated by the process and full of questions. Finally, Simeon came to a word that caused him to stop and wipe his pen.

"Daniel, I'm afraid I must stop now and bathe."

"But it is late at night, and you always bathe in the morning."

Simeon smiled and pointed to a word in the text. "Do you see the word 'YHVH', the most Holy Name of God? I am forbidden to write His name without washing first."

"Why?" Daniel asked.

"Ah, another good question. I suppose the practice began many generations ago with our forefather Moses, who God blessed with great knowledge of the Law, which requires us to diligently cleanse and purify our bodies, to make ourselves presentable to God before we dare to come into His presence."

"I guess I understand," he said with clear resignation in his voice.

Simeon laughed and said, "For now, until you are older, the important thing for you to know is that bathing is God's Law, and God wouldn't ask us to do it if it were not good for us." He ruffled Daniel's hair and added, "Now, off to bed. It is late."

They walked together back to the house, and before they entered, Daniel stopped and asked, "Can you teach me to be a scribe?"

"It is difficult, Daniel, and something that cannot be learned in a day. But if you are willing to work hard, I will teach you."

Daniel smiled. "I am willing."

On most mornings, Daniel helped his mother with the chores, and in the afternoons he would walk to a field and watch children play games. Azara urged him to join them, but because of his limp and even more because of his damaged self-esteem, he kept to himself. Every Sabbath, he and Azara walked with Raisa and Simeon to synagogue in Magdala, where many of the traditional Jewish families met to worship, pray and read the Scriptures together. Daniel would sit with his mother in the women's section behind the screen. When one of the boys in the inner circles invited him to join his family, Daniel refused the offer. He didn't want to make new friends. The hurt he felt over the loss of his father and best friend Baram was too great; he couldn't bear to go through it again.

Springtime had just become summer when Daniel turned thirteen years old. The fields were dotted with colorful flax blossoms and thickets of oleander trees in bloom. One morning, just after his morning prayers, Daniel made the long walk with his mother to the market in Tiberias. Hot and tired from the walk, they stopped to rest at the square, where the women gathered to fill their buckets with water while they shared the latest news and gossip.

Daniel liked to visit Tiberias, which was much larger than Magdala and located on the main road that led north and south. He would search the faces of the traveling tradesmen who passed him by in the streets or the men who gathered in the marketplace, hoping to see his father among them. He knew that it was unlikely that his father would show his face and risk capture, but still Daniel looked, on the oft chance that his father might be traveling in disguise – if in fact he was still alive. On this particular morning, just as Daniel and Azara reached the square, they had to stop and watch as a large crowd of people passed by, all following a small group of men walking purposely to the road that leads down to the lake. Daniel tugged at his mother's sleeve.

"What's happening, Mama?"

"It's Jesus, the Teacher," she replied, and Daniel could see her eyes fixed on one of the men who walked in front. They waited as the last of the crowd passed and then walked on to the well. While his mother drew water, he shaded his eyes and peered into the morning sun rising higher over the lake, where people said the Healer would often go and stand on a boat to speak to the crowds along the shore.

"How does he do the miracles?" Daniel asked his mother, who shrugged her shoulders and filled a second bucket.

"Bring me your bucket," she said, but Daniel walked past her and filled his bucket without her help. As he did, Azara noticed his limp. Daniel had been strong and resilient, like his father, but she knew the limp would limit him physically, probably for the rest of his life. "I don't know how he does the miracles. No one seems to know what to make of him, but now he's drawing the attention of the Romans. If the crowds grow much larger, they will stop him."

"He's just another foolish Zealot," a woman said from the other side of the well. Daniel turned to see the old woman, a widow he had seen before at the well and an opinionated woman who was always quick to spread news or gossip. "He's trying to gather people so he can build an army."

"But he preaches peace," Azara said.

"And he performs miracles," Daniel added. "How could he do that, unless he is the Messiah?"

The old woman waved him off. "You're too young to know. He's no Messiah. The Messiah will come from the skies, not from a carpenter's house. And in a blaze of fire, not wearing dirty sandals and smelling like those fishermen who follow him all day."

"Have you heard him speak?" my mother asked.

"No, I don't need to hear him," the woman replied. "He's just a clever Zealot, a troublemaker who uses smooth words to make people believe he is the Messiah."

"Maybe you would think differently about him if you heard him. Everyone I know who's heard him says he could be the One."

The old woman stood up slowly, her body too frail to move any faster. She faced Azara with a stern look. Daniel noticed the deep wrinkles in her face and wondered how her bony arms could lift a pail full of water.

"I'm an old woman," she said. "I've seen many men claim to be the One, but they were all liars. Meanwhile, we have become slaves to the Romans in our own country."

She pointed at Daniel and continued, "When I was your age, I believed the Messiah would come any day, but now I don't believe he will ever come. And if he does, it will be after I'm dead."

With that, the woman picked up her pail and walked slowly

away. Daniel's mother reached inside the pocket of her tunic, pulled out a small bread cake and tore off a piece for him.

"Why was that woman so mad?" Daniel asked his mother.

"She's seen a lot of misery in her many years, so it's understandable. After a while, after so many prayers to God for deliverance from Roman occupation, people become impatient, then frustrated and angry."

"Are you angry, Mother?"

"No, like your father, I believe God hears us and will come to save his people."

"When will that happen?"

"You ask a lot of questions, just like your father."

"Sorry."

"No, that's a good thing, Daniel. If your father were here…" Her voice trailed off, and Daniel could see tears forming in her eyes. Azara cried often, although not as much lately as she had in the first year since her husband disappeared. She brushed away the tears and smiled at him.

"If he were here, your father would answer your question by reminding you that we are Maccabeans, and we believe that God is gathering his angels right now, as he always has in difficult times. And he would tell you that no matter how bad things become, as long as there is one Jew in Judah who diligently follows the Law of Moses as God intended, as long as there is one who will rise every morning and offer up prayers and sacrifices to God, and lives a life of devotion to him, justice will prevail. God will deliver his people just as he has always done in the past. And one day – many are now saying it will happen soon – the Messiah will come, and salvation will come to God's people. And that will be the end of the age, a time when there will be no more murders in the streets or killing on the battlefields. There will be peace."

"Is Jesus the Messiah?" Daniel asked.

"I don't know," she said. "Maybe so, but I'll reserve judgment until I hear him speak and see him perform the miracles."

A few days later, Raisa came to the room where Azara was cleaning pots and cooking and asked if she and Daniel wanted to go with her and Simeon to the lake to hear Jesus speak. Azara reluctantly declined, saying she had agreed to spend the day caring for a sick neighbor, but after much pleading from Daniel, she finally agreed to let him go with them. In preparation for what would likely be a long afternoon, she packed a basket of fish and barley loaves and reminded him to share with his companions when they became hungry.

Brimming with excitement, Daniel walked with his aunt and uncle to the shores of Lake Galilee, only to discover that Jesus had retreated to a mountainside, surrounded by the same group of men who always traveled with him, men that Azara referred to as the Teacher's disciples. They joined the growing stream of people following Jesus, and Daniel marveled at the size of the crowd, more than he had ever seen or even imagined before, and all hungry to get close to the man who might be the Messiah. They blanketed the landscape in a circle round a large, protruding boulder that provided a perfect platform for Jesus to address his followers.

As the crowd settled in, Daniel ran ahead of his relatives and found an open spot close to the front, where other children had gathered around the boulder, literally at the feet of Jesus. At his first sight of Jesus, Daniel felt a twinge of disappointment. He seemed too plain and too calm to be the long-awaited Messiah. Dressed in white linen robes, he looked like any other rabbinical Jew. But as he studied him, Daniel recognized something in Jesus' countenance that was different. Maybe it was the compassion in his eyes as he watched people gather around him, or maybe it was his calm and confident manner as he conferred with his disciples.

The air was thick with anticipation and expectation, and Daniel could feel it, even if he did not fully understand it. As he sat on the grass just a few yards away, with his bent leg extended in front of him, Daniel knew he was now part of something hugely important, something unlike any other moment in his short life. He looked down the mountain at the mass of people murmuring and waiting for a prophetic message or another miracle. As he looked back to the boulder, Jesus was looking directly at him, smiling warmly at him with a nod before casting his gaze elsewhere. Daniel shivered as a wave of emotion swept through his body. There was something in that one brief moment of eye contact that reminded him of his father, Abram. It was a look of recognition, compassion, and assurance that he often got from Abram. It was a look that said he understood the painful sadness that often consumed him when he thought of his father.

Then Jesus stood, and a hush fell over the crowd. In a voice that resonated with authority, he spoke.

"Blessed are the poor in spirit, for theirs is the kingdom of heaven."

The kingdom of heaven. Daniel had heard plenty about the kingdom of heaven from his father when he read from the Torah at the synagogue and when the rabbis read from the scrolls. He and his best friend Baram had often talked about it, and they had often heard their fathers discussing it, or more often, arguing about it, as they did every point of Jewish scripture. And more recently, under Simeon's tutelage, he had read about the kingdom of heaven as he learned to write words from the Torah on the animal skins.

"Blessed are those who mourn, for they will be comforted," Jesus said, looking out across the mass of people in front of them, his eyes coming to rest on the children seated closest to him. Again, Jesus looked right at Daniel with the same knowing expression, and in that moment, Daniel was indeed comforted to know that this man who might be the Messiah was speaking to him and promising something he never thought possible.

"Blessed are the meek, for they will inherit the earth."

Daniel had never heard a rabbi speak this way, without reading from the scrolls, as if the ideas were his own. He remembered the old woman's words, that the Teacher used smooth words to deceive people into believing he was the Messiah. But Jesus wasn't talking about the Messiah at all; and he wasn't talking about the teachers of the law in the synagogue, or the wealthy Scribes or Pharisees. He was talking about ordinary people, people who had little, people who had experienced sadness to the point that they were brought to tears, people like him and Azara.

Daniel thought of his mother and wished that she was there to hear this man. He knew that she would like what he was saying. His words were soothing but not like the old woman had said.

"Blessed are those who hunger and thirst for righteousness, for they will be filled," Jesus continued. "Blessed are the merciful, for they will be shown mercy."

Daniel remembered that awful night when the Roman soldiers came to their house in Jerusalem, and how merciless the cruel captain had been. Was Jesus saying that God would judge him harshly for his cruelty? He hoped so. In his fitful dreams, which more often than not were about that terrifying night, Daniel would feel the fear and anguish again, and he would wish that he could be strong enough to kill the evil man who had sworn to kill his father.

"Blessed are the pure in heart, for they will see God."

Daniel thought of his father, and wondered if he was still alive, and if not, was he with God in Heaven?

"Blessed are the peacemakers, for they will be called sons of God. Blessed are those who are persecuted because of righteousness, for theirs is the kingdom of heaven."

Jesus spoke for a long time, and Daniel hung on every word. Although he couldn't understand it all, he tried to remember all that the Teacher said so he could tell his mother.

"Excuse me, boy," a man said as he leaned down to speak to

Daniel. "I am Andrew, one of the Teacher's followers. There are many people here today, and they are hungry. Jesus has asked if you would share some of the food in your basket with others."

Daniel was stunned, and without hesitation offered his basket to Andrew.

"Bless you, child," Andrew said, and Daniel watched in awe as the same basket that had been in his possession a few moments before was handed to Jesus. The disciples, acting on instructions from Jesus, told the people to sit. Then, raising the basket in the air, Jesus spoke a blessing of thanksgiving to the God of the Universe and distributed portions of the food to his disciples and those seated around him. To Daniel's utter amazement, the food that had been intended for a few people continued to be distributed to dozens of people, then tens of dozens. A murmur arose among the crowd as they watched the contents of the single basket of food increase with every morsel distributed, until everyone had been fed. And all from his basket!

"How many loaves and fishes were in your basket?" a man sitting beside Daniel asked when all had been fed.

"Five loaves and two small fish," Daniel replied.

"Look!" the man said, pointing at the group of men who followed Jesus. "Everyone has been fed, and they are filling a dozen baskets with leftover food."

"But how can that be?" Daniel asked.

"I don't know. He is a man of miracles. He heals the sick, he turns water into wine... and now feeding all of us from one basket. And he speaks with such authority, as if is speaking for God like the prophets."

Daniel looked up to see Jesus on the rock above him, scanning the crowd until his eyes finally came to rest on Daniel. The great teacher and healer, who was renowned throughout all of Israel and considered by many now to be the Messiah, was smiling at him with gratitude, and Daniel's heart leaped. He turned to the man beside him.

"He speaks with authority, because he is the One," Daniel said. "He is the Messiah."

Later that evening, as Daniel walked home with his relatives, Azara stared out the window, waiting anxiously for them to return. After all this time, she still worried about him when he was away, even when he was with Raisa. There were other people walking along the road leading back from Lake Galilee, and with each group that passed, she grew more anxious. But at last she spotted them off in the distance – first Raisa and her husband, walking together, and then behind them, walking briskly to keep up, Daniel.

Azara smiled, but then her smile faded as she noticed something very strange about the way that Daniel walked. It was a walk she had not seen in two years. A normal walk… a walk without a limp.

◆◆◆◆◆◆◆◆

NORTH GEORGIA, 2002 CE

On a crisp September Sunday in 2002, a black SUV with tinted windows pulled into the parking lot of a small church in North Georgia. While the hundred or so parishioners inside belted out an old familiar gospel hymn, "Jesus Saves," the driver of the SUV tilted his sunglasses up on his forehead and scanned the parked cars until he located the shiny white Cadillac Escapade. He stopped and left the engine running while he stepped out of the SUV with an iron tire tool in hand. The scene might have seemed strange enough to anyone who witnessed what happened next, but it was made all the more unusual because the slender, dark-haired middle-aged man wore the classic white collar of a priest.

As the hymn inside the church reached the chorus, and the singing grew louder, the strange-looking man in priestly garb sang the hymn out loud as he methodically cracked every window in the car with the tire tool before finally smashing the driver's side window until the glass shattered completely. Satisfied the hole in the window was large enough, he calmly reached inside, found the trunk release button and opened it. Still humming the melody of the hymn, he strolled to the rear of the car, reached inside the trunk and retrieved a black briefcase. Then, like a construction worker done for the day, he casually tossed the tire tool and briefcase into the back seat of his SUV, got in and drove away.

Inside the church a half-hour later, Dave Walker sat with his wife and eighteen-year-old son on the third row and struggled to stay engaged with the sermon. The topic was "The Way to Salvation," and during his forty-plus years of hearing sermons on that same subject, Dave already had a solid Christian understanding of what one must do to be saved. From church hymns to signs along the highway, the message that "Jesus Saves" was clear. To be saved meant one gains entrance to Heaven and avoids the nasty alternative of being cast into the Lake of Fire and eternally damned. To be rescued from the fires of Hell, one need only to believe in Jesus Christ, the Savior, who was not just sent by God, but was in fact God incarnated. Jesus, he had always been taught, was God manifested on earth so that He could walk among us and teach us the way to eternal salvation. And finally, he had always been assured that Jesus was coming again to gather up his flock and rescue them from the coming wrath of God upon the earth, an Armageddon-like ending that would literally destroy the earth. For all of his life, Dave had believed it all... that is, until lately.

In recent years, Dave had noticed that traditional Christian pastors preached less about hellfire and brimstone and more and more about Bible prophecies, especially those that point specifically to the last days and the portending destruction of the world. The "end times," they would say, is an imminent event, one that could very well come "any day now," but for sure within our generation's time. And one year after the tragic events of 9-11, those who predicted earth's imminent destruction were having a field day, pointing to that as just a prelude to the real devastation that is soon to come.

Not only were they preaching that message to growing audiences, many prophets of doom had taken to the airwaves and built non-profit "ministries" around the concept. Books on the subject proliferated, and several authors had become household names with their novels and non-fiction books dealing with end-times prophecies. All of that commercialization of a coming God-ordained event Dave found fascinating, especially because he didn't believe any of the biblical prophecies they used to support their claims would ever be fulfilled in the future. The reason for his disbelief was simple; he believed those prophecies had already been fulfilled two thousand years ago.

Dave taught physics at a local community college and after fifteen years had earned a reputation as an outstanding teacher. His students and academic peers all liked the man with the easy smile and engaging spirit, and they were always impressed by his sharp intellect and insights. He gave more to his subject and his students than was expected, mainly because he was so passionately immersed in his field of study. His lectures were energized by his excitement over new discoveries, particularly in the rapidly evolving study of quantum physics; a field of learning that he believed was taking modern science and institutional religion into new territories and revealing surprising connections between the two seemingly disparate fields of thought. For most of his career, Dave had nursed the notion that through its deeper research into quantum physics, science was only now catching up with what the great thinkers, philosophers and religious mystics understood intuitively and had been trying to explain for centuries.

Raised in a Christian church but teaching modern physics in a secular college had its share of inner conflict and tension, but lately Dave had begun to see that the apparent separation between his spiritual worldview and practical science was merging into a unified truth about the universe – a new understanding that at its most foundational level, deep into the cellular structure where particles and energy fields can now be observed, science was finding answers to long-held questions about our existence that no longer conflict with ancient wisdom – including, of course, the words of Christ, who often spoke of man's relationship with nature. And once his mind was open to that idea – that God is in the details of science, so to speak – his enthusiasm shifted into high gear.

Dave had always had a ravenous appetite for exploring the mysteries of life. It was a blessing and a curse, because it wasn't just a matter of *wanting* to know the truth. He *had* to know. And so far, none of the pastors he listened to were helping him with that, including the one he was trying to stay engaged with this morning.

Dave's impatient squirming elicited an occasional frown from his wife, Rebecca. She had long ago accepted Dave's relentless pursuit of the truth, and she enthusiastically supported his hours of study and research, even his plans for an excursion to Israel; but she did not support his fidgeting in church. Nor did she like the fact that their son, Clint, was nodding off in his seat. She gave him a solid poke in his ribs with her elbow to rouse him out of his slumber, and Dave gave thanks that Clint had wound up sitting between his parents. Otherwise, he might have gotten the poke instead.

Dave leaned over and whispered, "Good morning," in Clint's ear. Clint rubbed his eyes and tried to tune in to the preacher, but it was a hopeless cause. Within a minute, he was nodding off again, causing Rebecca to frown and Dave to chuckle. In almost every way, Clint had measured up to his father's expectations, achieving more than most of his peers scholastically and athletically. His strong arm in the outfield and his prowess at the plate earned him a baseball scholarship at Georgia Tech, where he hoped to pursue an engineering degree. Dave was proud of him but worried that Clint's first two weeks living on campus had drained his energy. All he had done since he had come home for the weekend was sleep, something he clearly was not getting enough of at school.

The sermon that morning was not helping matters. Even though the preacher spoke eloquently and with great conviction, Dave's thoughts continued to drift, and this time to an online video he had watched a few days before. In the video, Dr. Robert Eisman, a controversial university professor and prolific writer on the subject of the origins of Middle Eastern religion, had struck a chord by suggesting that the gospels should be looked at as Jewish *literature*, and not *documented history*, as many might believe. The distinction between the two, Dr. Eisman pointed out, was critical to understanding the intent of the gospel writers.

"What actually happened historically," he explained in the video, "is not necessarily what the 'poets' of literature tell us in their writings. Like any contemporary writer who recounts a tale, especially a tale he or she did not necessarily witness, the gospel writers recounted the story of Jesus through the lenses of their own particular perspectives and biases. In other words, the gospel writers – Paul in particular – were less concerned with historical accuracy than they were proving their point of view."

For most of his life Dave had never seriously questioned the historical accuracy of the Bible; he had always assumed there were logical explanations for any inconsistencies. As he pondered the points raised by the professor, however, he had to admit that he did not get much from the Bible in the way of geopolitical history. The more he looked it, the more he could see that if the gospel writers were writing to future generations, accurately recording dates or details of events and prominent historical players of that time was not their chief aim. That was unfortunate, Dave believed, because better understanding of history would provide a more accurate context for the gospel message. And that, in turn, would help him gain a deeper understanding of Christianity, the faith tradition into which he had been born and raised.

For better understanding of the environment in which the gospel writers penned their contributions to the New Testament, Dave had embarked on a period of self-study. He read the complete works of Flavius Josephus, the controversial but essential first-century Jewish historian. He read multiple books about the first-century Christians and watched documentaries about the ongoing debates over the origins of the Christian Church. That research led him to a series of books, online articles, videos and television documentaries about the mysterious – and deeply controversial – Dead Sea Scrolls, which were discovered at Qumran, Israel, in 1947 by a Bedouin shepherd. Qumran, he learned, was a wilderness community that relatively few Christians knew about, even though a growing contingency of scholars, archaeologists and other interested parties now believe it can rightly claim to be the birthplace of Christianity and the home base for the new religion's brain trust. If Jerusalem was the heart of the Christian movement, Qumran – as it turns out – was its head.

The more he read, the more Dave became intrigued with the ancient Qumran story and the people who lived and worked there. For decades, however, the controversial Catholic-sponsored team of experts charged with restoring and translating the damaged ancient texts had failed to share them with the broader scientific community. Over time, the right to know prevailed and the Scrolls finally became available to the public, even if the public – including most Christians – have generally ignored their existence or believed them to be irrelevant to their faith. But, as Dave would eventually discover, the real story of the early Christian Church – who its leaders were and what their mission was – is revealed in the texts of the mysterious scrolls, documents that were created in Qumran's scriptorium by generations of scribes. And for sure, they had a mission.

Much of what Dave learned about Qumran and the Dead Sea Scrolls came from lecture videos and documentaries that featured Dr. Eisman. As much as anyone, Eisman aggressively sought answers to questions about the Scrolls; i.e., who wrote them and for what purpose. Through the years, Eisman had played a pivotal role in pushing for their release to the public after decades of secrecy on the part of the École Biblique, the group that eventually controlled access to the Scrolls and kept them from public view.

The body of knowledge that Eisman had developed captured Dave's imagination. The more he learned about Eisman, the more he liked what he had to say, even if a few of the professor's findings challenged some of Dave's long-held fundamental beliefs. But if Dave was anything, he was open-minded and deeply interested in discovering the truth. In his research on the professor, Dave discovered that Eisman's fields of study also included engineering, physics and archaeology – all subjects that fed Dave's own fascination with the mysteries of the natural world and how they might be connected to the spiritual nature of man.

But now Dave was in church, and he tried again to pay attention to the sermon. The pastor was using a verse from Isaiah as his proof text, which was projected on the wall behind him. The verse, Isaiah 30:8, was God's instructions to the great prophet to "… go write it before them in a table, and note it in a book, that it may be for the time to come for ever and ever." Isaiah's message from God, the pastor said, was not just for the Jews of his day, but to us today as well.

"In Hebrew, the expression 'time to come' means 'the latter day'," the pastor explained. "Isaiah wrote his words on a tablet, or a book, if you will, so the message would be preserved for the latter days. And there is no doubt that we are living in the latter days, the end times. When Isaiah spoke of salvation, he wasn't just speaking to the Jews of his day; he was speaking to us today. All the signs are there, people. Earthquakes, famine, wars and rumors of wars… we are indeed living in the latter days."

A few members of the congregation nodded and an older gentleman seated behind Dave uttered an "Amen!" For most of his life, Dave had heard preachers and Bible teachers proclaim that we were living in the latter days, and that the prophets, the New Testament writers, and Jesus all spoke of a catastrophic destruction that would consume all but the new chosen people of God, i.e., Christians would be raptured first. As he matured, Dave struggled to believe the story anymore. Much of what was being said by the modern-day "prophets" just did not add up. Was Isaiah truly speaking to future events that would take place 2,000 years later? Or was he more likely referring to the "latter days" of his time, the period of biblical history when tensions were high between Jews and Romans, and military conflict seemed inevitable? Or were they possibly speaking to both?

"After 400 years of prophetic silence, God finally spoke through Zacharias!" shouted the preacher. Dave snapped to attention as the impassioned preacher continued, "And what Zacharias said that day two thousand years ago was surely meant for us today! He said that God was raising a horn of salvation for us in the House of David, and that God would redeem his people, and that God would remember his holy covenant with us and would deliver us from the hands of our enemies, so that we can serve Him without fear all the days of our lives! Those are some pretty strong promises, my friends, and they are just as much promises made to us today as they were to the Jews back then!"

Dave reflected on all he had learned about the political climate in the hundred or so years before and after Christ. The Romans held tight control throughout the region and beyond, and a fervent Zionist nationalism and pent-up hostility existed among many of the devout Jews who would not compromise their heritage or traditional beliefs in the face of Roman domination and influence. There was urgency in the warnings of the prophets and Jesus, and to say that they were issuing blanket promises for political situations that would occur thousands of years later seemed to diminish that urgency.

Whatever the answers to his questions might be, Dave had a

hunch he might gain fresh insight from the Dead Sea Scrolls, which were discovered over a half century ago, but were yet to be fully digested and understood. The fact that the scrolls had been lost for two thousand years, preserved in caves at Qumran, seemed highly significant. Did God have anything to do with their recent discovery? Maybe he orchestrated the events that led to them being stashed there, and maybe he wanted them to be found when they were. If so, Dave reasoned, maybe God is indeed speaking to us today with a fresh message delivered through the words found in the Dead Sea Scrolls.

The modern history of the Dead Sea Scrolls, Dave learned, began in the late 1940s and early 1950s, when nearly a thousand documents were discovered in caves around Qumran, a community on the northwest shore of the Dead Sea. Written in Hebrew, Aramaic and Greek, less than half of the content of the documents replicates biblical content while the balance of the content does not appear in the Bible. The documents have been dated somewhere between 150 BCE and 68 CE, although exactly when they were written and exactly by whom has long been a matter of debate. Many scholars believe they were written by the Essenes, a Jewish-Christian sect that flourished at that time.

Dave wanted to know more. Who were the Essenes, and what were their core beliefs? And what happened to them? Seeking answers to those questions over the years since the Scrolls were discovered has stirred a storm of controversy among biblical scholars, religious leaders, archaeologists, and the secular academic community. At stake was the very foundation upon which modern-day Christendom was built.

At the center of that controversy was the relentless Dr. Eisman. After personal visits to Israel and countless hours of research, Eisman concluded that the Scrolls provided evidence that the origins of the Christian church are not what most mainstream Christians today think they are. Even though Eisman's books, numerous articles and lectures were drawn from years of doctoral study and research, Dave noticed in the videos that Eisman's passion and emotional involvement seemed to reach deeper than academic pursuit. Dave could tell that the professor had made an earth-shattering discovery that, if understood through his lenses, would set Christendom on its heels. Eisman held a key to the mystery surrounding First Century Christians, and Dave knew that he had to make contact with him to find out more.

Dave tuned in to the preacher again, who had raised the decibel level in his delivery. On the one hand, talking louder proved irritating to Dave, as he felt the preacher was now trying to persuade through emotion rather than logic and reason. On the other hand, raising his voice meant the preacher was coming to the end of his sermon, and not a minute too soon as far as he was concerned. More than ever, as he tried to balance his teaching and family life with his research and self-study, Dave had become restless and impatient with his time. Lately, he had begun to feel as if he were being called to a mission, even if he didn't know exactly what that mission was. What he did know was that he was on a quest to find answers to his lingering questions, and the preacher's message was not helping at all. He would have to find them on his own.

"We don't need politicians telling us what to do to prepare for the future!" the preacher shouted, holding his Bible high in the air. "All we need is this! We don't need to hear from people in Washington, D.C. to know how to lead our lives; we need to hear from this, because hearing from this is hearing from God! Amen?"

At that moment, Dave got a call on his cell phone, and although he had remembered to turn off the ringer, the vibration mode still made a low buzzing noise that could be heard several rows away. Sheepishly, Dave got up and exited into the glassed-in front lobby of the church, but not before the call went to voicemail. The voicemail message only lasted a few seconds, so he stopped in a corner to retrieve it. He listened to an old familiar voice simply say, "New evidence. Call me."

Dave hung up the phone and stuffed it in his pocket, but as he was about to reenter the church, his phone buzzed again. He looked to see who it was, but the number was blocked. Thinking it odd to be getting a call on a Sunday morning, he decided to answer it. But after he said his "Hello?" there was nothing but silence on the other end.

"Hello? Anybody there?"

He was about to hang up when he thought he heard someone, a man, clearing his throat. And then the line went dead. Puzzled, Dave checked the number on his cell but it was blocked. He pocketed his phone and glanced out to the parking lot. For a moment, he thought his eyes were playing tricks on him, but then he realized that what he was seeing was real. Somebody had trashed his car!

Forty-five minutes later, Dave stood in the parking lot with Rebecca and Clint as the police officer concluded his investigation.

"So the only thing missing is the laptop?" the policeman asked.

"Yes."

"They must have wanted it pretty bad," the policeman said, as if waiting for a response from Dave.

"What do you mean?" Dave asked.

"Well, they didn't take about a thousand dollars worth of other items in your car including your golf clubs and those electronic devices in the back seat."

The policeman held up a wallet with the visible edges of twenty-dollar bills sticking out. "And they didn't take this, which at a glance looks like as much money as they are going to get for the laptop."

"That's mine," Clint admitted. "Probably not a good idea to leave it in the car."

"No," the policeman said, "and especially sitting out in plain view like that."

Dave frowned. "I don't know why they wanted the laptop. There's nothing on it of much importance to a thug."

"This wasn't the work of a thug," the policeman said. "The

perpetrator wasn't just stealing a laptop; he was also sending you a message by cracking all these windows. I'd say you've really pissed off somebody."

The next day, Monday, Dave stared out a classroom window to the courtyard of the community college where he taught physics. He stood silently for several awkward minutes as his students waited for him to resume teaching. But the events of the day before consumed his thoughts. He had laid awake most of the night trying to imagine who had attacked him and why. The timing of Randall's call and the curious phone call immediately afterward added to the mystery. He sensed a connection, but what? Although he had not bothered to get into it with the policeman, Dave knew that the thief must be interested in the data on that laptop, most of which was information he had been accumulating for years on the Dead Sea Scrolls and Qumran. Someone apparently wanted to know just how much he knew.

While the class waited, Dave remained transfixed until he noticed a couple of frisky squirrels scampering across the grass and scrambling up an old oak tree. His reverie broken, he turned back to see his students.

"Okay, class, I think that about does it for today," he said. "You're dismissed."

Although they were surprised that class was ending early, the students were nonetheless happy to escape. They gathered up their books and noisily left the classroom. As they left, Dave walked to the window and stared out onto the lawn, again deep in thought.

"Mr. Walker?" a voice behind him said. Dave turned to see that it was one of his students, a dark-skinned young man from India who frequently asked questions in class. In his fifteen years as a professor, Dave had never encountered a student so hungry to learn and so willing to ask the hard questions. It was a refreshing change from the majority of students who were anxious to leave the classroom as quickly as possible.

"Hi, Ravi, you have a question?"

"Yes sir," he replied. "In your lecture today, you mentioned John Stewart Bell's notion of superluminal communication, and you said that Einstein was not able to grasp the concept. Did you mean he couldn't accept it as theory, or that he couldn't accept it as empirically true?"

"Good question," Dave replied. "The problem with the superluminal communication concept is that, so far, all of the empirical evidence indicates that it is impossible in reality, while the phenomena used in experiments seem to give the appearance that they operate that way under certain conditions. So I think Einstein had to believe there was something to the theory, even if he couldn't get his arms around it."

"So what do you believe?"

Dave laughed. "Well, as I said earlier today, Bell was taken with Bohm's idea of hidden variables and nonlocality, and he formulated a mathematical construct that I believe is a huge development in physics; in fact, maybe the most important development ever."

"Wow, that's a big statement. Why do you say that?"

"Because Bell's theory proves that everything that happens in the universe comes from infinity, and it eliminates the principle of local cause. In other words, at the deepest and most fundamental level, what we always thought were separate parts of the universe are not separate at all but are very much connected by superluminal activity."

"So you think that because those phenomena give the appearance of acting in a superluminal fashion, we should continue to pursue the theory?"

"Absolutely. As physicists, isn't that what we're all about? To research and study, to postulate, and then to discover?"

Ravi grinned at him. "Yes sir. And thanks."

Dave nodded. "No problem. I'm glad you're interested enough

to ask; most of my students aren't."

"My curiosity arises from my fascination with the physical attributes of light," Ravi said. "In India, where I come from, we look at the natural world through the lenses of our Hindu eyes, and the more I studied light, the more fascinated I became with the parallels between the Hindu concepts of the physical world and the new science that's developing around relativity and quantum physics."

"That's interesting," Dave said. "As you know, I'm Christian, and the concept of light plays an important role in biblical texts – both Old and New Testaments."

Ravi broke into a grin. "Yes, I know about that. I know about Jesus on the mountain and glowing like a Jedi sword."

"Like a what?" Dave asked, then breaking into a grin. "Oh, you mean those light sabers in Star Wars."

Ravi laughed. "Yes, exactly. In India, we celebrate Diwali, the 'Festival of Lights' by the lighting of lamps that illuminate our homes and our hearts. It is the light that leads us out of the darkness and into a life where we can perform good deeds and draw closer to the divinity. I believe in the power of light to transform us in ways that no other energy can, and I also believe that everything in the universe is connected, even when it appears we are separate. As a Hindu, I've always believed that in a spiritual way, but now I am beginning to believe it scientifically. Anyway, thanks again."

"Sure."

Dave watched Ravi leave, and then turned again to look out the window. He repeated Ravi's statement in his head, "I've always believed that in a spiritual way, but now I am beginning to believe it scientifically." From the mouth of babes, he thought. As he continued to stare out the window, he noticed a middle-aged, dark-haired man standing beside the oak tree. On a campus where most of the students were in their early twenties and typically dressed in jeans or shorts, this man's dark suit and sunglasses were strangely out of place. Even stranger was the fact that the man seemed to be looking directly at him.

The bell rang in the hallway, and Dave jumped, nearly losing his balance and falling backward. He steadied himself by grabbing the corner of his desk, and when he looked back through the window, the man was gone. After regaining his composure, Dave laughed at his own awkwardness. He reckoned that the man, whoever he was, must have had a good reason to be there, and with the reflection off the glass, probably couldn't see him through the window anyway. He plopped down in his chair with a sigh, pulled his cell phone out of his pocket and made a call.

"Hello, this is Randall," said the voice on the other end.

"Hey, it's me, Dave. What's this new evidence? Is it from Qumran?"

"No, but I don't want to talk about it on the phone. Come down here as soon as you can."

"Okay, what's good for you?" Dave asked and immediately realized it was a foolish question. An ongoing bout with Multiple Sclerosis had left Randall partially debilitated, and he rarely ventured away from his home anymore, especially since his wife had passed away a few years earlier.

"Just come when you can," Randall said and hung up.

Dave smiled. Randall could be a bit grumpy at times, but he had a heart as big as Canada. It appeared he had learned of a new discovery, and he knew that was enough to get him hooked. Had it been anyone other than Randall making such a statement, Dave would have been skeptical, but this was Randall Cunningham, a man who Dave considered the smartest person he knew. And Dave knew a lot of smart people.

Before dawn the next morning, with repairs being made to his car, Dave drove a rental car along I-75 heading south out of Atlanta on his way to visit Randall. With no classes to teach on Tuesday, he had agreed to come right away. Early morning traffic, notoriously bad in Atlanta, was just beginning to build on the opposite side of the Interstate, and Dave thanked his lucky stars that he wasn't in it.

As he drove along the highway, he tuned in to the news on the radio, and none of it was good. One year after the events of 9-11, the economy was still reeling and Americans were still on edge, even though security measures had allowed the various commemorative ceremonies at Ground Zero; Shanksville, Pennsylvania; and at the Pentagon to proceed without incident. President Bush repeated his concerns about weapons of mass destruction in Iraq by presenting his case to the world in a speech delivered to the United Nations. And then there were the continued sniper shootings in and around Washington, D.C. and another major sex scandal in the Roman Catholic Church. The war in Afghanistan was showing signs that it would be a long and difficult struggle that would last for years, and Palestinian terrorist attacks in Israel resulted in a swift Israeli retaliation in Gaza and the West Bank, creating a circle of death and destruction in the region.

"You shouldn't listen to all of that bad news," Randall Cunningham said as he and Dave sat on his wide front porch and sipped coffee. It was mid-morning, and Dave had made it to Randall's two-story country home south of Macon just in time to grab the last buttermilk biscuit before Randall went for his fourth. Randall was getting old, and moved more slowly than the last time Dave had seen him, but his mind was as sharp as ever. The two men had been best of friends for many years, and Dave often sought him out for advice and counsel about business, family and spiritual matters.

Raised in a large family in South Georgia, Randall's ancestral roots in the area ran deep. His forebears were salt-of-the-earth, hardworking and religious people – and mostly fundamental Christian. Randall spoke with a South Georgia draw and dressed like a farmer in overalls and cotton shirts, but in fact he was a brilliant physicist who had only recently retired from a longtime consulting position for an international consortium. He was an avid biblical historian and an open-minded, deep thinker.

Along with everything else, Randall was also an amateur archaeologist, frequently traveling to the Holy Land to join excavation teams. After each trip, he would develop slide show presentations to explain to audiences his latest discoveries and their significance to our understanding world history, especially as that history relates to politics and religion. Lately, however, no one seemed interested in his findings, mainly because his ideas about early Christianity ran counter to the long-held traditional beliefs of mainstream Christian churches. As a result, he had eventually estranged himself from his fellow believers and retreated into his own private world. Most of the people from his former congregation now considered him a kook, and Dave was one of the few people who still considered him a friend.

"It's hard these days to hide from the news," Dave replied. "Radio, television and now the Internet. No matter where I turn, there it is. It's getting really bad out there."

Randall shrugged. "It's always been bad out there. We just hear about it more often because we're wired to the news. Which is one more reason the doomsayers are still going strong."

Years before, Randall had told all who would listen to him that mainstream Christian pastors and teachers misunderstand who the earliest Christians were and what happened to them, and that in turn has fed the misinterpretation of what the prophets and Jesus had to say about the latter days. Dave was sure that whatever new information Randall had uncovered would probably shed light on his point of view. After finishing their coffee, Randall motioned to Dave to follow him inside the old farmhouse and downstairs to a corner office that overlooked a pristine six-acre lake. He motioned Dave to a chair beside his cluttered desk, sat down and fished through his stacks of paper until he found a document. He handed it to Dave and watched as he read the headline from an online *National Geographic* article,

"Burial Box May Be That of Jesus's Brother, Expert Says."

"Is this for real?" Dave asked.

"They just found a 2,000-year-old ossuary, a burial box with bones that bears the inscription, 'James, son of Joseph, brother of Jesus.'"

Dave looked at Randall, who waited for him to understand the significance of the find, and when Dave didn't, he continued.

"This is huge, Dave. Until now, references to Jesus, Joseph and James have been found only in manuscripts."

"Josephus wrote about them," Dave said. "In his book, *Jewish Antiquities*, he has a whole paragraph about Jesus, the Messiah, and his crucifixion. And later he wrote about James being stoned to death."

"I know, but there are still a host of people who discount those references as Christian forgery. Josephus was our best historical source, but he doesn't get high marks for credibility. Anyway, now we have their names inscribed on a burial box, full of bones and with this inscription, proving without doubt that the three are in fact historical figures, not fabrications of a group of conspiratorial writers. This ossuary could be the most important find since the Dead Sea Scrolls."

"Ah, hard evidence," Dave said. "I can see why you're so excited."

"Well, what excites me most is not that they were real people," he explained. "I've always believed that. What I'm more excited about is that it proves to the skeptics that James was indeed the brother of Jesus. And that's important in light of my most recent theory about the early Christian church."

"Have I heard this before?" Dave asked.

"No, this is a theory that I believe will lead me to a big discovery, a discovery that will draw attention from people all around the world. And if it is proven to be scientifically and historically true, it will eclipse pretty much any other discovery since the beginning of recorded history."

"Are you pulling my leg?"

"No, I'm very serious, but it really is something that needs to be kept under wraps. If this gets out, it will be extremely controversial, and will draw anger from a lot of religious leaders."

"Why?"

Randall smiled wryly.

"Well, among other reasons, this discovery will challenge the traditional view of the early Christian church and likely piss off a lot of people throughout Christendom."

"You've already pissed off a lot of traditional Christians, Randall."

"Yeah, I know, but I'm saying that this one will go beyond that. Up to now, no one has taken me all that seriously, but this discovery will most certainly raise eyebrows in the most hallowed halls of Christianity."

"The Vatican?"

Randall laughed. "I know, it sounds like I've gone nuts on you. And maybe I have. But when you hear what I'm working on, you'll see."

"So are you going to tell me or not?"

"How long can you stay?"

"All day if that's what it takes," Dave said.

"Good. I'll brew another pot of coffee."

For an hour or so, Dave and Randall covered a lot of ground. While Dave had just begun to realize the significance of the Scrolls, Randall had long been immersed in the subject. His lifetime of studies in religious history and his more recent research into the Scrolls had led him to several unorthodox conclusions. He believed that the community of Messianic Jews at Qumran was for many years the training ground for Jesus and his brother James in their youth. He showed Dave how the Qumran scrolls used much of the same language that shows up in the Book of Acts.

"The Qumran scrolls," he said, "described a community there that practiced strict adherence to Jewish law and disciplines, but without the Roman influences and pretenses of the collaborative Jewish leaders in the Temple. They held all of their money and possessions in common, and they devoted themselves to a simple and regimented lifestyle. They rose at dawn to pray and greet the sun. They devoted themselves to purification through bathing, prayer and singing hymns to God."

But Randall was also convinced that the Jews at Qumran were on a very specific mission. "Historically, the Qumran community fits the profile of the Essenes, the broad group of separatist Jews who were scattered about the region in wilderness camps. But because of their strategic location on the northwest shore of the Dead Sea, just 17 miles from Jerusalem, the Qumran settlement was unique. Their mission went beyond communal living."

"When you say their mission, you mean their attempts to cleanse the Temple of Pharisaical teachings?" Dave asked.

"Yes, and that mission goes back farther than the Romans," Randall said. "Israel already had a long history of foreign intervention that dated way back to the destruction of Solomon's Temple and then Nehemiah's rebuilding of the walls around Jerusalem. During the reign of King Darius, the Temple was rebuilt, but according to the book of Maccabees, when it was completed, the people took a look at it and literally cried, it looked so bad. When Herod came along, he spent a lot of money to rebuild the Temple and gain favor with the Jews. That's why it was called 'Herod's Temple' and that's why the hardcore Jews – the Maccabeeans in particular – were so upset. Herod didn't really give a rip about purity, and allowed the Jewish fathers to sell forgiveness and pad their own pocketbooks."

Like Randall, Dave had a working knowledge of the Maccabean Dynasty that began around 165 BCE and claimed a lineage back to Moses, Noah and the first man, Adam. When Mattathias, a rural Jewish priest, refused to worship the Greek gods of the Seleucian Empire, all hell broke loose. Mattathias' son, Judah, led the revolt that ultimately led to the recapture of Jerusalem and subsequent cleansing of the Temple and restoration of traditional Jewish worship. The Maccabean Dynasty lasted until 37 BCE, when the Roman general Pompey conquered Jerusalem and Israel was again subjected to foreign rule – this time by the powerful Roman Empire.

"So," Randall continued, "the Jews at Qumran believed the Sanhedrin in Jerusalem had for too long yielded to Babylonian, Greek and Roman influence, and in so doing, had betrayed their devotion to God, were no longer adhering to the Law of Moses, and were giving up the God-given land of Israel to ungodly foreigners. I believe the Qumran community was headquarters for a Maccabean-like movement to restore Israel into the hands of God and away from the Herodian Priests in Jerusalem. It's become clear to me that they were the same sect in which both Jesus and his brother James trained to become leaders of the Jerusalem Church. So if you want to understand the origins of the Christian faith, you have to look at what happened at Qumran."

"So is that your discovery, that the Christian faith had its start at Qumran?" Dave asked.

"Yes, but there's much more, and it has to do with Qumran's connections to that mysterious character Melchizedek."

"Melchizedek?"

"Yes, the guy who shows up first in the Book of Genesis when he encounters Abraham. In later references, King David prophesies that the Messiah will be a priest forever *after the order of Melchizedek*, and Paul mentions him in his letter to the Hebrews, again referring to Jesus as 'a high priest forever *after the order of Melchizedek*.' But the biblical writers did not explain what that meant or exactly who they were talking about. He has remained a mystery down through the years, even to most biblical scholars. As it turns out, we now have convincing evidence that Melchizedek was not so mysterious after all. I believe the name refers to another character from scriptures – Noah's eldest son, Shem."

Randall based his belief on a number of deductions, starting with the logic that after the Flood, Noah's three sons were solely responsible for repopulating the world. The other two brothers, Japheth and Ham, lacked the spiritual leadership that distinguished their oldest brother, and over time, Shem emerged as God's priest on earth and the King of Salem. He was God's main man, as it were, and he remained so for many generations to follow, so many that he outlived eight succeeding generations of descendants. By the time his great-great-great-great-great-great-great-grandson Abraham came along, Shem was finally reaching his last days. All of his ancestors were long since dead as were generations of his descendants. And he was the living son of Noah the Righteous One, the pillar and foundation of the world after the Great Flood, which occurred over 500 years earlier! To the people of that day, Shem – or Melchizedek – seemed immortal, which explains why the biblical writers compared Christ's eternal nature to his – a "priest forever after the order of Melchizedek."

"So Melchizedek was Noah's son, Shem?"

"Yep," Randall said with conviction, "and he was the King of Salem, the ancient name for Jerusalem. His lifetime spanned hundreds of years, and over that time, generations of his descendants paid homage to him as God's man by bringing him offerings out of their own possessions. As a result, Shem – or Melchizedek – became the wealthiest man in the world, having accumulated vast amounts of treasure."

Dave was fascinated with Randall's revelation, even though for many years he had doubted the biblical story of the Flood. It wasn't so much a lack of historical documentation; he had long been aware that stories about a great flood were common in many cultures and religious traditions. The problem was more a matter of believing in such an occurrence in the physical sense. As a physicist, burning bushes, the parting of the Red Sea, and other miraculous moments from biblical accounts had always given him pause, and he questioned their plausibility in the physical world of which he knew so much. As much as he wanted to believe the story, the tale of Noah and the Great Flood just didn't make sense. But then, motivated by his insatiable need to get at the truth of any biblical event, he began to investigate the possible natural phenomena that would support the story, and in the process he came away with an astounding new awareness about the history of the planet.

Dave's hypothesis about the Flood was based on a shift that occurred in the rotation of planet Earth thousands of years ago. Before the Flood, he theorized, the earth spun on an axis perpendicular to the sun, and its entire surface was blanketed by a water-vapor canopy. The sun was shut out, and seasons did not exist. But the earth shifted, possibly due to a wobble, and began to spin on the tilted axis we experience today. The result was an earth that now felt the more direct rays of the sun at the Equator and less at the Polar Caps, causing the canopy to disappear. What followed was a month of constant rain and a great flood that left Noah and his family as the sole remnants of humanity. As the ark settled on dry land and the canopy began to disappear, the sun broke through for the first time, and the refracted light on the remaining water particles created a spectacular rainbow across the sky – an event that came to represent the promise of a better future.

For Dave, the significance of Noah's story had to do with God's motivation and how far he will go to fulfill his purposes for His people. If that meant tilting the earth a bit and wiping out all but a remnant, then so be it. The prophets of old had warned that God's judgment would come, and after those warnings were rejected, the door to salvation – the entrance to the ark – was shut. All through biblical history, God's pattern was to rain down judgment on his disobedient people, but leave a remnant to continue on. For that reason, both Dave and Randall agreed that there were Jewish Christians in Jerusalem – God's new "chosen people" – who had been spared. Many historians, including the oft-cited Flavius Josephus and Eusebius Pamphillus, write that sometime before Titus and his army of 50,000 soldiers advanced on Jerusalem in 70 A.D., the Jerusalem Christians escaped into the wilderness and into the mountains. But how they escaped and where they escaped to remained a mystery, although some later ecclesiastical historians believe they settled in Pella, located north of the Dead Sea on the eastern side of the Jordan River. Randall's ideas about the community of Qumran may have provided an answer.

"I believe there was an escape," Randall replied, "and I'm not sure how, but I am convinced that Qumran was the center of operations. And I believe they knew where the hidden treasure from Solomon's Temple was, and believing it was rightfully theirs, they took it with them."

"That would be a huge undertaking, moving all those people to safety and transporting all of that treasure. But if it's true, where did they go, and where is the treasure now?"

"Yes, that is indeed the question. If we could follow their trail, it would lead us to treasures from Solomon's Temple, and if we could follow the trail long enough, it would lead right back to Noah's Ark. I can't explain why, but I can feel it in my bones."

"So if you're right, the big question remains: Where is Noah's ark?" Dave said.

"Well, since you brought it up, think about this. Noah's descendants were the ancestors of all mankind from that day forward, and they all came out of northern Israel. What does that tell you? For one thing, it's more evidence that after the Great Flood, Noah's ark did not come down on Mt. Ararat in Turkey."

"What do you mean by *more* evidence?"

41

"Well, Mt. Ararat is the highest location in the ancient kingdom of Urartu, a region that covered thousands of square miles. The word Ararat is actually a bastardized version of Urartu, which Moses wrote about in the Hebrew Torah sometime around 1450 BCE. In that document, the word included only the consonants "r-r-t", but the Bible translators replaced it with a more complete word, "Ararat." After Urartu was destroyed sometime in the sixth century BCE by the Medes, the name Urartu vanished from history. The Bible doesn't actually state that Mount Ararat is the place where Noah's Ark landed; it simply says that the boat landed in the Urartian mountains, of which there are hundreds. Mt. Ararat is the highest, so most people have assumed that was the spot. But I don't think it was; I believe it settled somewhere in Israel, most likely on a mountain in northern Israel because the Ararat mountain range extends down that far."

"Do you have an idea which mountain?"

Randall smiled. "No, but I think we could nose around over there and find it."

"You've always said in the past that unless God wants it found, it won't be found," Dave reminded him.

"That's right. If I'm wrong about all of this, I won't find it. But if I'm right…"

"You'll upset a lot of people."

Randall cracked a grin. "I usually do."

Dave patted him on the back and stood up to leave. Randall walked with him to the edge of the porch.

"It's good to see you, Dave. And don't stay gone so long."

"I promise."

As Dave reached the bottom step, Randall noticed his car in the driveway.

"Hey, did you get a new car?"

"No, that's a loaner while my car is in the shop. I forgot to tell you that someone broke into my car while we were in church. They busted all my windows, took my briefcase with my laptop in it, but strangely enough, didn't take anything else."

Randall's face dropped. "Are you serious? Dave, I didn't tell you this because I didn't want you to worry, but someone broke into my house last week. Strangely enough, they didn't take anything either."

"Not even your computer?"

"Yeah, they took my old IBM, but they're going to be disappointed, because there's nothing on it anymore. I use a laptop now, and when I'm not using it, I keep it hidden under lock and key."

Dave furrowed his brow and rubbed his chin. "What's going on, Randall?"

Randall cracked a smile. "Like you said, we've pissed off somebody. Now get the hell out of here, and be careful."

On the return trip from Macon, Dave drove along in silence, contemplating all that he had learned from his visit with Randall. Like Dave, Randall viewed the world through two lenses, one colored by their shared interest in physics and the other their common faith as Christians. They also shared many of the same theological conclusions, many of which flew in the face of many long-held Christian beliefs that have been nurtured for centuries by mainstream Protestant churches and Catholicism. But mostly they shared a deep hunger to understand the truth about the origins of the early Christian Church, and they were both willing to explore and discover that truth even if it stirred up a little controversy, as this apparently had. The James ossuary finding was certainly intriguing and potentially another confirmation of their position, although Dave thought it best to wait for all the experts to weigh in before accepting it as authentic.

Halfway back to Atlanta, feeling a bit drowsy, Dave stopped at a truck-stop cafe for a coffee break. He found a counter seat and ordered coffee and a cinnamon roll, and then pulled an article from his briefcase that Randall had handed him just before they parted company. The subject was Qumran, and it was written by Randall, who was a regular contributor to an archaeological journal.

Dave was still on the first page of the article when he noticed a man taking the seat beside him. He glanced over to see that the man was dressed in black shirt and pants and wearing the white collar of a Catholic priest. He thought it strange to see a priest at a truck stop, and from the looks of the guy, with slick black hair and shiny black patent leather shoes, Dave thought he looked more like a pool shark than a priest.

"So what's good here?" the priest asked as he perused the menu. With no one else in earshot, Dave realized he was addressing him.

"I think it's all cooked in the same grease," Dave joked, "so it's either all good or all bad, depending on your seasoning preferences and your cholesterol level."

The priest laughed and said that maybe he would just get a cup of coffee. After he placed his order with the waitress, he turned to Dave and cleared his throat before speaking.

"So, are you on your way to Atlanta?" he asked.

"Yes, I am," Dave answered. "I was visiting an old friend in the Macon area."

"Well, I hope it was a good visit."

"Yes, it always is with Randall."

"Longtime friend of yours?"

"Yes, he was an elder in my church at one time before he became ill and moved out to the country. I don't see him as much as I used to, but when we get together, it doesn't take long for us to pick up where we left off."

"That's interesting," the priest said as the waitress brought him his coffee. He cleared his throat again and asked, "So, what sort of things do you guys usually talk about? Politics? Religion?"

"As a matter of fact, we do talk about politics and religion,"

Dave said.

"Well, as a priest, I would be very interested in knowing more about what you – and your friend – think about religion. Are you Protestant?"

Dave hesitated before answering, and the priest noticed.

"Forgive me, I ask too many questions," the priest said. He tugged at his white collar. "It goes with the territory. I'm a priest, but don't worry, I don't proselytize. I'm not one of those radical evangelical Catholics out to save you from hell. Truth is, I'm just curious."

"Well, I hesitated in answering your question because I'm not sure what category of Protestant I fit into anymore. I was raised in a traditional Christian environment, and I've belonged to several different Christian churches. Over time, my theology has been altered – or maybe I should say refined – as I've delved deeper into biblical history and science. Most recently, Randall and I both have been investigating the origins of the Christian movement around the time of Christ. Much of what we're finding has given us new insights about our long-held traditional beliefs."

The priest pointed his finger at Dave. "You know, too much of that academic pursuit and you'll become an atheist."

Dave laughed. "So what do you suggest I do instead, leave all the learning to you professionals in the Church, and just accept whatever interpretations you give us?"

"Actually, that's exactly what I would suggest. If you know your history, then you know that the Christian Church has stood the test of time. It is a solid oak tree, and it's futile to keep digging at the roots of it. To do so only damages the tree."

"That's an interesting analogy. But if you carry it out far enough, it falls apart. Oak trees eventually grow old and die, so you may not want to compare your religious institution to an oak tree. Trees die; that's the physical reality of plant life. But life does go on, and like you, I believe that God is the creator and sustainer of life. So I understand that there are questions that only God can answer – and will only answer in his time – but there's a place and a good reason for understanding the science of this world. The more I understand physical phenomena, from the celestial to the molecular, the closer I come to understanding God."

"So you just absolutely have to know all the answers, or you're not satisfied. Isn't that what the serpent told Eve in the Garden about the Tree of Knowledge – eat the fruit and you'll know as much as God?" the priest asked, sipping his coffee. "Like I said, you keep reading all that mumbo-jumbo in those books of yours and you'll be an atheist before you know it."

Dave shook his head. "No, if anything, I believe the discoveries we've made in science only strengthen my faith. Modern physics is taking us into new territories and making more discoveries that seem to connect with the biblical narrative. When we connect science with history, we get a clearer picture of what God wants for his creation. Where we get into trouble is when we rely one hundred percent on the Bible for our understanding, when the intent of the biblical authors was not history written for us today. They were clearly writing to an audience of that day, with a very specific message."

"And what do you believe that specific message was?"

"Well, no offense, but I believe it was specifically a message to the Jews in Israel at that time and not about Christians today."

"Why would I take offense at that?" the priest asked, pausing again to clear his throat.

"I assume, as a priest, that you accept the Bible as authoritative."

"And you don't?"

"I believe the accounts of Jesus and his followers are true, if not historically descriptive, and I believe that Jesus was – and is – the Christ. But I also believe there's much more to the story than what we have on the pages of the Bible. My theology differs quite a bit from mainline Catholic theology. However, if it's any consolation, it also differs from mainline Protestant theology in many respects; although I do think the early Protestants had it right when they offered the Bible to the masses in their own language and ended the day when interpretation was left only to the few clergymen who espoused their own narrow interpretations."

The priest narrowed his eyes and pointed at Dave for emphasis. "Yes, and now there are literally thousands of denominations, all with their own theologies, tenets and doctrines. Maybe the Catholics had it right, my friend, when they protected the biblical message – God's message – from the confusion that inevitably comes when truth is doled out to those who have little or no discernment. We become priests by learning and holding fast to the true church, the church that began with our first pope, St. Peter. As you know, Christ himself said that his church would be built upon a rock, and he was talking to Peter when he said it."

"I know," Dave said, "but I'm not so sure anymore that Christ was referring to Peter when he said that."

"I see," the priest said. "I get the picture. So let me ask you about your friend, Mr. Cunningham, does he feel the same way about the Catholic Church as you do?"

"Yes, Randall and I share the same basic theology."

Dave was about to elaborate but suddenly it dawned on him that the priest's habit of clearing his throat was a familiar sound. And then he was struck by another thought that made him feel very uncomfortable with this stranger, even if he was wearing a priest's collar.

"I'm sorry," the priest said, sensing the change in Dave. "Like I said, I ask too many questions."

"No, that's all right," Dave said, "but maybe you could answer a question from me."

The priest looked at his watch and smiled. "Well, maybe one. I just realized how late it's getting to be, and I have to get back to Atlanta before the fish fry tonight at the church. But go ahead, ask away."

"How did you know Randall's last name was Cunningham?"

"You told me."

"I told you his name was Randall; I didn't say his last name."

The priest smiled. "No, you didn't, but I saw his name on that article you have laying in front of you."

Dave looked down at the article and saw the byline, "Randall Cunningham," under the headline. He gave the priest a sheepish smile.

"Yes, well, there it is. You are very observant."

"Yes, another thing that goes with the territory."

The priest laid his money on the counter and stood to leave.

"Nice meeting you," he said. "Maybe I'll bump into you again sometime."

"Yeah, nice meeting you too."

The priest turned to leave, but Dave stopped him.

"Wait. One more quick question, please. Are you familiar with the Dead Sea Scrolls?"

The priest paused a moment before answering. "Of course I am, but I don't put much stock in them. Their value – or lack of it – has been settled decades ago. And if that's what you and your friend Randall have been talking about, you would be wise to forget about the Scrolls. There's nothing there for us; just another crazy sidetrack from the true mission of the Church."

"When you say the Church, do you mean the Catholic Church?"

The priest shook his head and said, "I'm sorry, my friend, but I did say just one question, and that's not a question that I could answer on my way out the door. Nor do I think it is the real question on your mind. The answer to the real question is that you will never know whether your suspicions about me are true, or if your suspicious nature is simply blinding you from recognizing the hand of providence. So I would love to chat some more, but I really have to go."

With that, the priest walked out, leaving his coffee cup three-quarters full and a five dollar bill to cover a dollar coffee purchase. Dave walked to the window but from his vantage point couldn't see the back of the parking lot. He waited a moment, knowing there was only one exit then watched a black SUV exiting the parking lot. The windows were tinted, and he couldn't see his face, but he had little doubt that the profile of the man in the driver's seat matched that of the priest.

Dave sat down at the counter to finish his coffee, but he could not shake a nagging feeling, the same pit in his stomach that he had felt when he discovered the assault on his car. There had to be a connection between that and the encounter with the priest. After all, how often do Catholic priests drive around in black SUVs but then stop to eat in roadside cafes like this? Had he been followed here and cleverly drawn into a probing conversation by the mysterious priest?

Back on the road, Dave mulled over the recent events, trying to make sense of it all. The more he thought about it, the more ridiculous it seemed that someone would find his and Randall's research to be a threat. But someone seemed to be worried about what they were doing. Dave realized he was becoming tense, so he breathed deep and tried to shrug it off, at least for the moment. He turned on the radio just in time to hear a newscast about more trouble in the Middle East, and he smiled to think that the world situation had not improved one bit since yesterday. But the sun was still in the sky, the earth was still spinning, and if his theories were correct, the world was *not* in imminent danger of coming to a tragic end.

Sensing a car following too closely, he glanced in his rear view mirror, and his smile instantly faded. Directly behind him was the same black SUV he had seen leaving the parking lot. He felt the hair on the back of his neck stiffen, and his heart began to race just as his phone rang. Hands shaking, he wrestled the phone from his pockets and looked to see it was another blocked caller. Tentatively, he answered it, but all he heard was silence.

"Hello? Anybody there?" he asked, but no one responded. He looked in the rear view mirror, but the SUV was no longer there. He had just passed a freeway exit, and when he looked back over his shoulder he could see the SUV heading up the ramp.

"What the hell is going on?" Dave asked the silent caller, but then he saw that the call had been disconnected. But not before he remembered what he had not been able to remember earlier, when he had first heard the priest clearing his throat. He had heard that same guttural sound before, just before the silent caller hung up.

Over the next few weeks, Dave worried that he might be in imminent danger or, worse yet, his family could be. But nothing unusual occurred, and he decided that if the priest was actually a henchman for some organization that wanted to suppress his research, the guy must have eventually concluded after digging through all of his computer files that he was no threat to whatever or whoever they were protecting. Most of the information in those files was research that anyone could gather, and other than a few opinionated articles from Randall and others, he didn't see any reason for whoever was checking him out to be overly concerned. It wasn't as if he -- or Randall, for that matter -- was trying to organize a movement. But no sooner had Dave come to that conclusion than he got a visit from the university's new chancellor, Dr. Horace Laurens.

A recent arrival from another college in the Midwest, Dr. Laurens had left an unfavorable impression on Dave when he first heard him speak to the faculty at an introductory luncheon a few months earlier. The new chancellor seemed far too austere and rigid for a contemporary and progressive-minded college; and unlike the previous chancellor, who had been friendly and engaging, the new guy's conversation was abrupt and his personality stiff, almost robotic. Dave made a point to steer clear of him. But then after his last class one day, as he was zipping up his briefcase and about to walk out of the classroom, Dave looked up to see Dr. Laurens walk in and close the door behind him.

"Before you leave, Mr. Walker," he said, "I have an important matter to discuss with you."

"Sure," Dave responded. "Would you like to get some coffee in the break room so we can sit and chat?"

"No, this will only take a minute."

"Okay."

"Mr. Walker, it has come to my attention that you are involved in research related to the Dead Sea Scrolls, and as a result, you have aligned yourself with certain people outside of academia who espouse extremely radical ideas about their relevance."

"If you're talking about Randall Cunningham, I can assure you…"

Laurens held up his hand. "Let me finish, please. It is not my intention to name names, nor is it my intention to tell you who you may or may not have relationships with. However, it is my intention to protect the academic integrity of this university, and I do not want our reputation tarnished by someone on our faculty espousing – or conspiring with others who are espousing – certain ideas that run contrary to mainstream academia and our traditions for academic excellence."

Dave gave him a quizzical look.

"I don't understand how my research into the Dead Sea Scrolls could damage the academic integrity of this university."

"Mr. Walker, I'm going to make this very simple, and I really don't want any further discussion after I say this. You will either stop this path you are on, or I can terminate your position… and without a good reference. It's your choice."

With that, Laurens turned on his heels and walked out of the room, leaving Dave in a state of shock. As he hoisted his briefcase to leave, he glanced out the window. There, leaning against the oak tree, was the same man in dark suit and sunglasses that he had seen a few weeks earlier. Once the man was certain that Dave had seen him, he turned and walked away.

ISRAEL, 33 CE

After Daniel's experience on the mountainside with Jesus, Azara eventually came to accept the fact that Daniel had genuinely been healed. Not only had his limp gone away, it seemed to her that his tendency to withdraw from others had also vanished. He no longer refused to play games with the other children, and he began to make friends again. She marveled at how athletic he suddenly had become, often winning foot races against the other boys and taking a keen interest in blacksmithing. His muscles were developing, as was his sharp mind and deep understanding of Jewish law. She had Simeon to thank for that, as Daniel spent hours at night with him learning how to be a scribe. In the process, Daniel naturally became intimately familiar with the Torah.

Azara and Daniel had become frequent visitors to the markets in Magdala and Tiberias, and Azara no longer worried that they would be recognized or hunted by the Romans. Although she never lost hope of finding her husband, Abram, she no longer asked about his whereabouts, believing that he must have perished. But she also believed that the mystery surrounding her husband's disappearance could only be solved in Jerusalem.

"Either he's dead or in chains," she told Raisa as they walked beside their produce cart along the dusty road leading to Jerusalem. She had convinced Raisa and Simeon to make the trip with her and

Daniel, and Raisa assured her that they would be able to stay with a friend she knew in the City. Although it was a long way to Jerusalem, Azara thought it important to go there to offer sacrifices for her husband Abram's sins, as was the custom when a relative died. She wasn't certain of her husband's death, but she did not want to leave anything to chance when it came to spiritual matters. And if he died in Jerusalem, then the sacrifices should be made at the Temple there.

Azara also wanted to see Jesus, who was reportedly on his way to Jerusalem too. When they finally reached the house of Raisa's friends, weary from a three-day trip in a cart, they were told they could stay there as long as they wanted. After a meal and some rest, they made their way to the Court of the Gentiles, located just outside the Temple. Azara shopped among the merchants for sacrificial doves, and just as she was about to make the exchange, a clamor arose across the courtyard. People began to run toward the area of the Golden Gate, the entranceway into Jerusalem known to Jews as *Sha'ar Harachamim*, the Gate of Mercy.

"It's Jesus!" a man shouted as he rushed toward the Gate. "He's come down from the Mount of Olives, and he's about to enter the City!"

Shouting to Raisa and Simeon that she would return to the courtyard later, Azara grabbed Daniel's hand again and hurried toward the Gate, anxious for an opportunity to thank Jesus for healing Daniel's leg. When they reached the Gate, Daniel and Azara climbed the wall and found a vantage point that allowed them to view the Kidron Valley below and the crowd of people who were surrounding Jesus, who sat astride a donkey being led toward the Gate. The atmosphere was thick with excitement, as people clamored for spots along the road to watch the man who many were now proclaiming to be the Messiah.

A man in tattered clothes who had rushed ahead of the crowd stopped at the wall and shouted excitedly to the people gathered there, "He's a miracle worker! I was blind, but he touched my eyes and now

I can see! I can see all of you! He healed me! He is the Messiah! They all saw it!"

The man rushed to find a spot close to the road that would soon lead Jesus to the Gate. As the crowd came closer, Daniel and Azara were finally able to see the Healer, many of his closest followers, as well as a contingent of Pharisees who were not pleased with the praise being heaped upon Jesus. People along the roadside cut palm leaves from trees and laid them in his path, and others shouted out to him as he passed, proclaiming him to be a great prophet from the House of King David. Daniel remembered the words of the old woman at the well who had said the Messiah would arrive on a great white horse wearing the armor of a conqueror and wielding a mighty sword. But this man rode the back of a small donkey wearing a simple white robe and wielding no sword.

As he neared the Gate, Jesus suddenly stopped the donkey, and a hush fell over the crowd. For a moment, his eyes were transfixed on the walls of the city, and then to everyone's amazement, he began to weep. The crowd murmured and soon realized that he was expressing his sorrow for Jerusalem, the city of his ancestors.

"The days are coming when your enemies will build an embankment against you and encircle you and hem you in on every side," he said, speaking through tears. "They will dash you to the ground, you and the children within your walls. They will not leave one stone on another, because you did not recognize the time of God's coming to you."

Then Jesus passed through the Gate. Azara grabbed Daniel's hand, and they hurried to the edge of the street, hoping for an opportunity to see him up close and possibly get the chance to speak to him. The crowds pressed in ahead of them and there was no space for them to reach the edge of the street. But Azara was determined, and clutching Daniel's hand, she raced ahead until they were finally able to squeeze through the crowd to reach the street. As Jesus approached,

Azara removed her scarf and laid it carefully on the dusty street. Daniel watched his mother's face as Jesus saw her.

"Thank you!" Azara cried out. "Thank you for healing my son!"

Jesus smiled at her and then at Daniel, standing in the street beside her. When Daniel looked into the eyes of Jesus, he recognized the same compassion that had captured him the first time he saw him speak and perform miracles on the mountainside, the day his leg was healed.

The donkey bearing Jesus continued to clop along the hard clay street, and as he passed Azara and Daniel, he reached out and touched Azara's hand. Daniel, swept up in the excitement of the moment, shouted, "Hosanna to the Son of David!" Jesus turned and smiled back at him. As the crowds continued to follow him into the City, Azara stood frozen in the street, and she began to cry.

"Mother, what's wrong?" Daniel asked.

Azara looked down at him and smiled through the tears. "Nothing is wrong, Daniel. These are tears of joy. I'm crying because he touched me."

They followed the crowds as Jesus made his way to the Temple courtyard. They found a high spot where they watched him dismount his donkey just as a gathering of Jewish leaders – the Sanhedrin – walked out to meet him. It appeared there would be a confrontation, but then Jesus walked to the area where the merchants were selling doves and exchanging money. To everyone's astonishment, the calm man whose very presence exuded peacefulness suddenly shouted angrily at the merchants that they had turned the holy Temple, "his Father's house," into a den of thieves. One by one, he turned over their money tables and benches, scattering their contents all over the courtyard grounds.

"Why did he do that?" Raisa's friend, Naomi, asked later that day after they had returned to their house.

"He was angry," Azara replied. "He said the Holy Scriptures teach us that the Temple is a holy place, a house of prayer, not a place for crooked merchants to make money."

"What happened then?" Naomi asked.

"Then he healed people," Daniel said, "just like he healed me. One man there had been blind all of his life, and Jesus just touched him and he could see."

"His touch," Azara said softly. "His touch carries the power of God. I felt it when he touched my hand."

"Then he got into an argument with the chief priests and elders of the Temple," Daniel said.

"The chief priests and teachers are jealous," Azara explained. "They didn't like it that we were showering Jesus with our hosannas and praising him for his kindness. They are afraid of him. Jesus left after that, and there were whispers that he was going to Bethpage for the night, but would return to the Temple again tomorrow. "

"Do you believe he is the Messiah?" Naomi asked.

Azara paused, lost in her thoughts for a long moment.

"I don't know," Azara finally answered. "Daniel has studied the writings of the prophets at the Temple school, and he believes that Jesus has already fulfilled many of their prophecies. Maybe he's the Messiah, or maybe he's another prophet. But I have to find out. Raisa, I'm going to stay in Jerusalem for a while. I want to go home."

Simeon shook his head. "You can't go back to your house. Someone else has probably moved into it by now, and it wouldn't be safe there anyway."

"It would only be for a while. Will you take care of Daniel for me?"

"I'm staying with you," Daniel said so emphatically that his mother knew he would not take no for an answer.

"Then it's settled," Azara said. "Daniel and I will go to our old neighborhood now. If we can't stay in our old house, we'll return here later tonight."

Raisa handed her basket to Azara.

"We will return to Tiberias tomorrow," she said. "There's enough bread in this basket for breakfast in the morning."

Azara thanked her and they embraced.

"Be careful, Azara," Raisa warned. "Jesus speaks boldly to the Temple leaders, and you know what happened to the prophets when they spoke too boldly."

Azara nodded solemnly. She thanked Raisa's friends for their hospitality, and she and Daniel headed off to their old neighborhood. They walked for a while before Daniel finally broke the silence.

"What was Raisa talking about? What happened to the prophets when they spoke too boldly?" Daniel asked.

Azara looked down at him, and he saw tears forming in her eyes and through quivering lips she answered him.

"They were stoned to death."

The sun had just barely settled below the walls of Jerusalem when Azara and Daniel reached their old neighborhood. They picked their way through alleys and streets until they reached the block where their old house still stood. As they approached it, they saw that it was dark and empty. Boards had been nailed across the door but they were able to crawl through them into the house. In the dim light, they were able to see that although the house was dusty and most of the furniture was gone, Daniel's bed was still there.

"We can stay here tonight," Azara said, "And tomorrow we will go to the Temple again to see Jesus."

Exhausted from the events of the day, Azara fell asleep quickly but Daniel found it difficult to close his eyes. He flashed back to that terrifying night when the Romans came to their house. He recalled the fear that had so engulfed him, and his body involuntarily shivered, waking Azara.

"We'll be okay," Azara said, wrapping her arms around him

and holding him close. It was enough to calm Daniel long enough for him to finally fall asleep.

At morning's first light, Daniel woke to the sound of Azara walking in the front door, carrying a bucket of water.

"Good morning, sleepyhead," she said. "I found the bucket I kept in storage and fetched us some water. After you wash, we can share the bread Raisa left with us."

"When will we go to the Temple?"

"At noon."

"What will we do until then?"

Azara looked around the room. The house was dusty, and it was apparent that no one had lived there since they left. If they could go and come from the house when the streets were deserted, she reasoned, they could stay there a while, at least long enough for Azara to meet Jesus and tell him that she wanted to be one of his followers.

"I think we will clean up this house until then," she said.

Daniel looked around the room. The house that had been so much a part of his life as a small child now seemed a strange place.

"It doesn't feel like home anymore," he said. "I don't want to stay here."

"It's just for a little while," she said. "I promise."

Daniel helped his mother sweep the floors and clean the cobwebs from the corners, and by noon the house was transformed into a semblance of its former state. Azara wiped her brow and Daniel saw that she was pleased with the results of their efforts.

"What do you think?" she asked.

A notion formed in Daniel's mind that he had not considered before. This had been his mother's home for many years even before he was born. It had served her and his father well, and it was clear that she dearly longed to live here again.

"I think we could stay here a while, if you want," he answered. "And maybe I can reopen the blacksmith shop. We'll need to earn money somehow."

Azara gave him a hug. "Thank you."

By the time Daniel and Azara reached the Temple courtyard, crowds had already begun to gather. There was a palpable atmosphere of anticipation. And standing just outside the doors to the Temple were the chief priests and elders, who also appeared to be anxious about the imminent arrival of Jesus and his disciples. Finally, a group of young men rushed into the courtyard shouting, "Jesus is coming! He's on his way into the City!"

Azara and Daniel moved to a short wall near the Temple steps, and Azara lifted him up to a spot where he could see. More people entered the courtyard including one man who spoke to the crowds excitedly.

"It was amazing!" he said. "Jesus spoke to a fig tree and cursed it for not bearing fruit. Then it withered instantly, right before our very eyes!"

The crowd of people murmured amongst themselves, and one of the chief priests addressed the man.

"He uses tricks to deceive you," he said. "Can't you see that he is trying to fool you into following him?"

"It was no trick," the man said. "I was there and saw it myself."

Then all heads turned when a crowd of people entered the courtyard and someone shouted, "He's here!" With Azara steadying him, Daniel stood on the wall to see. He recognized Andrew and the other disciples who helped part the crowd so Jesus could walk through the courtyard to the Temple steps. There the chief priests accosted him.

"We have questions for you," one said. "By what authority are you doing these things?"

"And who gave you this authority?" another asked.

In his characteristically calm manner, Jesus answered, "I will ask you one question. If you answer me, I will tell you by what authority I am doing these things. John's baptism, where did it come from? Was it from heaven, or from men?"

The crowd that gathered around them all waited for their response, but the chief priests found it a difficult question, one that required them to confer at length with each other. Finally, one spoke up and said, "We don't know." Jesus nodded and said, "Neither will I tell you by what authority I am doing these things." Then Jesus asked them another question.

"What do you think? There was a man who had two sons. He went to the first and said, 'Son, go and work today in the vineyard.' 'I will not,' he answered, but later he changed his mind and went. Then the father went to the other son and said the same thing. He answered, 'I will, sir,' but he did not go. Which of the two did what his father wanted?"

Like everyone else in the Temple courtyard, Daniel formed his answer in his mind just before he heard Azara whisper, "The first!" And when the chief priests answered the same, Jesus shocked them all with his next words: "I tell you the truth, the tax collectors and the prostitutes are entering the kingdom of God ahead of you."

A collective gasp went up in the courtyard, but that was just the beginning. One after another, Jesus used parables to communicate his messages to the gathering of Jews, and he held nothing back in his warnings to the rabbinical leaders in the Temple. After one parable, he confronted them with this bold statement: "Therefore I tell you that the kingdom of God will be taken away from you and given to a people who will produce its fruit."

Daniel didn't understand what the warning meant, but he was sure that it was directed at the chief priests who were questioning Jesus, and he was also sure they did not like what he was saying.

"What's happening now?" Daniel asked his mother.

"They are angry and want to have the Teacher removed from the courtyard, but they know the people here all came to see and hear him, so they don't know what to do. They're afraid of him."

Daniel wrinkled his eyebrows. "I'm not afraid of him. He healed me. I don't understand why they are so angry."

"Because they want money and prestige more than they want the truth," she explained, "and they hear Jesus say that will be taken away from them."

They listened as Jesus began to tell them another parable, in which he compared the kingdom of heaven to a king who prepared a wedding banquet for his son. When the king sent his servants out with invitations, people refused to come. He sent his servants out again with a second invitation, reminding the people that he had prepared a great feast for dinner. And again they paid no attention, except for a few who seized the servants and killed them. The angry king, of course, sent his army out to destroy the murderers and burn their city. Then he sent servants out again, except this time out into the streets to invite anyone they could find. The result was a wedding hall filled with guests.

As Jesus continued the parable, Daniel noticed that everyone in the courtyard was hanging on every word, especially Azara.

"But when the king came in to see the guests," Jesus said, "he noticed a man there who was not wearing wedding clothes. 'Friend,' he asked, 'how did you get in here without wedding clothes?' The man was speechless. Then the king told the attendants, 'Tie him hand and foot, and throw him outside, in the darkness, where there will be weeping and gnashing of teeth.'"

Then Jesus looked directly at the group of chief priests and said, "For many are invited, but few are chosen."

As the day went on, Jesus continued to speak to the crowds using parables, and he continued to field questions thrown at him by the Pharisees, questions that were clearly intended to trip him into answers that would give them ammunition to have him discredited. But Jesus continued to astound them and the crowds with his sharp intellect, his deep knowledge of Scripture and his stern warnings. The Sadducees confronted Jesus too, but again he confounded them with his answers, chastising them for their lack of understanding about the Scriptures and the power of God. After a while the Pharisees and Sadducees in the Temple, realizing that their attempts to trick Jesus had backfired, ended their questions and left him. Jesus turned to his disciples and the Jews gathered around him and spoke about the Temple leaders.

"You must obey them," he said, "but do not do what they do, because they do not practice what they preach."

Azara and Daniel listened as Jesus described the deceit and hypocrisy of the Temple leaders.

"He is angry with them," Azara whispered to Daniel. "Just like your father was."

Jesus ended his denunciation of the Temple leaders by comparing them to snakes and reminding his followers that it was they who denounced the prophets and had them pursued and killed.

Azara began to weep, realizing that it was those same Temple leaders who had likely turned against her husband and informed the Romans of his anti-Herodian stances. Then Jesus uttered his own prophecy regarding the Jewish leaders: "And so upon you will come all the righteous blood that has been shed on earth, from the blood of righteous Abel to the blood of Zechariah son of Berekiah, whom you murdered between the temple and the altar. I tell you the truth; all this will come upon *this generation.*"

Then Jesus paused, as if to allow his anger time to pass, and as he did, Daniel noticed that his mother was crying. Jesus paused, looking through the crowd until he noticed Azara weeping. Then he spoke again but this time in a voice full of compassion – the same tone that Daniel remembered from the day on the mountainside when Jesus healed him.

"O Jerusalem, Jerusalem, you who kill the prophets and stone those sent to you, how often I have longed to gather your children together, as a hen gathers her chicks under her wings, but you were not willing."

The following day, Azara met an older man at the well who listened as she recounted the events that had taken place the day before in the Temple courtyard. His name was Nathan, and he asked if she and Daniel would like to join the Jerusalem church, the mostly underground movement of Jews who were now following the teachings of Jesus and his disciples. Zealous for God and fed up with the tainted, Herodian version of Judaism that had become the mainstream, the new followers of Christ met secretly in small groups in houses where they would offer prayers to God, read the Scriptures and share a meal together. Afterwards, the adults would engage in spirited discussions while the children played together in another room or on the rooftop.

"We will be gathering tonight in my home, and I hope you and your son will join us," Nathan said. Azara readily accepted, and that night they visited Nathan's home church. The reception from others was warm, and by the end of the night, Azara and Daniel both felt they they had become part of a new family. The women offered to bring food to them to help them get re-established in their old neighborhood, and a few of the men, especially Nathan, agreed to help Daniel restart his father's blacksmith business.

Then, just two nights later, as Daniel sat at the table polishing off a hearty meal of bread and fruit, they heard a knock at the door. It was Nathan, who asked if he could talk to them.

"Join us at the table," Azara offered as she poured a cup of wine for him.

Nathan sat down and stared solemnly across the table at them. Daniel munched on a carrot and Azara pushed a bowl of fruit across the table to Nathan, who shook his head.

"Thank you, but not now," he said. Azara could tell by his tone of voice that he had come to tell them something they didn't want to hear. "I'm sorry to be the one to tell you this, but I have news of your husband, Abram. One of the men who worked at the Roman stables knew him. He was there when the Roman soldiers brought Abram and another man, your neighbor across the street."

"They killed them, didn't they?" Azara asked with a quiver in her voice.

"Yes."

"How?" Daniel asked angrily, his fists clenching involuntarily.

"I don't know all the details, but…"

Nathan bowed his head and issued a long sigh.

"It was brutal."

Azara began to weep uncontrollably. For so long she had held out hope, and now that hope was gone. Nathan reached across the table and took her hand to console her, but it was no use. Daniel listened to her sobs and saw the pain etched in her face, and it made him angry. He pounded his fist on the table.

"I hate them! I spit on them like my father, and I vow…"

Azara grabbed his arms and shouted, "You vow what?! To resist them and die like your father? We must wait and allow God to perform his judgment in his time."

"If all we do is wait, the Romans will never leave. Maybe it's time to resist. Maybe God wants us to stand up and fight them before it's too late."

Nathan nodded calmly. "I understand how you feel, but Azara is right. I didn't know your father, but from all I have been told about him, I believe I know what he would say to you now, if he could. Judgment is coming soon, although it will not be against the Romans. Do you remember the day that Jesus left the temple? His disciples asked him about the buildings in Jerusalem, and he answered them saying that not one stone would be left on another. He warned us that the destruction of Jerusalem is drawing near, and to be ready to flee to the mountains when it happens."

Daniel and Azara were silent, soaking in what they feared to be true.

"The Romans are only an instrument of God's judgment," Nathan said. "Their motives are clear, and one day they too will reap their reward for all their godlessness. But judgment on Jerusalem is coming because the people have listened to the false teachers in the Temple, who have perverted the Law of Moses."

"When will this happen?" Daniel asked.

"There are signs already," Nathan answered.

"But didn't Jesus also speak of salvation for us if we followed him?" Azara asked.

"Yes, there will be salvation from the coming destruction for those who listen and follow the path Jesus has laid out for us. And that leads me to the other reason I've come tonight. The men at Qumran are laying the groundwork for the Jerusalem church to grow, as many are being added to our numbers every day. To be successful, we need help from everyone in the church, Daniel, including you. The brethren have asked me to come to you to ask you to join our community at Qumran."

"Why me?" Daniel asked. He and Azara had heard others in the church talk about the wilderness camps that were scattered across Israel, and they had also heard that Jesus and his brother James were part of the Qumran community.

"Because you are Maccabean, a direct descendant of Judas Maccabee who led the army that recaptured Jerusalem from the Syrians years ago. Daniel, you have been touched by the hand of God, and you have been blessed with a sharp mind. You have learned the Scriptures well and have become a skilled blacksmith, like your father, and another blacksmith is needed at Qumran. But we also know that you have learned from Simeon the difficult task of a scribe. We want you to come there and perfect your skills as a scribe and train with us for the day that is coming, the Day of Judgment."

Over the next few days, Daniel pondered Nathan's request. For reasons beyond his own understanding, his heart had leapt at the idea of joining the group that was now following Jesus. He realized that he had become like his disciples, willing to follow him anywhere, even into the wilderness. And he missed his training with Simeon to become a scribe. To learn from the master scribes at Qumran would be an honor. Were it not for his mother, the decision would have been easy, but leaving her alone was something he could not do. For her part, Azara had assured him that she would be fine if he chose to go, and reminded him that she would still see him often, as the Qumran camp was only fourteen miles away in the mountains near the Dead Sea.

"There will be work for me to do here in Jerusalem," she added. "We all have a part in carrying out the plan."

"I'll think about it," Daniel said, ending the conversation.

Less than a week after Jesus' encounter with the Temple priests, as Azara was heading out to get water, she heard that armed men sent by the chief priests and elders had arrested Jesus the night before and taken him in to the Temple for questioning. Stricken with fear, Azara ran back inside to get Daniel, and they hurried to Nathan's house to find out more. Talia greeted them and said that Nathan had already gone to the Temple to investigate. Without hesitation, Azara and Daniel rushed to the Temple courtyard where a crowd had gathered. They searched until they found Nathan among them.

"Last evening, they brought him in to see Caiaphas," Nathan said in a trembling voice. "I believe he is in great danger because the chief priests have accused him of blasphemy, a very serious charge, and many in this crowd are in agreement. And those of us who have followed Jesus are afraid that the Romans will remember and arrest us too."

"What will happen now?" Azara asked.

"I'm not sure," Nathan said, and at that moment they heard a commotion and watched fearfully as a bound and closely guarded Jesus was led away from the Temple. Azara, Daniel and

Nathan followed the crowd as Jesus was taken to Pontius Pilate, the governor. Word quickly spread among the Jews that the chief priests had condemned Jesus to death, and now his fate rested in the hands of Pilate. After waiting anxiously, Daniel, Azara and Nathan were shocked to hear shouts from the crowd inside to crucify Jesus. Then, after an agonizing wait to see what would happen, they watched from the roadside as Jesus was led away to be crucified. It was a terrible sight, as he had been severely flogged and was bleeding profusely from a crude crown of thorns that soldiers had placed on his head. They followed Jesus to the hillside where he was nailed to a wooden cross and left there to die.

For several hours, Daniel, Azara and Nathan huddled together and waited and watched. In the crowds of people who gathered to witness the crucifixion were Mary, the mother of Jesus, and James, his brother. Azara could see the torture on their faces, and she wept for the woman whose son was being ridiculed and viciously tortured. While Azara wept and Nathan prayed, Daniel felt sick to his stomach. Finally, he stood and said, "I don't want to stay here any longer, Mother. Let's go home."

Reluctantly, Azara agreed, and they left Nathan there and walked away from the awful scene. After they had gone a short distance, they heard a loud wailing from the women who had come to watch and looked back to see that Jesus' body had gone limp. And while Daniel stared at the sight, Azara slumped to the ground. Daniel rushed to help her up, and together they made their way back home. As they walked together in silence, he saw how much the tragic event had hurt his mother, and as he thought about the injustice of the chief priests and the brutality of the Roman soldiers, he felt his anger boiling up inside him, and once again he made a vow that somehow, someday he would get revenge.

After the crucifixion of Jesus, Daniel and Azara barely left their house for several days. An atmosphere of fear and uncertainty had gripped the Jerusalem Church, and from their own experience, they were keenly aware that the Romans might seek out those who followed Jesus. Then one night, Nathan paid them a visit and brought astonishing news.

"Many of us have been meeting secretly in an upstairs room," Nathan said. "We were meeting there last night, when he just walked in."

"Who?" Azara asked.

"Jesus."

"But we saw him die," Daniel said.

"I know. Many of us were witnesses. But the third day, after they took his body to Joseph's tomb, he appeared to Mary and others who were near his grave. Then yesterday, the twelve – minus Judas Iscariot – were praying together in their upstairs room when suddenly Jesus was standing there among them. They were so astonished that Thomas accused him of being an imposter, until Jesus showed him the nail scars and the wound in his side."

Azara sat on the bed and began to weep.

"So… he's… alive," she whispered. She looked at Daniel, wiped away the tears and broke into a grin. "He's alive!"

"Yes, he's alive," Nathan said. "But he told us that he would not be with us for long. He says the Kingdom of God is drawing near, and for us to wait here in Jerusalem to receive the gift he has been speaking to us about. He said that when it comes, we will be bathed in his Holy Spirit."

"How long did he say we will have to wait?" Daniel asked.

Nathan shook his head. "He said that would be up to God."

Nathan put a hand on Daniel's shoulder and asked, "Daniel, we still need you at Qumran. James has asked about you and hopes you will join us. We all want you to come. Have you made your decision yet?"

"I should stay here in Jerusalem with my mother," he said. "I can reopen my father's blacksmith shop and earn money."

"There's no need," Nathan said. "All that we have, we share. The community of believers will care for her."

Daniel looked at his mother, who nodded and said, "I believe your father would want it. If God wills it, go and make him proud."

Daniel saw that they were both waiting for his answer, but he remained uncertain. He still felt hatred toward the Romans, and now that it was clear that the chief priests and elders were collaborating with Herod, he hated them too. In spite of his prayers and meditation, and even though Jesus had clearly said he must demonstrate love even to his enemies, he still hated them all. They were responsible for the murders of his father and Baram's father, as well as the abduction of Baram and his mother and sister, who were most certainly taken to a foreign land to become slaves. And they were also responsible for the death of Jesus, the powerfully tender man who had healed his body. How could he not hate them for the heinous acts they had committed against the people he loved the most?

"Will you come?" Nathan asked.

Daniel looked again at his mother and shook his head.

"No, I'll stay here."

Over the next few weeks, Daniel and Azara ventured out more frequently into the city. They rejoined the Jerusalem Christians who continued to report the news that Jesus had appeared to his many of his followers. Nathan continued to visit often, and always with a basket of food and wine. And after he left, Azara would find money that he had secretly placed under a cup or bread basket. Daniel felt guilty about receiving so much without giving anything in return. He remembered his father's words about an honest day's labor and knew that he would not want his wife and child to be so dependent on charity.

"When I get blacksmith work, I will pay you back," he told Nathan on one of his visits.

"In that case," Nathan said, "come to my house tomorrow and I will give you work. I have a bridle that needs repair."

The next day Daniel knocked on the door to Nathan's house, which was located near the house where Jesus' followers lived. Nathan opened the door and let him in.

"I have news," he said. "Jesus was meeting with his disciples last evening when he was suddenly taken up into the air, right before their eyes. He disappeared behind a cloud. Then two men in white, angels of God, I think, appeared to them and said that Jesus had been taken into heaven."

"Are you saying he's gone?" Daniel asked. "My mother and I had hoped we would see him again."

Nathan smiled and said, "It's okay, Daniel. His body is gone, but not his spirit."

Daniel remembered again the words of the old woman at the well who said that the Messiah would return in "power and glory." The disciples' accounts of meeting a very calm, resurrected Jesus still dressed in his linen robes didn't match that description at all.

"Here's the broken bridle," Nathan said, and proceeded to show Daniel the problem and what was needed to repair it. Daniel had watched his father make similar repairs a hundred times before, and assured Nathan that it was a simple fix.

"You have the confidence of your father," Nathan said. "You are strong in mind and body, Daniel. I wish you would reconsider James' request to join the community at Qumran."

Daniel shook his head and said that he had not changed his mind. Nathan was disappointed but over the next few days, he brought Daniel more blacksmith work, along with repairs that were needed by others who belonged to the Church.

And then came the day that changed Daniel's life. It started early one morning, just ten days after Jesus' miraculous ascension. Daniel was on his way to return a tool he had repaired for Nathan when he saw a commotion down the street. He hurried there and searched among a murmuring crowd of a hundred or more people until he found Nathan.

"What's going on?" Daniel asked.

"The Eleven were meeting in the upstairs room of their house when suddenly there was a great roar of wind that filled the room The disciples say that shafts of fire fell upon them and caused them to speak all at once in foreign tongues. I don't know what it means, but..."

"It means they are all drunk!" a man standing next to him shouted, causing many in the crowd to laugh.

But then the crowd grew quiet when they saw one of the disciples, Peter, stand up before them, indicating that he wanted to speak.

"They're not drunk!" Peter said in a loud voice. "It's only nine in the morning! No, this is what was spoken by the prophet Joel."

Peter continued to preach to the crowd, explaining that Jesus had been raised from the grave, lived among them and then ascended to heaven.

"He has been exalted to the right hand of God," Peter proclaimed, "and received from the Father the promised Holy Spirit and has poured out what you now see and hear."

As Peter continued to preach, Daniel was overcome by a familiar sensation in his spirit, a feeling that reminded him of the time that Jesus prayed over him and healed his body. In a flash, he felt as if the gates of Heaven had swung wide open – and just for the purpose of inviting him inside. And in that same instant, he suddenly knew what he must do.

A loud murmur arose among the others in the crowd, as they too experienced a rush of the Holy Spirit. Many fell to their knees, and one man shouted up to Peter, "What do we do now?"

Without hesitation, Peter said, "Repent and be baptized, every one of you, in the name of Jesus Christ for the forgiveness of your sins. And you will receive the gift of the Holy Spirit."

Many people in the crowd came to Peter and the other followers to be baptized that day. Later, Nathan reported that as many as three thousand people followed Peter's instructions and were added to the Jerusalem Church. As Daniel and Nathan walked back to Nathan's house in silence, Daniel finally stopped and handed the repaired tool to Nathan.

"Can I ask you a question?" Daniel asked.

"Of course."

"Do you think that Jesus, if he were still among us, would want me to go to Qumran?"

Without hesitation, Nathan said, "I'm sure of it."

Daniel issued a long sigh.

"Then I will go."

NORTH GEORGIA, 2008 CE

Six years had passed since Dave was confronted by the University Chancellor, and unwilling to risk his position, he had heeded the warning and discontinued his aggressive research into the Dead Sea Scrolls – at least publicly. After a rough start in his freshman year, Clint had finally made the adjustment and earned an engineering degree from Tech. After careful consideration and a job offer from a prestigious engineering firm in Atlanta, he decided against a baseball career and went to work full time. He lived in the suburbs, had a steady girl, but rarely came to visit Dave and Rebecca on weekends as he had done in college. Dave missed seeing him but knew he was busy.

During that same six years, Dave had completely lost contact with Randall, who was angry about the Chancellor's ultimatum and even angrier at Dave for not fighting them on the issue.

"You should tell them to take the job and shove it," Randall had said during their last phone conversation. "This is your life's mission, and it's not fair for them to take that away from you. Stand your ground, Dave. You can get another position elsewhere."

The remainder of the phone conversation was brief. Dave tried to explain the practical issues involved – his benefits package, losing his tenure, etc. – but Randall wouldn't have it. He accused Dave of being a coward and hung up the phone. The comment stung, and though Dave knew that Randall could fly off the handle too quickly sometimes, he felt he had gone too far this time. And for six years, the two men didn't speak, both too stubborn to call and clear the air between them.

In the meantime, during his free time, Dave continued to search the web for the latest journals and updates from archaeologists and biblical scholars, and he especially monitored the latest online articles and lectures from Professor Eisman. He immersed himself in the history – biblical and otherwise – of Qumran, the Dead Sea Scrolls, the Temple in Jerusalem, and the early Christian Church. Finally, halfway through another hot summer in 2008, while vacationing at St. Simon's Island on the Georgia coast, a chance encounter took place that became a turning point.

It was his first morning on the beach, and always the early riser, he reached the water just as the sun peaked over the horizon of the Atlantic Ocean. With a slight breeze in his face, Dave strolled along the shoreline searching for shells and nodding an occasional hello to joggers and other early morning walkers. By the time he reached the pier he had worked up an appetite, and the faint aroma of bacon sizzling on a grill somewhere in the village drew him in that direction. He found the breakfast café and settled at a table just outside the front door. He was studying the menu when he heard a voice behind him.

"Professor Walker!"

Dave turned to see a familiar face. It was Ravi, his former student, dressed in bathing suit, t-shirt and sandals and holding a take-home tray with two cups of tea. Dave stood to shake hands.

"Ravi, so good to see you. Care to join me?"

"I would love to, sir, but I have to get back to the hotel. My wife is waiting for me to return with tea. She couldn't come with me because the baby is still sleeping."

"So you're married and have a baby. That's terrific, Ravi. Did you finish school yet? The last I heard you were working on your masters' degree."

"Yes, I received my masters' degree four years ago and now I'm working on my doctorate in physics. Hopefully I can complete that by this time next year."

"That's fantastic," Dave said, "but I'm not surprised. I have to say, Ravi, after all these years, you are still the brightest student in any of my classes."

"And you are still my favorite professor," Ravi said. "I remember how willing you were to stay after class to answer all of my questions. By the way, how is your research coming along on the Dead Sea Scrolls? Have you written your book yet?"

Dave looked at him blankly. "My book?"

Ravi laughed. "Well, you were so immersed in the subject, I just assumed that one day you would write about it."

Dave hung his head. "No, to be honest, I discontinued my research into all of that."

Ravi was noticeably surprised. "But why? You were so enthusiastic about your latest discoveries, and you were planning a trip to Israel with your friend in Macon. What happened?"

"Well, it turns out that the university didn't share my enthusiasm, and for reasons I have yet to understand, they asked me to stop."

"I see. That's too bad. But sir, surely you will continue someday in the future… and soon, I hope. There is mystery at Qumran; you told me so yourself, and there is much to be learned from the

Scrolls that were discovered in the caves there. You can't stop when there is so much to discover. Do you remember what you once told me about my own research and discovery? You said that as physicists, our mission in life is to research and study, to postulate and then discover."

Dave nodded and said, "Yes, I did say that, and I still believe it, but I had to put that on hold for a while. I didn't want to lose my job, and…"

Dave paused before continuing. In the six years since it happened, he had spoken to no one about his strange encounter with the priest, or being followed by SUVs with tinted windows, or the threatening appearances of the man in black outside his classroom window. And now, standing face-to-face with this former student who was just starting out with his career and a new family, Dave realized that Ravi didn't need to hear all of his anxieties about the future or his personal conspiracy theories.

"You know, Ravi, you are absolutely right. It's time for me to get back to work on that. I've put it off too long. And I will indeed get to work on a book. That's a great idea."

"As I recall, you were also hoping to put together a video presentation about your findings. Did you complete that?"

"No, I never got to first base on that."

"Would you like my help? As part of my doctoral work, I have become quite an accomplished video producer."

"That would be great, but I really don't have money…"

"Oh, not for money, sir," Ravi interjected. "I just want to know what you know, and I think it would be a great learning experience for me."

"You're serious, aren't you?"

"Serious as a train wreck, as you used to say."

Dave extended his hand and they shook. "You, my friend, are an angel."

Ravi smiled and dug a card out of his wallet.

"I wish I could stay and talk more, Mr. Walker, but here's my contact information. I can get started anytime you're ready. And when you finish your book, I'll be the first in line to buy a copy."

After saying goodbyes, Ravi left, and Dave ordered breakfast. While he ate, he enjoyed the spectacular view of the ocean and the cool morning air. A breeze kicked up and he closed his eyes. Ravi had touched something inside, maybe his soul, and he realized that for six years, out of fear that he shouldn't rock the boat, he had abandoned his mission, maybe even his life's calling. He heard the tinkling of chimes hanging from oak trees in the restaurant's front yard; and they seemed to be sounding a gentle alarm to wake up, cast aside his fears and get moving again.

A week later, energized by his week at the beach and even more so by his encounter with Ravi, Dave drove to his first class and began to develop his strategy going forward. His first order of business would perhaps be the most difficult. Like it or not, he would have to confront Chancellor Laurens and tell him he was renewing his research, even if it meant his dismissal from the university. What happened after that would depend on the response; if he was forced to leave his faculty position, his loss of income until he found another position would force a change of lifestyle. So he decided to settle that issue first before turning Ravi loose on a video production.

After he reached his desk, and looked around the room that had served for so many years as his classroom, he suddenly felt familiar pangs of fear and anxiety. Was he nuts to be doing this? For a moment, he felt his resolve fading away, and he realized just how comfortable he had become. He had a great salary with benefits and retirement plans, and he had enjoyed a reputation in the academic community as an outstanding physics professor. Was he really going to walk down that hall to the chancellor's office and throw it all away? He looked out the window at the old oak tree and remembered that other problem – the warnings of danger from Randall and the mysterious men who had seemed to be threatening him with dire consequences if he continued to pursue the truth revealed in the Dead Sea Scrolls about the origins of the early Christian church. In that moment, Dave realized he was at a crossroads and that the easiest move he could make would be no move at all.

But then he remembered his encounter with Ravi. He remembered the message that seemed God-sent at the time, a message that had prompted him to risk everything for the sake of knowing the truth. His resolve returned, and he strode down the hall and walked into the administration offices just as Dr. Laurens was walking out of his office pushing a cart ahead of him loaded with the contents of his desk. Dave's timing could not have been better for inserting himself into an awkward moment. Laurens was leaving the University, and it was obvious from the scowl on his face that he was not happy about it.

As he passed Dave on his way out, he stopped and locked eyes with him.

"I can't believe it. They fired me!" he said.

"I'm sorry," Dave said weakly.

"They claim it's about budget cuts but I think somebody has blackballed me. If I find out who…"

Dave shrugged his shoulders and without thinking said, "Don't look at me."

Laurens gave him a "harrumph" and continued pushing his cart out into the hallway. Dave watched in stunned silence for a moment, and then turned to see Laurens' administrative assistant, who tried to suppress a smile.

"Is he really leaving?" Dave asked. "What happened? I had no idea."

"It's been in the works for some time," she explained. "The board finally had enough of him and voted him out. The newspapers have already started calling, so you can read all about it tomorrow. In the meantime, let me just say that this is starting out to be a great day for me and a great day for this university."

Dave laughed at the relief written on her face. "Yeah, I guess I can say the same. So who will be his replacement?"

"The word I'm getting is that the position will not be filled right away. For a while, his assistant, Mr. Cartwright, will step in as interim. I can't wait; he's a wonderful man and the opposite of Laurens in just about every way imaginable."

"Yes, John Cartwright is perfect for the position. I wouldn't mind if he wound up there permanently."

"You and a lot of other people. So, Mr. Walker, now that the monster is gone, what can I do for you?"

Dave grinned at her. "Nothing. I think the board has already taken care of my problem."

Back at his desk, Dave leaned back in his chair and marveled at what was happening. Just a week after the encounter with Ravi and his subsequent recommitment to resuming his research, and now the ouster of Laurens, it seemed to Dave that God was smiling on his decision to move forward. His enthusiasm renewed, he decided that his next step would be to review all of his old notes and develop a hit list of places he would need to visit and people he would need to connect with for additional insight. He remembered that before their last phone call six years ago, he and Randall had planned to visit Israel. Whether Randall would forgive and forget was yet to be determined, and whether he would go with him was therefore in doubt, but for sure a trip to Qumran would be critical.

For the rest of that day, Dave taught his classes as usual but struggled to stay engaged. His juices were flowing again, and he couldn't wait until his last class was over so he could dive back into the mysteries of Qumran. When the time finally came, and he began to review his notes, he noticed an article copied from Professor Eisman's website, an article that debunked the authenticity of the James Ossuary that had been discovered years earlier and that Randall had been so excited about.

Of all the people studying the first century community at Qumran, none had produced as much information and detailed analyses as Eisman. Dave wrote his name at the top of his hit list of people to contact. And as he leaned back and thought about it, he was suddenly struck with a crazy idea. He looked at his watch and realized that it was still mid-afternoon on the west coast where Eisman lived.

"I'll just call the guy," he said to himself, and after digging up Eisman's phone number, he placed the call. To his surprise, Eisman answered right away, but he was straightforwardly blunt and hesitant to agree to Dave's request to an interview.

"Are you a treasure hunter?" he asked.

"No, I'm a physics professor by profession, but my avocation is researching and writing about biblical history, especially the centuries before and after Christ. I've read all of your articles online and watched your videos, and I would like to ask a few quick questions. I won't take much of your time."

"What do you plan to do with my answers?"

"I've started developing a story that I plan to turn into a book," Dave said. "Over the past decade or so, I've become convinced that there's a story waiting to be told about Qumran and its role in the history of the early Christian church."

Impressed with the answer, Eisman agreed to a few minutes. Because Dave knew of Eisman's insistence that James was the brother of Jesus and the key figure in the formation of the Early Church, his first question was in reference to the discovery of the James ossuary that Randall had been so excited about.

"I read your article about the James ossuary, and…"

"It's a fake," Eisman said interrupting. "As I wrote in the article, there were a few characteristics that made me suspicious about its authenticity, but the best evidence against it is the inscription itself, which reads, 'Jacob the son of Joseph, the brother of Jesus.' If the inscription had been written at that time, it would not have been so explicit about the relationship between James and Jesus. It was not uncommon to write the deceased's name as the son of someone, but to inscribe that he was the brother of someone... well, it just wasn't done. The more you look at that inscription, the more it seems as if it were inscribed to prove something to a modern audience, people like us who are schooled in the gospels. If it had simply said 'Jacob son of Joseph', it might have passed muster, although there are problems with that too. So forget about the ossuary; it doesn't matter anyway. James and Jesus were historical figures, they were brothers, and whether the ossuary is real or not doesn't change that."

"That's a great answer," Dave said. "Like you, I'm more convinced than ever that they were brothers, and that they spent their early years at Qumran, training for ministry."

"That's possible. So is that what your book will be about, Jesus and James?"

"Like I said, I'm still fishing and not sure what my thesis is; I only know that as I continue my research, the story will emerge. A great writer once said, 'Stories are not made up; they are discovered.' I'm still in the discovery mode."

"Have you discovered the Copper Scroll yet?"

"Yes, I've discussed that with my good friend, Randall. He knows biblical history like the back of his hand and has been a great help to me in my research and discovery. He told me about the Copper Scroll, and has his own theories."

"Is he a treasure hunter?"

"No, he's retired and lives out in the country. In fact, his health is failing and he never travels. You're really worried about treasure hunters, aren't you?"

"Yes, I am. And you should be too. I'm not a conspiracy theorist, but I also recognize the power of wealth. Not only are there a number of veteran treasure hunters interested in the Scrolls, so are a lot of very wealthy individuals and religious institutions that worry about being in second place in the hunt. If there's real treasure to be found, and if the Copper Scroll is the map, they will stop at nothing to find it first. There's a lot more at stake than the value of the treasure, though."

"What do you mean?" Dave asked.

"The institutional church discounts the significance of Qumran in early Christian history and prefers to bury what happened there. The story of the Dead Sea Scrolls includes conspiracy of the highest order and involves some of the most powerful people and organizations in the world."

Dave flashed back to the strange events six years ago – the theft of his laptop and smashed windows, the man in black under the tree, the priest at the roadside cafe, the black SUV that was tailing him on the highway.

"Have you been threatened in the past because of your views?" he asked.

"Yes, plenty of times, and my wife worries about that. But at the end of the day, not enough people are paying attention to this stuff for it to matter. I've rattled the cage some with all of my writings, but I'm just a ripple in a huge ocean. Now if you're going after the treasure, that's another story. That might get their interest."

"I'm not interested in the treasure to become wealthy," Dave said. "I'm in good shape financially. My mission is to learn the truth about the Early Church, which will help me fully understand my Christian heritage. My only interest in the treasure is its relevance to that mission. If my research takes me down a trail that leads to the treasure, then it will only be because God wants it to be found."

"Well that all sounds fine, but I still don't understand exactly what you're up to," Eisman said.

"Frankly, I'm not exactly certain myself. I just know that I need to keep digging, so to speak, and keep putting pieces of the puzzle together. And I believe you can help me understand better how some of those pieces fit. Is there any chance that you can come to Atlanta for a weekend and let me interview you on camera?"

"Are you serious?" he asked.

"Serious as a train wreck," Dave answered. "You can stay at our house here on the lake. There's plenty of room and my wife will feed you some of the best Southern cooking you've ever had. And of course I'll pay your airfare."

"All of that sounds tempting," he said. "But I have to tell you, I get a lot of calls from some real religious nut cases. Of course, they don't usually offer to fly me from L.A. to Atlanta."

"So you'll come?"

"Well, I'm getting to the age where flying is such a hassle and sitting cramped up for so long is difficult."

"Would it help if I bought Business Class seats?"

"Okay, book it."

During the few weeks before Eisman's scheduled visit, Dave worked with Ravi to assimilate all of the information he had gathered over the years, and they videotaped a mock presentation with Dave outlining his findings and conclusions on camera. While it was clearly just a beginning, the video was well-produced, thanks to Ravi. And it was Ravi who challenged Dave to broaden the scope of the presentation by videotaping other experts in early church history. Dave realized he was right, and after getting Eisman's consent, he called Ravi to ask if he would videotape the interviews. Dave's son, Clint, now twenty-four, had stopped by for a visit and overheard the conversation with Ravi.

"Dad, I can do PA if it's on the weekend," he said while Dave was discussing details of the shoot.

Dave nodded and said, "Ravi, my son Clint says he'll do PA. I don't know what that is exactly, but I'm sure he's good at it."

Two weeks later, Dave picked up Eisman at the Atlanta Airport and drove him to his house at Lake Lanier. He introduced him to

Rebecca and Clint, who was spending the weekend at his parents' house. After Dave and Clint took the professor on a quick boat ride around the lake, the group spent the remainder of the afternoon in deep discussion about topics as scientifically far-reaching as quantum physics and as folkish as bass fishing in the South. By evening, the dialog had shifted completely to the key issues and controversies surrounding the Dead Sea Scrolls.

"I hate to cut this conversation short," Dave said just as Eisman was getting cranked up, "but let's save this for tomorrow when the camera is rolling."

The following day turned out to be a bright and beautiful fall Saturday. Clearly excited about the opportunity, Ravi arrived early with his camera and set about staging the interview locations. But the smell of bacon cooking wafted down the hall and drew him away from his duties just in time to come face to face with a sleepy-eyed Clint, who had just ambled out of his bedroom.

"Hiya, you must be Ravi."

"And you must be Clint."

"Are you as crazy as my father about all this Qumran stuff?"

"Yes, maybe more so. The more I learn, the more I want to know."

Clint scratched his head. "I guess that's a good thing."

After a hearty breakfast, Dave decided to take Eisman on another boat ride, but this time with the video crew. Before the cameras rolled, however, Eisman wanted clarification.

"I still don't understand exactly what you're planning to say in your book or documentary," Eisman said. "I mean, I don't know what slant you're going to take and how you want to use me in this. And before I keep spouting off, I think I need to get a better understanding about that."

"Fair enough," Dave said. "It's my belief that the Jewish Christians at Qumran were indeed the architects of a first century movement that formed the foundations of the Christian faith. And for a lot of reasons, I believe it is important for all Christians to have a clear understanding about that. And the more I dig into the Scrolls and first century history, the more convinced I am that there is an important message for all of us, Christians or otherwise."

"I hope you're not one of those nuts who say we're living in the last days," Eisman said.

"No, just the opposite, actually. I believe the last days that the prophets and Jesus referred to occurred in the first century before Rome destroyed Jerusalem in 70 AD. And that puts me at odds with mainstream Christian theology, especially those churches that preach and teach that the Second Coming of Christ is imminent, that the world is teetering on the brink of disaster, and that Christians will be rescued through a mysterious rapture."

"Well, I certainly don't go for all of that, but I have to say that my general view of world history – past and future – is not very pretty. But that has nothing to do with prophecy; I just don't believe that God is or ever has been in the business of saving souls or saving us from our own human tendencies to self-destruct."

"In light of world events, I understand your pessimism," Dave said. "Do you mind if we roll the camera now?"

Eisman nodded a yes, and Ravi got the two of them together in the shot and gave Dave a thumbs up.

"So you were saying the Apocalypse could happen before we get back to the dock?" Dave joked.

Eisman laughed, but then furrowed his eyebrows. "Apocalyptic thinking is at the core of most Middle Eastern religions. Even today in the 21st Century, huge numbers of otherwise sane people still believe the end of the world is drawing near in accordance with the prophecies of their ancient religious leaders. And of course the extremists in those religions are all busy doing their part to bring about the end. That's been going on all the way back to Old Testament days.

"And it was true in the century before Christ, but the trouble for Jews then was as much political and nationalistic in nature as it was about religion. A century-and-a-half before Christ, Israel was once again under foreign domination, this time Greek. And a schism developed among the Jewish leadership between the 'Hellenized' Jews and the devout orthodox Jews who would die before bending their knee to a Greek god."

"Good for them," Dave said.

"If you say so," Eisman said. "Anyway, not long after the recapture of Jerusalem around 165 BCE by the Maccabees, some of the more militant of the victors, led by Judas Maccabee, wanted to press on and extend their political and religious influence to foreigners. Others took the view that the revolt was about religious freedom, and were satisfied with cleansing the Temple and re-dedicating themselves to traditional worship. Those differing views became a rift that continued until Judas died and his younger brother, Jonathan, who was high priest, also became commander of the army. But he wasn't the fighter his brother was, and he set about making treaties with foreigners, and the rift became an ongoing schism."

"I'm familiar with the Maccabees," Dave said. "Was there a clear connection between the Maccabees and Qumran?"

"Yes, I believe there was, but the best person to talk to you about all that is Victor Jones. He's the old guy in Texas who a lot of people say Indiana Jones was based on. Actually, he was formerly a Baptist preacher who now calls himself a non-Jewish believer in Judaism. He became fascinated by all of this stuff, became a sort of biblical archaeologist, and started digging in the Judean Desert around Qumran. He believes that the Scrolls were written by Maccabean Jews."

"He sounds fascinating," Dave said.

"He's a character, but he's brilliant. And he's got credibility. He and others believe the list in the Copper Scroll is an account of

treasures from the First Temple, which were hidden by the prophet
Jeremiah and his contemporaries before Nebuchadnezzar and the
Babylonians sacked Jerusalem around 500 BCE. Victor's crew found
a jug of anointing oil in one of his digs at the Cave of the Column
that was proven to be the same oil used as the ritual incense of the
First Temple. He believed he was hot on the trail of finding the rest
of the treasure, including the Ark of the Covenant, when the Israeli
authorities halted his work."

"You're right, I need to talk to him," Dave said.

"I'll give you his phone number."

"Hey guys, the camera's still rolling," Ravi said. "Let's get
back on point."

"So, Professor Eisman," Dave said, "as we said at the
beginning of this interview, my mission is to gain a better
understanding of the Qumran community, because I believe what
happened there is the key to understanding our Christian roots, if you
will. And after looking at some of the evidence, and putting two and
two together, I believe that during the years when we know nothing
historically or biblically about the life of Jesus, between age 12 and 30,
he was there at Qumran training."

"We don't have a record of it, but he could have been," Eisman
said. "If you read my books, then you know that I believe his brother
James to be the Righteous Teacher mentioned in the Dead Sea Scrolls
found at Qumran."

"I did read your book," Dave said, "and I agree with you that
James was the Righteous Teacher. But what were he and the others at
Qumran up to? What was their mission? From the descriptions of daily
life at Qumran, it sounds like they spent all their time praying and
singing hymns and such. And of course, writing the Scrolls. But I just
believe there's a lot more to them than meets the eye; certainly a lot
more than most Christians know about them."

"Well, if you really want to understand what they were up to,"

Eisman said. "then you have to look at the historical context. Then you have to look at what was important to the Jews who lived in the wilderness and desert camps, and why they were out there in the first place. They were religious and pious and all that, but I wouldn't describe them as passive or practicing the 'love-your-enemies' kind of theology that is credited to Jesus. That's more of a Hellenistic, Aristotlean idea anyway."

"So how would you describe the Jews at Qumran?"

"In the Scrolls, it's clear that they were big on purity, and we know that was a rule in all the wilderness camps. It was hugely important. And here's why. In the War Scroll, there are references to the wrath of God, the battle of God, and so on. They weren't just sitting idly by out there and happy to turn the other cheek to the Romans. No, they desperately wanted the Romans driven out of Israel, so they could regain control of their land and reestablish their 'undefiled' Jewish traditions in the Temple."

"So among other things, you think they were also preparing for battle?" Dave asked.

"Yes, but not in the traditional sense. They knew they were no match for the Roman army, but they thought they had a secret weapon, an atomic bomb, if you will."

"And what was that?"

"Holy angels. Around chapters 7, 8 or 9, the War Scroll gets very serious about maintaining purity in the camps, with restrictions on menstruating women in the camp or male ejaculations or anything that would keep the camp from being perfectly pure. They had this crazy idea that the holy angels could not abide with human pollution, but if they kept the camps perfectly pure, then the holy angels would come and fight with them, granting them the ultimate victory."

"So, the group at Qumran believed that holy angels would actually appear in their camps to help them wage war against the Romans?" Dave asked.

"Yes, you have to remember that they were messianic and believed in all that stuff. The War Scroll cites the Star Prophecy, the whole thing about a Star that rises from Jacob with a scepter that will rule the world. That Star Prophecy shows up several times in the Scrolls. For Christians, Jesus is the Star, of course, and that's why there's a star over Bethlehem when he is born. But James' interpretation of the Star Prophecy describes an angelic host that comes down out of the clouds."

"So do you think the War Scroll is written from James' point of view?"

"I think the War Scroll is what the Early Church writers were trying to present as James' proclamation of the Son of Man coming on the clouds of heaven. And the clouds of heaven are the angelic host. The imagery that's used in the Scrolls to describe these angels mirrors what is written in the Book of James. He says their coming will be like a torrent of rain that will come down out of the clouds and spread judgment on all of the people of the world – both the righteous and the evil ones. So these are not the meek and mild angels we usually think of when we imagine angels. No, these angels are coming down to engage in a holy war, like the Four Horsemen of the Apocalypse."

After the videotaping session, Rebecca called everyone to the table. Ravi packed his gear and reluctantly said his goodbyes, disappointed that he couldn't stay through dinner. To Dave's surprise, Clint asked during the meal if he could ride along when Dave took Eisman back to the airport.

"I'll do one better," Dave replied, "You can drive."

Halfway through the meal, Clint tried to steer the conversation back to Qumran, but Rebecca wouldn't have it.

"Give the man a break," she said as she served a second helping of mashed potatoes on Eisman's plate. Conversation for the rest of meal centered around Eisman's family life and his world travels. Afterwards, Eisman gathered his belongings, said goodby to Rebecca, and the three men climbed into the car with Clint at the wheel and Eisman in the passenger seat.

"I'm fascinated by your findings, Professor," Clint admitted after they were on the road.

"What part of it is most fascinating to you?" Eisman asked.

"I guess it would be what I would call the 'real time' factor. Clearly, the writers of the Scrolls were writing to the people of that time, and I can't accept that their warnings were intended for us two thousands years later. And I especially can't accept the modern-day Christian writers and television personalities who have built empires around their 'last days' theologies."

"Yes, it's become big business," Eisman said. "Millions of dollars are at stake if they are proven wrong and our version makes its way into the mainstream. What we're saying makes them very angry."

"Angry enough to threaten us, you think?" Dave asked.

"Or worse," Eisman replied. "They're all lunatics anyway."

As they neared the airport, Dave reminded the professor that while he had given him a whole lot more pieces to the Qumran puzzle, he still didn't have all the answers.

"I'd like call on you in the future and possibly work together, even if our individual purposes are in different directions. In fact, I want to go to Israel with a video crew, and it would be great if you came along."

"Count me in," Eisman said. "But only if you buy Business Class tickets again."

With the videotaped Eisman interviews "in the can," Dave's thoughts turned to his friend and colleague Randall. A few days later, he dialed Randall's number, and got an answer after the second ring.

"Hello, Dave," Randall said. "Are you calling to apologize?"

"If that's what it takes, yes. I'd like to come down today. Do you have time for a visit?"

Randall laughed. "Time is about all I have. See you when you get here."

When Dave pulled up to the front of the house two hours later, he saw Randall already on the front porch waiting for him.

"You don't look a day older than the last time I saw you," Dave said as he gave his old friend a bear hug and took a chair across from him.

"You do," Randall said. "Look, I'm sorry for being such an old cuss back then, but…"

Dave cut him off. "Randall, there's no need for apologies. You were right; I abandoned my mission because I was afraid, but things have changed, and now I want to get back to work. And I want to work with you again, if you're still interested in pursuing this."

"Hell yeah, I'm interested. I never stopped pursuing it. Unlike you, I don't have anything to lose, although for a while there, I did get a little nervous that somebody was out to hurt me over this."

"What happened?"

"Well, it wasn't long after your last visit. I had a few phone calls from someone who kept hanging up, and then I ran into this Catholic priest one day…"

"Don't tell me it was at a restaurant!"

"No, I don't go out to eat much. I was at the grocery store, his cart bumped into mine, and the next thing I knew he was buying me coffee at McDonald's. He was a nice fellow at first, but then he got real strange at the end there when I starting talking about the Jewish Christians."

"Randall, that's the same guy that followed me into a restaurant at an Interstate exit after I left here the last time. Did you see him anymore after that?"

"No, and at first that didn't bother me. As you know, I'm pretty good at pissing people off, so I just chalked it up to that. But then, the more I thought about him and the questions he was asking, the more I started thinking that running into him that day was no accident."

"It wasn't an accident, Randall. There are some people out there, and they may be backed by some very powerful people and organizations, who must have gotten wind of you – probably through those presentations you used to make and the articles you've had published. And I think that guy was sent to check us out."

"Who do you think they are?"

"He was Catholic, so I have to think maybe some organization connected with the Catholic Church. But I suppose that could have been a front. The fact that we haven't heard anything out of them since tells me they don't consider us a threat anymore."

"That's too bad," Randall said, shaking his head. "That means we haven't been doing our job. And it's true. Frankly, I'm getting to a place physically where I can't get out to speaking engagements anymore, and when the heat was turned up on you, you… well… you know."

Dave laughed. "Yeah, I turned chicken. Look, I'm back on the case, and I hope you'll come back too."

"I never left."

Dave acknowledged his point with a nod.

"What now?" Randall asked.

"First, I'm going to Texas to visit Indiana Jones."

"What?"

"His real name is Victor Jones, the guy that Robert Eisman told me about who has done a lot of excavation and research in Israel. I plan to videotape that, and maybe you can help me develop some questions to ask. And after that, I want to go to Israel. I know you've been there plenty, but I feel a very strong pull to go there and see it for myself."

"Count me in, partner. I think I've got one more trip in me."

On the drive home, Dave felt good about himself and the progress he was now making. He felt he had regained much of the momentum and was once again on a mission, one that was becoming clearer with each passing day. Then, to his utter amazement, his cell phone rang, and when he looked at the display, the number was blocked. He answered it, and his heart skipped a beat. There was no one on the other line, but just like six years ago, a second before the line went dead, he heard a man clearing his throat.

"That does it," Dave said to himself. He pulled off the road, parked his car and searched his cell phone contacts for a name, and finding it, called the number. He got an answer right away.

"Harold, this is Dave Walker. I think I need your help."

QUMRAN, 55 CE

The early morning sun peaked over the shadowy cliffs that lined the eastern shore of the Dead Sea. Brilliant rays of sunlight reached the spot where Daniel, now a strong and weathered man of thirty-seven years, knelt on a rocky outcrop overlooking the Qumran compound, deeply immersed in his morning prayers. A rooster crowed somewhere in the distance, but otherwise all was silent except the whisper of his voice.

I give thanks to You, O Lord, for you establish my foot upon level ground, You have set me by a fountain which flows on a dry land, a spring of water in a desolate land, a well-watered garden and a pool. And you, my God, have helped my soul, and You have exalted my horn on high. I shine forth in sevenfold light, in light which You have established for Your glory.

After a moment of quiet mediation, Daniel opened his eyes and gathered in the expansive view that lay before him. In the near distance he could see the craggy cliffs that stretched away from him into a half-circle before their sandy-bronze slopes descended to the shores of the sea. Across the sea and beyond the starkly chiseled shores was the barren land of Jordan. He shielded his eyes and watched the sunlight's reflections dancing on the blue surface of earth's saltiest sea. During his years with the "saints" at Qumran, he had faithfully risen every morning and recited his thanksgiving prayers at this same spot, in keeping with the covenant and traditions of the Community Rule that outlined the daily routines of members who lived there.

Like others who had chosen the solemn, disciplined life at Qumran, Daniel had dedicated himself to the monastic life at Qumran, and he had subscribed to every discipline and followed every directive from his instructors. Unlike the others, he had risen quickly through the ranks and become one of the Righteous Teacher's most trusted scribes. Most importantly, Daniel had just the day before reached a milestone in his development on his way to becoming a high priest, having successfully completed the seven steps that defined a high priest at Qumran.

Daniel raised his arms to the heavens, closed his eyes and meditated on the seven spiritual virtues that now described him – humility, patience, abundant compassion, perpetual goodness, insight, understanding and wisdom. Soon he would be elevated to the position of high priest, after which he would be recognized by the rest of the community as a saint of the highest order, worthy to lead others out of the darkness in the world and into the light of God's eternal salvation.

"God's light is eternal," James had said in his talks to the gathered community, "and it will never go away. As my brother said, 'All who come to God will be received into that light and will not perish when the destruction comes'."

As he had every morning, Daniel ended his prayers with thoughts of his mother, Azara, and he remembered her telling him as a boy that God would spare the Jews if just one remained faithful to the Law of Moses. And in Qumran, there were many who had done so. He had not seen her in many years, and it saddened him that she had lived all these years alone. On occasion, he would hear how she was faring from the Qumran leaders who frequently visited the churches in Jerusalem to distribute scrolls and receive support from them. Still, hearing was not enough; he yearned to see her in person. And today, finally, he would. James, the Righteous Teacher and brother of Jesus, after talking it over with the other priests, had granted him permission to visit her for a few days.

His prayers ended, Daniel returned to the central area at Qumran where he drew water out of the cistern and bathed before retreating to the inner scriptorium. It was there that he and the other scribes performed their tedious tasks of copying sacred scrolls, which would be distributed to the saints who were scattered throughout Palestine and beyond. It was arduous and exacting work, as the requirements for creating perfect documents were stringent. Although the Qumran community constituted the unofficial headquarters for the Jewish Christian movement, they nevertheless maintained their adherence to the disciplines and requirements handed down from the days of Moses. And though they believed that their Messiah had established a new law, the Law of Christ, they continued to believe they would honor God by following the Jewish traditions to the letter.

"I did not come to abolish the law or the prophets," Jesus had said on the mountain that day when the Healer smiled on Daniel and healed his leg. "I did not come to abolish them, I came to fulfill them."

So Daniel and the other scribes performed their tasks precisely as Jewish custom prescribed. Before a scroll could be written, the animal skin had to be thoroughly cleansed. Each column of writing could have no less than forty-eight and no more sixty lines. The ink had to be black and specially prepared. Every word written had to be spoken aloud as they were written, and as Daniel had learned years earlier from Simeon, his pen had to be wiped and his entire body washed before writing the most holy name of God, YHVH.

Within thirty days of being written, each scroll had to be inspected, and if as many as three pages required correction, it had to be completely rewritten. If two letters touched each other anywhere in the document, it had to be rewritten. Each letter, word and paragraph had to be counted, and the middle paragraph, word and letter had to correspond exactly to those of the original document. When it was finally completed, the document could only be stored in sacred locations such as a synagogue.

With such reverence given to the creation of the scrolls, and in such a solemn environment as the scriptorium, it is no wonder that the Jewish Christians considered the documents to be holy literature. They were direct links to God, who inspired the leaders of the movement to spread His message that Jesus was the fulfillment of His promise for salvation. And it was up to the scribes to produce enough scrolls to accommodate the growing numbers of converts who were spreading across the region and beyond.

But on that day, Daniel's excitement about making the visit to Azara would make it difficult for him to focus on his work. It had been so long, and news of late had been sparing because of increased tension between the Jewish Christians and the Temple leaders. Just a week earlier, there had been threats from the Temple leaders about James and his followers. As he walked across the courtyard to the scriptorium, he heard his name and turned to see James motioning him over to sit with him in the shade of the tent.

These were the moments he cherished, when the Righteous Teacher would talk to him one-on-one. No one knew Daniel's heart better than James, and he was honored that the revered leader at Qumran took such an interest in him. He hurried to his tent and sat cross-legged facing the Righteous Teacher, who offered him a piece of bread. He took the bread, and they ate together silently for a moment. Like his brother Jesus, James had dark, penetrating eyes that were both searching and compassionate, and like Jesus, he alternated between meditative silence and reflective discourse.

"You have come a long way here," James said. "You have risen through the ranks as quickly as anyone has before."

"Surely not as quickly as your brother," Daniel said. "I've heard the story of his visit to the Temple when he was twelve, and how he amazed the teachers with his knowledge of the Scriptures."

James nodded and laughed. "No, you're right. Maybe not as quickly as Jesus, but every year since you first joined us here and were initiated into the Covenant, you have been judged by the saints to have gained great knowledge and understanding of the Laws of Moses. Your conduct has remained pure and undefiled, and your work as blacksmith and scribe has been exemplary. By every measure, you have grown into a great man of God and worthy of becoming a high priest."

James dipped his cup in a bucket of water and offered it to Daniel.

"I've just received word from Paul in Ephesus. There are many more being added to the church, and with that comes a growing responsibility to prepare more scrolls for them."

"Teacher, did you know Paul before his conversion, when his name was Saul?"

James laughed. "Every Jew in Jerusalem knew Saul. He was chief henchman for the Temple Guard, a villain who stood by and watched while our brother Stephen was stoned. And just two years later, he left me for dead at the bottom of those steps."

James placed a hand on Daniel's shoulder. "Then, after he learned that you and the others had rescued and taken me into the wilderness alive, he convinced the high priest at the Temple to grant him permission to seek us out. He was angry that I had survived the fall and thought he would find me in Damascus."

"But you were here."

"Yes, he followed the wrong road, the one leading to Damascus. Daniel, some are saying that Paul is not teaching the truth. They find it hard to believe that someone so cruel to our brothers and sisters can be trusted. But I tell you now that Paul is living proof that God will work out his plan in his own way, using whoever he chooses to accomplish that plan. Because he made that wrong turn, Paul was struck by a blinding light that illuminated his soul and brought him into the presence of the risen Christ. At that very moment, his eyes were opened – really opened – for the first time, allowing him to see what we often sing about in our 'Songs of the Sabbath Sacrifice,' that this life is only a pale reflection of the unseen greater reality that awaits all of us."

"Was the light Yahweh?"

James hesitated, then stood up and motioned to Daniel to follow him.

"Come with me; I want to show you something."

Daniel followed him to a high rock that overlooked Qumran, a point where they could see much of Israel's geography in every direction. After catching his breath, James pointed to the north, where the dawn's early light illuminated the snow-capped eastern face of the farthest mountain, creating the illusion that it was being spotlighted.

"Yahweh is the light, the same light that shone so brilliantly on the Holy Mountain when my brother was transfigured. Sometimes, when I look in that direction at night, I see that light still emanating from its peak."

James paused and looked northward toward to brilliant light emanating from a distant mountain.. "Just before that mysterious night, Daniel, my brother Jesus stood at the foot of the mountain, and told Peter, James and John that he would build his church on the great rock that towered behind him. On that mountain, Yahweh revealed to my brother a well-kept secret, one that he has revealed to me and I will soon reveal to you, the moment that you have completed your final step to becoming a priest."

James placed his hands on Daniel's shoulders. Daniel sensed a new urgency in his voice, and his penetrating eyes and solemn expression indicated the importance of his next words.

"There is much work to be done before then. While you are in

Jerusalem, go to visit Nathan. He will be your contact with the leaders of the underground churches there. But first, visit with your mother, who I have seen many times at the Temple courtyard. She is a devoted woman of God, a devout follower of the Laws of Moses. The Temple of God is made of such strong saints, Daniel, but the Temple no longer resides within the walls of a structure in Jerusalem. As my brother said so often, those walls will soon be crumbling, and there will not be one stone left on another. But God's Temple will still exist in the hearts and minds of those who are rescued."

"What about this place? Will Qumran stand, or will it fall too."

"For many years, Qumran has been a temporary way station on the path to righteousness. My brother, and John the Baptist before him, came here not to make it their homes but to prepare for their ministries. Qumran will not stand, but if we remain diligent in our preparations, the Roman soldiers will find no one here to conquer."

Daniel looked up to see that James was smiling.

"Go see your mother," he said. "And give her my love."

By mid-morning Daniel was on his way to Jerusalem, and though he had walked the 14-mile stretch a dozen times over the past 20 years, and though he was returning to the city of his youth, he still felt like a visitor on his way to a strange place he didn't know. Azara still lived in the same small house in one of Jerusalem's poorer districts, but to Daniel it didn't seem poor at all. As he turned the corner and saw the house, he was flooded with memories from his youth. This was where he had played in the streets with his friend, Baram. It was where his father had been a proud, hardworking blacksmith and devout follower of the Law of Moses. But it was also in that house that the Romans had come in the middle of the night and forever changed his life and the lives of those who were closest to him.

Before the images of that terrible night had time to sink in, Daniel's heart leaped at the sight of his mother standing in the doorway. Overcome with joy, she ran to greet him in the street, and as she held him as tight as her frail arms allowed, she burst into tears. Then, gathering her composure, she held him at arm's length to get a better look.

"You have become your father!" she said. She pulled on his beard and laughed. "He would have been proud of you."

Daniel could see that her face was lined with deep wrinkles and her shoulders appeared a bit more slumped than the last time he had visited. But her eyes still sparkled and her mind was still sharp.

"You look well," Daniel said as they walked together into the house.

"I'm old," she said, "but I'm getting along all right. I'm still sewing to make a little money, and the Christians who meet at Nathan's home come by every other day to check on me."

Although his visit with Azara was short, he savored every moment of it. For three full days he walked with her to the well in the mornings and visited the small group of Christians who met at Nathan's house. Nathan was old now and had lost much of his strength, but his mind was still sharp. No longer able to perform manual labor, he had become a skilled leatherworker, scratching out a living for himself and his wife, and always finding enough extra to share with Azara.

"I don't leave the house very often," he told Daniel, "but it just means I have more time to study the Scriptures."

Daniel received a warm welcome from the Jerusalem church, and they drowned him with questions about his experiences at Qumran. He explained to them that in his first year he had served the community as a blacksmith while he began his studies to become a scribe. James the brother of Jesus had noticed his aptitude for writing and encouraged him to apprentice under the other scribes. In short time he had developed his craft to the point that he devoted most of his time during the day drafting scrolls or copying existing ones. When Nathan handed him one of the scrolls given to his small group, they were thrilled to learn that it had been penned by his hand.

"Daniel is being modest in his account," Nathan said. "His extraordinary faith and diligence has strengthened the great work that is being done at Qumran. Following in the footsteps of the Righteous Teacher, he has completed the seven steps required to become a high priest, and is now chief among us tonight. I've known him since he was a boy, and I'm proud that James has sent him to us with an urgent message."

Nathan turned to Daniel and nodded.

"James sends his greetings," Daniel said to the group, "and has asked me to remind you of his brother's warnings. The time is drawing near when judgment will come for those in the Temple who have defiled the Law of Moses."

"What should we do to prepare?" Nathan asked.

"Continue in your prayers and scripture reading," Daniel replied, "and continue to share all that you own. Remember the message given to us through Jesus that we are to love God and each other, and if we are faithful, we will experience salvation. Even now, preparations are underway for the Church to escape the imminent destruction."

On the morning of his departure, Daniel ate his last meal with Azara. While she had been thrilled to see him, she couldn't hide her sadness, knowing she wouldn't see her son again for a long while. The visit had been brief, but long enough for Daniel to feel satisfied that his mother was living comfortably and being cared for by the Jewish Christians who met at Nathan's house. After a long hug and promises that he would return within a year, he left her standing in the doorway, smiling through her tears.

On his way out of Jerusalem, he stopped by one more time to visit with Nathan, who was working on a leather piece for a woman who was waiting just outside his door. She looked up as Daniel approached and broke into a broad smile that seemed strangely familiar to him.

"Good morning, Daniel!" Nathan said.

"Good morning. I came to say goodbye and to thank you again for taking such good care of my mother."

"She is a good woman and no trouble at all," Nathan said, then pointing to the woman added, "By the way, say hello to my friend, Leah."

"Hi Daniel," she said. "You don't remember me, do you?"

He studied her for a moment but couldn't make the connection.

"I am Leah, Baram's little sister."

Daniel was stunned. A flood of memories washed over him, and all he could do was stare.

"I wouldn't expect you to remember," she said. "It was so long ago."

"Leah! Of course I remember you. But I thought you had been…"

"Yes, I was made a slave, and so was Baram but in another household. Many years ago, Baram escaped and came for me. We left in the middle of the night and found our way into the hills where we lived in caves for a long time with others who were hiding from the Romans. A year later, when I felt it was safe, I returned to Jerusalem. But no one knows who I am, other than the people in Nathan's church. I live with his cousin not far from here and tell anyone who asks that I am a part of their family."

As she talked, Daniel stared at her, marveling at how she had retained her youthful appearance in spite of her years and all that she had endured. She caught his stare and blushed.

"And Baram?" Daniel asked. "Is he in Jerusalem too?"

"No, it's not safe for him here. He still lives in the hill country, with rebels who are planning to rise up and fight the Romans."

"Our battle is not with the Romans," Nathan said but then spit on the ground and added, "not that I wouldn't enjoy spitting on the graves of the men who took your families away in the middle of the night."

"Nathan's right," Daniel said. "It was hard to see that when I was young. I've always hated the Romans, but my mind has been illuminated by the truth of the Scriptures. The story of our people has reached a turning point. The great storm that Jesus warned us about is at our doorstep, and the people of Israel are not prepared because they blame the Romans. As James says to us so often, 'We don't need to worry about the Romans because God's holy angels will defeat them when the time is right.'"

"I know," Leah said, "but Baram and the other men around him are too angry with the Romans to see it. They believe they are the instruments of God, his Holy Army, and they are training for battle. Baram believes that the day of reckoning is at hand, as Jesus prophesied, but he believes salvation depends on how well they prepare for battle."

"Where do they live? How do they survive?" Daniel asked.

Leah bowed her head before speaking. "They live in caves, and they depend on farmers and family to bring them food occasionally. When they have to, they eat berries and insects. It is a miserable existence, even if it is a noble one."

Daniel looked distressed, but Leah said, "He's okay, Daniel. He's where he wants to be – just like you in Qumran. And he's strong."

"How did you know I was in Qumran?"

"Nathan has told me all about you."

Nathan looked up from his work and laughed. "And she has told me all about you when you were a young boy."

"I have nothing but good memories of you," Leah said. "Even as a little boy you were kind to me. I remember once when Baram was making fun of me, you made him stop. I never forgot it."

It was Daniel's turn to blush. Lost for words, they were rescued by Nathan. "I've got a pot of stew and some fresh bread. There's plenty for all of us."

"I should go," Daniel said. "I am expected back at Qumran."

Nathan read the disappointment on Leah's face. He held up the pouch.

"I am finished with this," he said. "Perhaps Daniel could walk with you back to your home. I'm sure the two of you have some catching up to do."

Daniel smiled knowingly at his old friend. Nathan rose and gave him a bear hug.

"Seeing you again has warmed my heart," he said. "Go in peace and may God be with you."

"And peace be with you as well," Daniel said.

Leah gave Nathan a hug, and she and Daniel set out for her neighborhood. They walked in silence for a while, both shyly avoiding the sudden attraction they felt for each other.

"Will you stay at Qumran for the rest of your days?" she asked.

"I don't know. I believe my mission is there, and I suppose I will stay as long as God wills it. James says that Israel will soon be scattered and that our mission is vital to God's plan for its salvation."

"What is your mission?" Leah asked.

"To be prepared and to help all of those who believe the Messiah's warnings to be prepared as well."

"Does that mean you will be coming to Jerusalem more often?" Leah asked.

Daniel smiled. "Yes, I hope so. James says there is much to do before the day of destruction comes."

Leah looked up at Daniel and felt an attraction that she had begun to think would never happen in her life. As a child slave, she was never allowed to spend time with boys at all, unless it was the son of a Roman centurion who wanted her for pleasure.

"When do you think it will happen?"

"I don't know. Jesus said no one knows the day. Are you afraid,

Leah?"

"No, I've been through too much to be afraid. God has rescued me once, and when the walls of the Temple come down, and the battle begins, I believe God will rescue me again. But I am worried about Baram. I didn't tell you before, but the truth is that Baram and his band of Zealots often steal from the Romans by robbing their wagons and storehouses. I'm afraid that any day, they might be discovered and killed for their actions against Rome."

Daniel nodded, and they continued walking in silence for a while. Suddenly, Leah stopped and grabbed Daniel's arm.

"Daniel, I have an idea," she said. "Would you go to the hills with me to see Baram? He would be so happy to see you again!"

Daniel hesitated, and Leah noticed.

"I don't understand," she said. "You speak so fondly of Baram, and you say your heart was broken when the Romans carried him away. So why don't you want to see him now?"

"I do want to see him, but…"

"But what?"

"I don't know. Our lives are so different now, and I don't believe his way is the way of the Lord."

"I understand," she said, "but just to see him, if only for an hour."

Daniel could see how important the idea was to her, so he nodded his agreement but added, "I'll need to talk to the brothers at Qumran first. If they say I should go, I will go."

The two walked in silence for a few moments before Daniel asked, "By the way, Leah, do you know what happened to your mother?"

She brightened. "Oh, yes, she has been a slave in the family of a Roman soldier for years. Just last week, Nathan heard from someone who had traveled from Caesarea Maritima that the soldier had been transferred to Caesaria Philippi, where Agrippa II is building a palace.

He's not sure yet, but he thinks my mother may have gone there, too."

"Caesaria Philippi," Daniel repeated. He looked northward toward the mountains that were barely visible in the far distance. He did not know why, but the news of Leah's mother, Naomi, being taken there seemed to be significant.

They walked in silence a while until Leah asked, "Daniel, I have dreams that I will see my mother again. I don't know how, or when, but I feel it in my spirit."

"I believe you will see her," Daniel said, "and maybe very soon."

NORTH GEORGIA, 2008 CE

Harold Cappos was a retired FBI agent whose expertise in finding missing children had helped him build a successful second career as a private investigator. An unassuming man in appearance – he looked more like an accountant than FBI agent – Harold was nonetheless one of the brightest and best. He knew all the tricks of the trade and then some. Dave considered him to be one of his most trusted friends, dating back to a time years earlier when he had sought Harold's help with a missing child case. The parents were family friends, and Harold had worked tirelessly to find the girl. And he eventually did, only to learn – as he often did, unfortunately – that the girl had willingly left with her "kidnapper" boyfriend and was not in favor of returning home.

"I get paid to find out the truth," Harold often said, "and sometimes the truth hurts."

After his intimidating brushes with the mysterious man dressed as a priest, and after the phone calls and the incident on the highway, Dave decided to give Harold a call, and Harold was happy to hear from him.

"Hey, I hope you're calling to catch up and not because you have a problem," Harold said.

"I do want to catch up," Dave said, "but you're right, I have a problem."

After he explained the events of the past few years and his most recent phone call on the way back from seeing Randall, Harold pressed Dave for more details. Dave was somewhat embarrassed that he couldn't recall much beyond a general description.

"I'm not trained to look for details like you guys," Dave said.

"The devil's in the details," Harold said. "From now on, try like hell to get a tag number, make and model of the car, what kind of clothes he was wearing, what kind of shoes..."

"Oh, I know what kind of shoes he was wearing," Dave said, excited that he finally did remember a detail. "They were real shiny brogans, really well-polished. I noticed them right away, because they looked like the military dress shoes I had to wear in ROTC in college. Hated those shoes."

"Interesting," Harold said. "Okay, look, I'll make some calls and give this some thought. In the meantime, if you remember anything else, let me know. And call me anytime if you bump into him again."

"Or if he bumps into me," Dave corrected.

"Look, I don't think this guy is necessarily dangerous," Harold said. "Or if he is, it's not the kind of danger you would expect from the Catholic Church. They don't intimidate like this; they don't have to. This sounds more like some kind of religious kook trying to scare you guys away from something he's after."

"You mean the treasure?" Dave asked.

"Sure," Harold said. "And maybe he's not trying to stop you from looking for it; maybe he's just trying to get you to hurry up and find it. And when and if you do find it, that's when you better be looking over your shoulder.'

"Roger that," Dave said. "And thanks for the advice. I'll keep you posted."

In spite of the new sense of danger around his efforts, Dave remained encouraged by his visit with Professor Eisman and subsequent reunion with Randall. He plowed into his research again. He continued a dialog by email with Eisman, and he called Randall regularly to discuss his discoveries and ideas. And he made a phone call to Victor Jones, the Texas preacher who had converted to Judaism and become an expert on the Dead Sea Scrolls. Eisman had assured him that Jones would be a great resource for gaining clarity about the mysterious text contained in the Copper Scroll. And though he hated to admit it, Eisman considered Jones' archaeological finds significant confirmations that there was a lot more to Qumran than meets the eye, certainly a lot more than mainstream Christianity wanted to give it.

Talking to Victor Jones proved to be a difficult task, due to the fact that the old guy's health was failing rapidly. His wife fielded his phone calls and did a poor job of communicating the purpose of Dave's call. When he finally received a return call two weeks after his first call, Dave wasted no time getting to the point.

"Thanks for calling me back," he said. "Your wife tells me that you get a lot of calls from people with bad intentions, and I want to assure you that my only intention is to learn the truth about what happened at Qumran. I'm not after treasure, except as it will prove or disprove any of our current beliefs about the earliest Christians."

"They were Jews," Jones said. "They were striving to be perfect Jews, and that's really what we should do as well."

"But were they the first Christians?"

"Absolutely. They were the authors of Christianity. The first Christians, the ones we read about in the Book of Acts, were induced to lead lifestyles that were simple, pure and holy, just as the men at Qumran did. They were encouraged to worship and practice many of the Jewish traditions; and of course, they shared everything in common. Yes, they were the first Christians."

"Do you think they escaped the Roman army in 70 A.D.?"

"Of course they did, but how and where they went, I don't know. That's why I was over there and digging around for clues. But my time has run out, my friend."

"Well, I had hoped to come visit you…"

"No, don't do that. Tell me again, why do you want to talk to me? What do you think you'll learn that you don't already know from reading my books or visiting my website?"

Dave pondered the question. "Truthfully, I don't know. But I've been on this trail for a while now… years, in fact… and without sounding too presumptuous, I hope, I believe I am supposed to keep following the trail until I find the answer."

"The answer to what?"

"Where they went."

"Why is that so important?"

"Because I believe the escape was in the planning stages as early as the time that Jesus was around, and that his warnings to the Jews and new believers was to be ready to go; and that where they were going was a 'mansion with many rooms.'"

Dave paused to let Jones respond, but there was only silence for a moment. And when he did finally speak, the old guy whispered into the phone, "I think you got it, my friend. I think you do. Give me your mailing address."

Dave gave him the address and waited to hear why Jones wanted it. But suddenly, Jones cut the conversation short.

"I have to go. Bye." And he hung up.

Dave stared at the phone and laughed. "Ooookay… bye."

After the strange exchange with Jones, Dave monitored his mailbox for a delivery from Jones, but after two weeks he decided to give him a call, on the pretense that he had another question. But his call went to voicemail, and he left an extended message. Again he got no response, until a week later, when he did finally receive a call from Texas. Only it wasn't Victor Jones. Instead, it was Jones' wife, who reported that her husband had finally succumbed to terminal cancer. Dave explained his reasons for calling and offered his condolences.

"Also," he said, "Your husband took down my address, but I never received anything from him. Do you happen to know what he was going to send me?"

"No, I don't know anything about that," she said, "but I'll look around. Victor left stuff laying all over the place… things he meant to do. If I find it, I'll send it on. If you don't get anything, you'll know I didn't find it."

"Thanks," Dave said. "That's all I can ask."

"You're welcome," she said, "I'm sorry I can't help you any more than that. I know Victor would have enjoyed talking to you; he loved talking to people who were as interested in the Scrolls as he was. Which reminds me, you may want to contact Jim Barfield in Oklahoma. He and Victor had many discussions and shared a lot of information. Jim was raised a Christian, but he has now become a leader in a congregation of Messianic Jews."

"Thanks," Dave said, "can you tell me how to reach him?"

"I have his number right here."

After he hung up the phone, Dave immediately searched and found Jim Barfield's website. What he discovered was another rich source on the Scrolls, Qumran and the early Christian church. Barfield, as it turned out, had recently retired from a successful career as a fire investigator. His fascination with the Dead Sea Scrolls had led him to the Copper Scroll and inspired him to make several trips to Israel to find the treasures described there. His knowledge of investigating physical evidence helped him develop a few theories that resonated in many ways with Dave's. It was immediately clear to Dave that he had to meet him, and as he had learned with Eisman, it was best to do so face to face.

Two weeks later, Dave landed in Oklahoma City and drove a rental car south to Lawton, where arrangements had been made to conduct an on-camera interview with Jim Barfield. They got to know each other first over lunch, and Dave explained that his mission was simply to discover the true origins of the Christian church, and he ended his story with learning about the death of Victor Jones.

"I really liked working with Victor," Barfield said. "We didn't always agree on the details and we often came to very different conclusions. His methods were more mystical than mine. He trusted his instincts more than me. Because of my background, I tend to be more straightforward and strategic in putting pieces of the puzzle together. And that's what the Copper Scroll is, essentially, a puzzle that we're all trying figure out. But Victor was a great man, and more than anyone else, he opened my eyes to the true nature of the Copper Scroll. I came to realize that there is a whole lot more to that document than most scholars are willing to concede."

"What do you mean by that?" Dave asked.

"Well, it's more than just a list of gold and silver. It's not just a treasure map; I believe there's a deeper significance attached to those items that directly relates to the story of the Bible, and the foundation of the Christian church. If we find that treasure, a mystery that's been buried for two thousand years will be solved."

"And the world will know the truth," Dave said.

"Yes, the world will know the truth."

Barfield's enthusiasm and knowledge made his on-camera interview both entertaining and enlightening.

"I have to say, Jim, after reading through your website and watching your videos on the site, you astound me with your knowledge and insight."

Barfield laughed. "I know. People aren't used to a retired fire inspector being an authority on anything other than fires. But I became interested in this because, just like you, I believe we've been led astray as Christians about the origins of our faith. I applaud your efforts to get at the truth, and I'm happy to tell you everything I know, if you think it will help."

"I believe it will," Dave said. "Let me start by asking general questions about the Dead Sea Scrolls found at Qumran. When do you think those scrolls were written?"

"The standard answer is between 200 BCE and 100 CE, but it's possible they could have been written centuries prior and re-copied over and over again. And here's how I come at that. When a scroll becomes out of date, or worn out, the Jewish people will roll it up and store it away in a place of honor, which protects them for future generations. But it also takes them out of circulation, and that means that copies of those scrolls for continued distribution and use had to be made by scribes. The documents at Qumran were clearly produced around the first century, but some of them could have been copies of originals that were written well before then, and if you ask me, as far back as the time of Jeremiah. At the end of the Community Rule scroll, for example, it says that these things were dictated by Jeremiah and written by his scribe Baruch. So why would he be mentioned in there, if the documents had been written by the guys at Qumran? Were they using his name to give the documents more clout? I don't think so; these were very devout men of extreme integrity with no motivation for proving anything."

"Interesting," Dave said. "Those original writings, then, were real treasures to the people at Qumran. And maybe they were hidden at Qumran for us to find all these many years later."

"That's very possible."

Dave continued. "That fits with my belief that the men at Qumran were the architects of the Christian faith, which in their eyes was a return to the pure religion given by God to his people through Moses and handed down through the ages from one generation to the next."

"Yes, and Jesus was the continuation of the line of Jews who were chosen by God to speak his truth to his people. I believe Qumran was in operation from the time of Samuel, and then there was about 70 years when it was not occupied, but then it was in full operation when the Messiah came along. The Jews at Qumran were unhappy with the compromises made by the Herodian Jews and the Temple leaders. They knew it would all be destroyed soon, as Jesus predicted, and they considered it their mission from God to rebuild the faith. I am of the absolute opinion that Jesus and John the Baptist and James were from a particular sect called 'carpenters', or 'builders', or 'the way.' They were also called the Sons of Light, all names attributed to the earliest Christians. And there are many parallels between what was going on at Qumran and what was going on in the early Jewish Christian church.

"And you think Jesus was at Qumran?"

"Remember the story of Jesus at age twelve conferring with the priests? And his mom and dad went back for him. At twelve, Jewish parents would have their boy trained under teachers like the ones at Qumran. And they would receive training until they were ready to take up their rightful place as a priest at the age of 30. That's when Jesus shows up the second time in the Bible. Six months prior to Jesus showing up, John the Baptist (who was six months older) showed up saying to make straight the way of the Lord. According to the Scrolls, John was born at Passover, which is when they expected Elijah to show up. Every year at Passover, the Jewish families would set a plate for Elijah, and during the meal, the kids go to the front door to welcome him in.

"On the cross, Jesus says that John the Baptist is Elijah; and the people below thought he was calling out to Elijah. Fifty days after that came Pentecost, when tongues of fire came down as they did with Moses on Mt. Sinai and at other times. In other words, Jesus comes on the scene exactly when he's supposed to. And it's very possible that he received his training at Qumran."

"Let's shift gears for a minute," Dave said. "You said earlier that Jesus was the continuation of a line of men who heard from God, and I read something on your website where you quote the phrase from the Bible describing Jesus as being 'in the order of Melchizedek.' Can you give me your understanding of that phrase?"

"Sure, here's what I think. The word Melchizedek translated is 'messenger' or 'angel.' I think Melchizedek was a righteous messenger who also was known as a Righteous Teacher. But there was more than one person who can claim the title of Melchizedek. According to the Scrolls, Noah was the eighth teacher of righteous. And the New Testament confirms that Melchizedek was not just one man, and that the next Righteous Teacher, the next Melchizedek, was Noah's son, Shem. Jewish people have known that all along."

"So, if there were a line of men who were known as Melchizedek, who was the first? Adam?"

Barfield grinned. "Yep."

"Okay, now let's talk about your favorite subject," Dave said. "The Copper Scroll."

"Yes, you believe that the Copper Scroll is an authentic list of valuable items, much of it gold and silver and precious gems, and through research and investigation, you have actually identified locations for many of those items. What exactly are those items, and I have to ask of course, is the Ark of the Covenant part of the treasure?"

Barfield nodded in the affirmative. "I believe the items listed there are treasures from the Tabernacle of Moses and include the Ephod of the High Priest, vast quantities of gold and silver, massive amounts of Tabernacle service vessels and gems of tremendous value. More importantly, though, I believe I have learned the location of a buried cave that contains the Tabernacle of Moses, the altar of incense, and the Ark of the Covenant. After the Babylonians conquered Israel, they returned to Babylon with their captured slaves. Among those was Jeremiah, who found great favor with Nebuchadnezzar and his generals. According to the Book of Maccabees, Jeremiah was given valuable gifts because he was speaking the words that God had told him to say, which essentially was to pack his bags, go with them back to Babylon to make retribution for the seventy years that the Israelites had failed to keep the Sabbath."

"Is the treasure described in the Copper Scroll still there at Qumran?" Dave asked. "And if so, is there a good chance it will be found?"

Barfield paused a moment and then shrugged his shoulders. "We now have enough evidence to believe that it was hidden by the Jews before Jerusalem fell to Nebuchadnezzar, and I believe it is most likely in the Qumran area. On the other hand, many have been hunting for it, but as yet there has not been a significant find. Will it ever be found? God only knows; and I mean that sincerely. I would be honored to be the one to find it, but those items will only be found when God wants them to be found and by whomever He chooses. In the meantime, I keep searching."

"If you find the treasure, what will you do with it?"

"I want those items to go to the Jewish leaders in Israel. They should be cleansed and properly handled by the Jewish priests, the Levites. If we find anything, it will go to them."

"That's good to hear," Dave said. "So you think the treasure was hidden somewhere in the area around Qumran, but is there a possibility that it may have been moved at a later date?"

"Yes, it's possible," Barfield answered. "It would be silly to say otherwise. But we're talking about a lot of stuff, so if it was moved elsewhere, it would have been a huge undertaking requiring a lot of coordination. There is certainly precedence for that. In his day, Solomon had a plan in case the Jews were overrun, a way to hide or protect the items in the Temple, especially the most holy items including the Ark of the Covenant. Those items were taken to a place where they could be hidden from the Babylonians. It says in the II

Maccabees that they took the treasure to Mt. Nebo, and Qumran is right on the way there. And the Copper Scroll says that they put a lot of treasure there and buried the entrance.

"In the Copper Scroll, the writer mentions what is now called the Silver Scroll by researchers. I do believe it's the key to finding silver, but I can't prove it, and no one has found it. And here's the possible explanation why. Copper is spiritually symbolic of judgment, and silver is symbolically portrayed as redemption. So what I'm thinking is that the Copper Scroll was found in the fifties, and it was a message that there's judgment coming on us – on the whole world, in fact. So the Copper Scroll was left open, and is there for us to see. But to prove that document is correct, there's another sealed document, the Silver Scroll that is yet to be found. And it will reveal the path we need to follow for redemption."

"That's interesting," Dave said. "By the way, do you think you could put a dollar amount on the treasure you mentioned earlier? It must be valuable."

Barfield laughed. "Are you kidding? I could never put a monetary value on it; it's off the charts. It's priceless!"

"In 70 CE, when the Romans sacked Jerusalem, why didn't they find the treasure?

"As I said before, all those things were hidden from the time of Jeremiah. God made sure they were hidden so they would survive all these years. And I believe God will determine when they are to be found."

"Let's change gears again," Dave said. "You mentioned Baruch, who wrote about the last days, or the last times. Do you think we are in the last days?"

"From my studies, 'last days' doesn't mean the end of the world; it means the end of an age, or the end of an era… like the end of the Jubilee period. So it's a designated amount of time, and the first century Jews, especially the Jews at Qumran, were expecting the

Messiah to come back at a certain time. And he did, but only to usher in a new age. That has happened throughout biblical history, as it did when Noah and his family ushered in a new age after God's judgment literally rained down on the earth. I'm not trying to disparage current day preachers who say we're living in the last times, but I think they have it wrong. I don't believe the world is about to come to an end, but I do believe we are close to the end of an age, and on the verge of a new one."

"One last question, Jim. Do you believe your research and findings fly in the face of modern day Christianity?

Barfield laughed. "Yes, I've angered a few religious leaders, if that's what you mean, particularly those Christian institutions that have so much invested in the traditional view of Christianity's origins. I've been threatened, and on our last dig in Israel, just when I thought we were a few feet away from finding items in the Copper Scroll, I was suddenly shut down by the authorities with no explanation. Everything had been going so well up to that point, but somebody way up the chain of command wanted to stop us. And they did."

"This will be a strange question perhaps," Dave said, "but I have to ask it. Have you had an encounter lately with a stranger dressed as a Catholic priest?"

"Yes, that is a strange question," Barfield replied. "And the answer is no. In fact, the only time I talked with a Catholic priest was a few years ago when I was asked to give a lecture on my findings at a local Catholic Church. There were a dozen or so priests in attendance that night."

"Did you have any discussions with any of them after the lecture?"

"Yes, several of them actually. They were all very interested."

Barfield scratched his head and added, "You know, now that you mention it, there was one guy who stayed after everyone else had gone and pounded me with questions. I finally told him I had to leave, and later, when I pulled out of the parking lot, I noticed him watching me from his car."

"Black SUV?" Dave asked.

"Yes, as a matter of fact, I believe it was."

On the flight home the next day, Dave gazed out the window of the jet and pondered all that he had learned during his visit with Barfield. It seemed that the more he knew, the more convinced he was that he was following a trail that would lead to some very important answers to his questions. More than ever, he felt he was on a mission, and the fact that there was someone following his steps, as well as others like Barfield and Eisman, convinced him that he needed to press forward courageously. And it became as clear as a ringing bell that his next stop on the trail would take him right to the source – Qumran! He decided that the moment he landed, he would make a phone call to Randall and tell him it was time to embark on a journey to the Promised Land.

ISRAEL, 55 CE

As Daniel walked across the valley outside Jerusalem on his way back to Qumran after visiting his mother, he stopped beside a fig tree, remembering that day when Jesus had entered the city and later the Temple courtyard. He looked back at the walls of the great city and understood what Jesus must have felt when he wept over the city. It wasn't just the walls, which would one day crumble; it was the people of Israel who broke his heart and brought him to tears. And like Jesus, Daniel looked beyond the walls to the people he loved on the other side – his mother, Nathan and the other members of his church. He felt connected again to a family, and realized how much he loved them. And then there was the matter of meeting Leah. She had stirred something inside him that had long been ignored, and while he could not deny his attraction to her, he prayed that God would help him understand how to deal with his desire to see her again.

Daniel arrived at Qumran after darkness had fallen over the compound. He went straightaway to his straw mattress, but as tired as he was from the day's journey, he could not sleep. The visit had also stirred many uncomfortable memories, especially that awful night when the Romans had come to his house in the night. Following the strict commands of his teachers at Qumran, Daniel had prayed daily for God to remove his hatred for the Romans and the Herodian Jews, in keeping with the teachings of Jesus. And until that visit, he had come to believe that he had been delivered. But after stepping inside his father's old blacksmith shop, the old familiar feelings of anger and hostility rose to the surface again, and hearing that his best friend Baram was preparing for battle with the Romans made him wonder about his mission at Qumran. His only weapon was the pen and scroll, and a part of him that he had buried years ago wanted to wield a sword instead.

As he lay awake and stared at the rock ceiling over his head, Daniel reflected back on his life at Qumran. For so long, he had focused all of his attention on the details of his work in the scriptorium writing the Scrolls. During his first few years, before he had achieved his higher rank among the brethren, he had served most of his time working as a laborer, first as a blacksmith but also helping to maintain the aqueducts or tending and harvesting barley crops and date palms. Today, however, he would spend most of his day working on the Scrolls, which required great concentration and collaboration with the priests and elders. And already he knew that staying focused on the task at hand would be a challenge.

Not long after he first came to Qumran, he had willed himself to forget about his past life in Jerusalem. Although he often had thoughts of his mother, he had long ago yielded his worry for her welfare to God through meditation and prayer. And over time, with guidance from the Qumran teachers – especially James – he had accepted his lifelong mission to serve the Church. This was a critical time in the history of God's people, they said, and he had been privileged to be among those chosen to help fulfill a vital mission. But still, after his recent visit with his mother, his mind kept flashing back to his old home in Jerusalem. He could not lose the image of Azara waving goodbye to him with tears streaming down her face. He wondered if he would see his friend Nathan again, knowing that his old friend was aging and nearing the end of his life. He thought about the Christians in Nathan's church, who had befriended his mother and taken her in, and he thanked God for them. But mostly he thought about Leah, and he wondered if she had been as drawn to him as he had been to her. He remembered her radiant smile, and he fought an urge to think of what it would be like to have her as his wife.

And then he thought about Baram and Leah's suggestion that he visit him. She had seemed so insistent, and though he longed to see his childhood friend, he knew that such a visit could spell trouble. James would most likely disapprove anyway. More importantly, he wasn't sure that God would approve, either.

As dawn came, Daniel looked over at the man stirring from his sleep nearby. While Daniel had risen quickly through the ranks in the Qumran community, the aging Mishael had remained content to serve as a field hand and baker his whole life with no aspirations for priesthood. More than anyone, Mishael knew Daniel's story, and more than anyone including James, he understood and sympathized with Daniel's hatred of the Romans.

Daniel reached for a scarf lying beside his mat and tossed it onto Mishael's chest.

"You're back!" Mishael said, sitting up and rubbing his eyes. "What's this?"

"My mother made that for you. It's a gift, she says, for being such a good friend to me."

Mishael wrapped the scarf around his neck and buried his hands in the folds.

"I'm so grateful," he said, his voice cracking with emotion. "It's the best gift ever."

"That's what you always say, Mishael."

In the distance, they heard the familiar sound of the ram's horn, heralding the dawning of a new day. Daniel smiled and said, "Assembly."

Along with the other men spilling out of their tents and caves, he and Mishael made their way down the side of the hill to the community center that rested on the plateau overlooking the Dead Sea. They stopped at a cistern where they washed their hands in preparation for the Morning Prayer.

"So," Mishael whispered, "what was it like to return to your childhood home? Did you meet a lot of people? Did you see any of your old friends?"

"It felt strange at first, but after meeting my new brothers and sisters in the Jersualem Church, and reuniting with Nathan and his family, and..."

Daniel hesitated, his mind drifting to thoughts of Leah.

"And what?" Mishael whispered, waving his hand to help snap Daniel out of his reverie.

"And, yes, I did see an old friend. From my childhood."

"Oh, was it your friend across the street? I thought he was taken by the Romans."

"He was, but he escaped and now lives in the hills with the rebels. It wasn't Baram that I saw in Jerusalem; it was his sister, Leah."

Mishael raised an eyebrow and cracked a smile. "Ohhhh, a woman."

Daniel frowned at him. "Yes, a woman, but just a friend from long ago. Nothing else."

"If you say so," Mishael said with a shrug as they dried their hands and continued the walk to the assembly area. There they joined the hundred or so men who stood together facing east toward the rising sun. For nearly a half an hour, they met in quiet, prayerful mediation, until finally the sun peaked over the distant mountains on the eastern shores of the Dead Sea. Then they listened to the distinctively deep voice of James the Righteous Teacher as he began to lead them in a worshipful psalm:

"We give thanks to You, O Lord, who places understanding in the hearts of your servants..."

As James continued his prayer, Daniel tried to follow his words and make them his prayer, too, but he struggled to stay engaged. His thoughts continued to drift back to Leah. James continued his psalm:

"...And we know by the abundance of your goodness, and by the oaths that we have made, that we should not sin against you, nor do anything which is evil in your eyes."

Suddenly stung by the sharp words of James, Daniel looked up suddenly at the rays of sunlight that streaked across the waters, as if God were pointing – and speaking – directly to him. In that moment he felt convicted. He had allowed his flesh to intervene and create a distraction from his purpose at Qumran. Quietly, he uttered a prayer of repentance, and asked God to help him keep his mind on his mission.

As the congregation of men broke after the Morning Prayer, each setting off in different directions to conduct their daily work responsibilities, Daniel walked through the compound toward the Scriptorium. Before he had gone far, however, he heard James calling his name and beckoning him to join him as he walked toward the edge of the compound.

"Walk with me to the palm grove," James said as they started down the hillside, passing through goat herds and barley fields to the grove of date palm trees. They walked quietly at first, and Daniel worried that the Righteous Teacher was in some way disappointed with him. At times, men in the Qumran community had received rebukes from the Assembly of the Congregation, and Daniel often worried that he would fail somehow in his duties and be reprimanded.

"Teacher, have I made a mistake with the Scroll?" he finally asked.

James slowed his pace and put his arm around Daniel's shoulder, like a father would his son.

"No, Daniel, your work has been more than satisfactory up to now," James said. "How was your visit to Jerusalem?"

Daniel hesitated. He wanted to share with James all the thoughts running through his mind, including his encounter with Leah, but he was also afraid that James might not approve. And if he didn't, he would most likely forbid him from visiting Jerusalem in the future. And if he couldn't visit Jerusalem, he couldn't see his mother, or Nathan, or Leah.

"I worry about my mother," Daniel said.

"Of course, that is only natural," James said. "But you know she is well cared for by the Christians in her church; you said so yourself. Is there something else?"

They walked quietly for a moment until finally Daniel sighed deeply, deciding that it was time to tell him everything.

"I met a woman at Nathan's house, someone from my childhood," he began, noting that James raised his eyebrows. "We only talked, nothing more. Her older brother Baram was my best friend as a young boy. On the night the Romans came to my house, they bound Baram and Leah and their mother and carried them away to become slaves. Baram escaped and now lives in the hills with a small band of men who hope to raise an army…"

James held up his hand and interrupted, "I know, an army to fight the Romans. I've heard of them and others who believe our battle is with Rome."

"Leah asked me to go to him, to try and convince him to leave his cave in the hills."

"And did you tell her you would go?" James asked.

Daniel shook his head. "I told her I would talk to you and the Assembly here to get your counsel. But I believe I already know the answer, and I won't go."

James studied him a moment, and then said, "Daniel, I can see that you are troubled, and I suppose it is because of your past experiences with ruthless Romans. I know of your hatred for them."

"But I've prayed that God would free me from that, and I thought He had. But seeing Leah and being reminded of what happened to all of us has stirred up old feelings."

James nodded his understanding and let him continue. By this time, the two men had reached the date palm grove. James looked up to the top of the palm where one of the young men from the community, skilled at picking fruit, tossed a date to James, then picked another and tossed it to Daniel.

"We have a good crop today," he shouted down. "Perfectly ripe. See for yourself."

James and Daniel both took bites out of their dates and nodded their agreement.

"I remember how much Baram loved dates. I was sure I would never see him again, and hearing that he lives only a day's journey from here brings me joy, but it also makes me fearful. I want to see him again, but I'm afraid of who he has become, and afraid that he won't like who I've become."

"Then you must go see him," James said without hesitation. "You are carrying a burden that can only be lifted by removing the doubt in your mind."

"You would let me go?" Daniel asked. "But you've said many times that the work here is most important; that we must persevere in our diligence because the time is drawing near."

"I did, and it is still true. But until you deal with this matter, you will be distracted, a double-minded man who is no longer clear about your mission here. So go and meet this long-lost friend. Embrace him and listen to his story, and demonstrate your love for him, the love of Jesus my brother. But remember your oath to return with all of your heart and soul to every commandment of the Law of Moses… and to separate from all the men of falsehood. God will let you know when others are speaking falsehood, and they will know that you are speaking His truth."

James smiled at him. "Now go and visit your childhood friend, Baram, and see if he would become one of us."

The following day, Daniel journeyed north through the wilderness to the craggy slopes and hills beyond Tiberias. Through messengers, Leah provided him a map to the hideout where Baram had last camped with his ragged band of rebels. Still lean and fit for a man his age, he found the long trip across valleys and winding mountain paths more invigorating than tiring. The countryside and a cool breeze across the hillsides gave him a sense of freedom and adventure that he had not experienced since he was a child on the farm in Tiberias. For so long, he had totally devoted his life to the work and disciplines at Qumran, and other than a few visits to Jerusalem, he had yet to come this far away from the compound.

As he neared Tiberias, the memories of his childhood there came flooding back. He remembered running freely through fields of grain and palm groves, and he thanked God for Raisa and Simeon, who had risked their lives to provide a home for his mother and him. He recalled that day on the mountainside, when Jesus fed the people with his basket of bread and fish and talked to them about the things of God. He remembered the tender moment afterward when Jesus, who had spoken so authoritatively to the crowds moments earlier, personally brought his basket to him and humbly thanked him for sharing his food. Tears came to Daniel's eyes as he recalled how Jesus had placed a hand on his forehead and whispered that his love and kindness had healed him.

Flooded with these memories, Daniel felt an urge to pay a visit to Raisa and Simeon below, but he decided against it. Resolved to complete his mission and find his long-lost friend, Baram, he pressed on through the countryside, following Leah's map that led deep into the mountains. As he passed through a mountain gap that led him into a dark, steep-sloped ravine, he realized that he was drawing near to Baram's hideout. Suddenly he felt a twinge of fear and doubt about his visit. How would Baram react to his arrival after all of these years? What about the others in his small army; how would they respond to a stranger?

Winded from the climb, he stopped to rest on a rock and drink from his water pouch. He heard movement behind him, and when he turned to investigate, he saw the blur of a large stick as it struck him on the side of his head. The blow knocked him out and he fell face down on the dusty path, out cold.

An hour later, Daniel woke to find himself lying on a mat just inside a cave dwelling. His head throbbed and his vision was blurred.

"You're awake," a voice said, and Daniel turned to see the rough and weathered face of a man who came and kneeled at his side. Daniel blinked and tried focus, but the sharp pain on the back of his head caused him to wince and close his eyes.

"Where am I?" he asked.

"Leah's map was accurate, Daniel. You are at our camp."

Daniel forced himself up onto his elbows and stared at the man in front of him. Then they both broke into smiles.

"Baram!"

Baram helped him sit up, and in spite of the throbbing pain in his head and his blurred vision, he looked around in an effort to get his bearings. The cave was crude and ill-equipped and full of weaponry.

"I am sorry that you were clubbed," Baram said. "We have many enemies now, and they come without warning, so some of the men here believe it's better to attack and ask questions later. Come with me and we'll tend to that wound."

Baram led him down the slope from the cave to a stream where a small band of men had made camp. Daniel sat on the bank with his feet in the stream and washed his head wound. After wrapping the wound in a cloth headband, Baram offered him wine, and Daniel drank it eagerly.

"Leah said you might come," Baram said, "but I didn't believe you would. I know the leaders at Qumran do not approve of our mission."

"That is true, if your mission is to defeat the Roman army."

"Jerusalem belongs to the Jews, Daniel. God willing, we will drive out all foreigners and restore the city to its former power."

Daniel shook his head. "It's too late for that kind of thinking. The Temple leaders have so profaned the Law of Moses that God's hand is no longer on our people. Jerusalem will fall to the Romans, and as Jesus prophesied, the Temple and the city itself will be destroyed. When they come, the Roman army will be ruthless, and many will be slaughtered."

"So what would you have us do then, wait for them to come and not give them a fight? Your father and my father died as rebels who defied Rome, and before I will bow to their edicts, I and my brothers here will fight until our last breath."

Daniel realized that Baram's mind was made up. He laid a hand on his old friend's shoulder and smiled.

"Do you remember when you and I would pretend to fight the Romans with sticks in the street? We were such great warriors, and we would always win the battle."

"I remember. We made a pact that we would never yield to the evil Romans, and we believed – as I still do – that God would lead us into battle and give us the victory. Are you telling me, Daniel, that you no longer trust God to give us the victory?"

"God will give us the victory, but not as you see it. We cannot stand against the Roman army, but there is salvation, an escape, for those who follow the plan laid out by the Messiah, Jesus of Nazareth."

Baram hung his head. "An escape? To where? Why should we leave our homeland, the land that God has ordained as ours since the time of Moses? We will not run from the enemy; God would not have us give up Israel without a fight. Come, I want you to meet someone."

Still aching from his head wound, Daniel followed Baram to the entrance of a cave where a large, weathered man sat on a rock alongside his arsenal of clubs and swords. As the two approached, the man studied Daniel carefully while he sharpened one of his swords. Baram motioned for Daniel to sit, and they both sat cross-legged on straw mat.

"Rami, this is Daniel, the one I told you about," Baram said.

Rami continued to sharpen his sword without acknowledging Daniel, then after an awkward moment of silence he spoke in a quiet voice.

"From Qumran?"

"Yes," Daniel answered.

"Then you are one of the Christ-followers."

"Yes."

Rami sighed. "And you have come here because you want to convert Baram to your way of thinking."

"No," Baram said, interrupting. "Daniel and I were friends when we were children, and..."

Rami held up his hand to stop Baram. "I know your histories... both of you. I know how the Roman dogs came in the middle of the night, and I know how your fathers were murdered. Believe me when I say that I have felt that much suffering and more. But there's no need to talk of things in the past. We have no control over that."

Rami leaned forward and narrowed his eyes, at the same time bringing the point of his sword noticeably close and pointing directly at Daniel.

"But with God's help, we can control what happens in the future. Not by preaching the radical ideas of your Jesus and his brother at Qumran. Not by laying down our swords and turning the other cheek to the Romans. No, it is time to fight for Israel, and nothing can change that."

"You cannot defeat the Roman army," Daniel said.

The comment brought fire to Rami's eyes, and he leaned in to within inches of Daniel's face.

"So says a scribe from Qumran. With God on my side, I could defeat the Romans by myself. Perhaps you should read the Scriptures as you copy them. God has never failed to deliver His people from the hands of our enemies, and he will not fail us this time. Let the Romans come, and watch as we wipe them out."

Rami glared at Daniel as he spit on the ground to emphasize his spite for the Romans. Daniel looked at Baram, who also spit on the ground.

"I understand your hatred of the Romans," Daniel said quietly. "And in days gone by, I would have eagerly joined you in the fight. But the Romans are not the enemy; they are only instruments in the hands of God, who is about to root out the real enemy that has defiled the Temple from within."

Rami snorted and began to sharpen his sword again, but Daniel continued.

"Israel is facing a great day of destruction, in spite of your mistaken belief that you can stand against Rome. Change is coming to the House of Israel. There will soon be a new order, one that Jesus proclaimed on the first day that I met him, the same day that he healed my twisted leg and invited me to follow him."

"If you are trying to convince us that we should become Christ-followers," Baram said, "you will be disappointed. Jesus is dead, and while his words were inspiring, he cannot save us from the grave."

"He is not dead, because the grave could not contain his divinity," Daniel said. "And if you walk with us in the way that Jesus has prepared, you will indeed be saved from the coming destruction."

Rami shook his head. "Foolish words. There is no escape for Jews, no place to hide. When the Romans come, all of you Christ-followers in Qumran will die like sheep at the slaughter, unless you sharpen your swords and join us. Fighting is our only choice."

Daniel rubbed his aching head and narrowed his eyes at Rami.

"You are right. Fighting is indeed your choice, but it will be to no avail. We have reached the end of an age, and all of Israel is about to be wiped out, except for those who follow the sons of light. The City of Jerusalem will be destroyed and no stone will be left standing. Millions will die, and no one can stop it including your small group of rebels. But Jesus promised a way out for those who trust his words."

Daniel looked at Baram as he spoke his last few words. For a moment, he saw a hint of understanding in his eyes, but then Rami interrupted.

"I trust God, and no one else," Rami muttered, and then he stood as if to say it was time for Daniel to leave. Daniel nodded his understanding.

"Come, I'll walk with you a ways," Baram said.

As they walked across the camp, they passed Baram's cave.

"I have some bread for your trip," he said as he reached into his cache and handed a loaf to Daniel, who stuffed it in his pocket.

"Baram, come with me. There is much work to do for the escape, and you could help us prepare. It's not just me; Leah wants you to come as well."

Baram lowered his eyes and shook his head. "No, I'm needed here."

Daniel nodded and the two embraced.

"But please, if you see my mother, tell her I love her and I am okay."

Daniel paused thoughtfully, then said, "I will give her your love. But I won't tell her you are okay, because you are not. If you change your mind, Baram, you can find me at Qumran. But I must warn you again. Time is growing short."

As he turned to pick his way down the rocky slopes to the road leading back, he realized that this would likely be the last time he saw Baram. James had been clear that the day of destruction was coming very soon. Daniel knew that the Righteous Teacher was speaking the truth, but he could not bring himself to imagine how or when it would happen. But one thing he did know; when the time came, he would be ready.

HIGH ABOVE THE MEDITERRANEAN OCEAN, 2008 CE

Two months after Dave's visit with Jim Barfield in Oklahoma, he and Randall boarded a Boeing 747 bound for the Middle East. Dave had planned the trip that he hoped would turn out to be a major fact-finding adventure. Clint, who had traveled a week earlier to Europe to visit a college buddy, had agreed to videotape the experience, but his plane would not arrive in Israel until the next morning. Randall had jumped at the opportunity, and reluctantly agreed not to complain about the food, the flight or the accommodations. All the details had fallen into place very nicely, including a lecture on Qumran at the Israel Museum that fit nicely into their itinerary in Jerusalem.

The only hitch – if it actually was a hitch – had been at the very last minute, when Dave kissed Rebecca goodby and headed to his car.

"Oh, by the way," she had said nonchalantly, "yesterday at the grocery store, I saw this guy dressed like a Catholic priest."

A sudden wave of anxiety swept over Dave. "Italian looking guy with dark hair? Was he following you?"

"Well, I think he had dark hair," she had replied, but then she had seemed to doubt herself, saying "maybe it was dark brown. Look, it may have been absolutely nothing. It's just that after hearing your run-ins with that guy, I always notice guys in black with a collar. I mean, there's a Catholic church almost across the street from the store, so..."

Dave relaxed a bit. "Do me a favor, will you? Call Harold Coppas and tell him what you told me. And give him the addresses where I'll be staying while we're in Israel, just in case. And you keep your eyes open. You're right, it's probably nothing, but be alert anyway."

Rebecca had promised to call Harold and assured him she would be fine. Dave and Randall had boarded without incident, and now they were somewhere over the Mediterranean Ocean. As the morning sun peeped over the distant horizon and light filtered in through the cabin windows, Dave watched with interest the large contingent of Orthodox Jewish families on board. Many of them had donned their tallit prayer shawls, and some wore tefillin boxes strapped to their forehead. It was time for their daily morning prayers, and as Christians, Dave and Randall found themselves for once in the minority.

As he watched the Jews engage in their prayers, Dave reflected on his final conversation with Eisman and his meeting with Barfield. Both men had arrived at many of the same conclusions even if they were following separate paths and came from different religious perspectives. One point of intersection was on the subject of personal responsibility. Although Eisman confessed that he was not religious, and though Barfield was a devout messianic Jew, both men had agreed with Dave that the Jews at Qumran, who followed the rules of the community and dedicated themselves to the disciplines of morning prayers and singing praises, exemplified the kind of devotion to personal purity that would go a long way today toward making the world a better place to live today. *Maybe they had it right,* he thought.

131

There's some connection between purity and light. Leading a life of purity allows the light of God to illuminate the soul without fear of being discovered as an evildoer.

Dave looked over at Randall, still sleeping with his head resting awkwardly on a small airline pillow. Feeling the urge, he unbuckled and made his way to the lavatory behind him, and as he passed the last row, he noticed a man sitting in the aisle seat reading a magazine. He would have thought nothing of it, except that even in the dim light, he could see that the magazine was upside down. For whatever reason, it appeared that the man was pretending to read.

On his return trip to his seat, Dave passed by again, but the man had turned off his overhead light, drawn his blanket up and turned his head so that Dave couldn't get a good look at him. He tried to get a look at his shoes, but in the darkness he couldn't see them. When he reached his seat, he shook Randall awake.

"Are we there?" Randall asked, rubbing his bleary eyes.

"No, but I have a question?"

"Couldn't it wait until I was awake?"

"Did you tell anyone about this trip?"

Randall shrugged. "Not really, just a few people at my church. Now, can I go back to sleep?"

Dave laughed and nodded. Randall closed his eyes, then opened them again and turned to Dave.

"Oh, and I did mention it on my website. Why do you ask?"

"I'll tell you later," Dave said. "Go back to sleep."

After landing in Tel Aviv and exiting the plane, Dave stopped Randall before they began their walk to baggage claim.

"Hold on a minute," Dave said, watching the passengers from the rows behind him exit. "There was a man in the last row..."

Randall could see that Dave was worried, and the two waited until it appeared all the passengers had deplaned.

"So, didn't see him?"

Dave looked up and down the walkway, but the man was nowhere in sight.

"No, I guess I missed him."

Randall nudged him. "Well, let's get going. I think you might be imagining things."

"Yeah, maybe I am."

After gathering up their luggage at the carousel, Dave and Randall rented a car and drove to Jerusalem, arriving late that night at their Ramada Hotel. After checking in, Dave told Randall to go up to the room without him.

"I just want to make sure we're not being followed," he explained.

Randall agreed to the plan and caught an elevator. Dave rolled his bag to the far end of the empty hotel lobby and watched the doors and exits. It might have been a good plan except for the observant bellhop, who mistook Dave's sitting down as exhaustion.

"Sir, can I help you carry your bags to your room?"

"No, thanks."

"Is there anything else I can do for you? Would you like something to drink? Water, perhaps?"

"No, thanks."

"Please, when you have rested, let me know, and I'll be happy to help you with your travel bags."

Dave looked across the lobby, saw no one suspicious, and decided to abandon his plan. He thanked the bellhop one more time as he stood and made his way to the elevator. After the door opened, he stepped inside and turned to get a last look at the entrance to the hotel. And just as the doors were nearly closed, he saw someone entering the lobby. Quickly, he thrust his arm between the doors to stop them from closing, and the noise caught the attention of the hotel clerk and the new arrival. The doors sprang back to the open position, and Dave stood facing them both with a sheepish look. To make his embarrassment even more pronounced, it was clear at a glance that the new hotel guest was not the man from the airplane but rather a very well-dressed woman looking very concerned about his strange behavior.

"I think you're right," Dave told Randall when he got to the room. "I may be imagining trouble that's not really there."

"Better safe than sorry," Randall said.

The next morning, the two men joined Clint for breakfast downstairs at the hotel restaurant, and then they piled into a rented SUV and headed out. Dave had planned to spend their first day visiting the familiar sights in and around Jerusalem, an excursion that Randall had made many times but an experience that would be the first for both Dave and Clint. Because Randall spoke a little Arabic and seemed familiar with the map, Dave trusted him to guide them to their intended destinations.

The trip was a thrill for Dave, who had for all of his life read about the Holy Land. Traveling across desert countryside and viewing the distant mountains, he felt energized and confirmed that he was on a very important mission. With Randall adding commentary and historical context, and Clint adding tidbits he read on the internet, Dave visited sites that had only lived in his imagination until this point. They visited the spot where the Ascension had reportedly occurred, then made their way back to a point overlooking the Kidron Valley. Across the way, they could take in the whole city of Jerusalem, a view that Dave had seen so many times in photographs. Randall unfolded his map and spread it out on the hood of the car, and he and Clint – armed with his GPS map on his cell phone – argued about the best route to take to their next destination.

Finally acquiescing to Randall's insistence, they loaded up and struck out for the Golden Gate, but just a few miles into the drive, the car suffered a flat tire. Clint pulled the car to the side of the road, and all three got out and stood on the shoulder to get a look at the flat tire.

"Now what?" Randall asked.

"No problem," Clint said, bending down to get a close look at the tire. "Shouldn't be too hard to change. I'll get the spare."

"No problem, he says," Randall said grumpily. "Glad you brought him along, because I don't think my back would hold up long enough to change a tire."

"Uh-oh!" Clint muttered from the back of the SUV. "There's no spare."

"Now what?" Randall asked.

Dave scratched his head, and Clint retreated to the car to retrieve the phone number of the rental car agency. But while he was fishing through papers for the number, a young twenty-something Arab on his bicycle stopped beside the car.

"Sir, can I help you?"

"We have a flat tire, and there is no spare," Clint explained. "So I'm calling the rental car agency to have them bring us one. Or better yet, a new car."

"That will take hours," the Arab said as he laid his bike down and inspected the tire. He ran his hand along the treads until he found what he was looking for.

"The tire has been punctured. You will need a new one. My brother is a mechanic and his shop is just down the road. I can call him and he can replace the tire, and have you on your way in just a few minutes."

"That's very kind of you to offer that," Clint said.

The Arab grinned. "I am like the Good Samaritan, except I am actually the Good Muslim. But I will need money to convince my brother to come. Twenty U.S. dollars should be enough."

"Why should we trust you?" Randall asked bluntly.

The Arab grinned again. "Because after we replace the tire, you will owe another twenty dollars. I am Muslim, but you can trust me."

"How long before you return?" Dave asked as he extracted a

five-dollar bill from his wallet.

"Five minutes. You'll see."

Dave handed him the money, and they watched as he disappeared around the curve on his bike.

Dave looked at Clint and Randall and asked, "Did we just get taken?"

Randall shrugged and said, "Don't ask me."

Over Randall's shoulder, Dave noticed a black car driving toward them very slowly. He peered in the window as it passed and saw a familiar face in the driver's seat. For a moment, he and the driver locked eyes, and then the car eased on by. Then, just before he reached the curve in the road, the driver steered the car onto the shoulder a 100 yards or so in front of them.

"That's the guy on the airplane," Dave said, his heart racing. He hurried to his car and pulled pen and paper from his briefcase.

"Are you sure that's him?" Randall asked.

"Positive," Dave said. "I'm writing down his license plate number."

"That won't do much good," Clint said. "It's probably a rental. You would have to get through a lot of red tape to track him down, even if you were in the States, but especially here."

They watched for a moment, but no one emerged from the car.

"Think we should call the police?" Clint asked.

Dave scratched his head and said, "Maybe, but what do we tell them?"

Clint snapped his fingers. "I have an idea. I'll call the rental car company and tell them we're stranded and someone is stealing parts off the car. Maybe that would get the police here faster, anyway."

"Not a bad idea, actually," Randall said, "but look!"

They looked past the parked car and saw a truck coming toward them, and as it pulled onto the shoulder beside their car, they could see the young Arab in the passenger seat and his brother driving the truck. Both men climbed out, and without saying a word, the Arab's brother grabbed a tire from the back of his truck and went right to work changing the tire.

"I am the Good Samaritan, don't you think?" the young Arab asked with a grin.

Dave looked up ahead and saw the mysterious black car drive away.

"More than you know, my friend."

Within a few minutes, the two brothers had made the swap and tossed the flat tire – rim and all – into the back of his truck. Dave handed him another twenty dollars, and they watched as the truck sped away.

"Let's get going," Clint said. "Maybe we'll see that guy in the black car up ahead."

"And if we do?" Dave asked.

"Don't ask me," Clint said with a shrug.

"Go ahead and crank up," Dave said. "I need to make a quick call to Harold Cappos. I think I have a few more details for him this time."

The call to Harold went to voicemail, and Dave gave him a quick run-down on the events up to that moment, as well as the license plate number and a description of the car, noting at the end of the voicemail, "The guy has a thing for black. Black hair, always dresses in black, and always drives a black car, even if it's a rental."

After driving a few miles in silence, Clint made a turn on to the road that led to their next destination, the Golden Gate. As they were approaching the famous landmark, Dave noticed how much larger it appeared in person than it did in the many photographs he had seen over the years. Making it even more imposing were the Arab soldiers standing guard at the Gate, armed with machine guns and prepared for any disturbances. Clint pulled the SUV into a parking area so he and Dave could get out and take the walkway up from the Wailing Wall to the Temple Mound. Randall wasn't sure he wanted to make the trek anyway, so he offered to drive the SUV and meet them later at the Dome of the Rock. When Dave and Clint reached the spot, Randall was waiting for them. While they rested, he explained to Clint that they were standing at the spot where the sun shines directly on what would have been the Holy of Holies, a phenomenon that occurs during the Spring Equinox.

"This is where James was thrown down the Temple steps, while Saul looked on," Dave said. "That was about 36 A.D., a couple of years after Saul witnessed Stephen being stoned to death. But as it turned out, James was only 'mostly dead', and some of the men from Qumran rescued him and took him back to the compound."

"A lot happened in those years after Jesus," Randall said. "Paul returned to Jerusalem in 54 A.D. after his third missionary journey, and the Jews mobbed and bound him for preaching the Gospel. But he appealed to Caesar, and because he was a Roman citizen, he was freed and went to Caesaria Maritima around 58 A.D. That's about the time when he met up with Agrippa II, who listened and had him sent to Rome."

"Meanwhile," Dave continued, "as James became more prominent as the leader of the Christian church, the Jewish Temple leaders decided it was time to kill him. And this time, they didn't leave anything to chance; they stoned him and then clubbed him to death."

"When was that?" Clint asked.

"James was murdered in 62 A.D.," Dave replied.

"Just a few years before Rome sacked Jerusalem, then," Clint noted.

"Yeah, things were heating up around that time," Randall said. "Nero had become Emperor, and he was a lunatic, as you know. Tensions between Rome and Israel had deepened dramatically, and a Jewish Revolt was brewing."

"So what happened after James was killed? Who became the

leader of the Christian church?"

Dave snapped his fingers and pointed at Clint. "That is the sixty-four-thousand-dollar question, because it was just a few years later that the Roman army advanced on Jerusalem; and someone must have been in charge of the escape. Coordinating tens of thousands of Christians in secret would require good leadership, I would think. James must have passed that mantle on to someone. But who?"

JERUSALEM, 62 A.D.

As the months and years passed, the Christians at Qumran worked tirelessly on the Scrolls and preparing the growing number of Christians for the day of reckoning that lay ahead. One morning, after his prayers were ended and the sun peeked over the distant mountaintops, Daniel raised his ram's horn to signal the beginning of the new day. As he lowered the horn, he noticed that one mountain appeared to glow as if it were magically illuminated.

"That is the Holy Mountain," a voice behind him said. Daniel turned to see James, who came to his side and stood with him as they marveled at the sight.

"What does it mean, Teacher?" Daniel asked.

"It is a sign," James said, "like the star that shone on the night that my brother Jesus was born. It is the same light that caused him to shine so brightly on that same mountain. It is the same light that blinded our brother Paul when he was on his way to Damascus seeking to kill me. It is a sign that a change is coming to Israel, a change that is imminent."

James held out his hand and dangled a leather strand on which he had tied two very large metal keys.

"Take this. These are the keys that will unlock the doors that lead to freedom for those who follow our way. Soon, very soon, I will suffer a similar fate as that of my brother, Jesus, after which you can be sure that the last days he spoke of are at hand. Sometime after that, you must begin to lead our brothers and sisters to their salvation."

"Where is the lock that this key will fit?"

"There," James said, pointing northward toward the mountains. "And soon you will go there to help prepare a place of refuge from the coming destruction."

James stood face-to-face with Daniel and placed his hands on his shoulders, as if to stress the importance of his next words.

"You have completed the seven steps and earned God's blessing as High Priest. It is time for you to know a great mystery, one that only the angels know. As you have written in the Scrolls, my brother Jesus was a High Priest after the order of Melchizedek, following our ancestor, Adam, then Noah, whose oldest son, Shem, lived so many years he seemed to have no beginning or end. He outlived generations of descendants after him until he eventually became the only living survivor of the Great Flood. He became King of Salem and the most wealthy and influential man of all. And it was Shem who has always guarded the secret of the Ark and its whereabouts."

"I've heard you speak of the secret of the Ark, but only that it remains intact somewhere in the sides of the north."

"Yes, buried underground atop the Holy Mountain where it came to rest after the waters receded. Come to the scriptorium; I want to show you something."

They walked down the slopes to the compound and entered the chamber where the scribes worked so hard for many hours every day, transcribing the scrolls for distribution to the churches. James located the scroll he wanted, unrolled it, and laid it out on the table before him and Daniel.

"As you know from your duties as a scribe, this scroll foretells the coming of Melchizedek, who will carry out the vengeance of God."

James read from the scroll: "As Isaiah has prophesied, 'How beautiful on the mountains are the feet of the messenger who brings good news, who announces salvation."

James closed the scroll and placed his hand on Daniel's shoulder. "Daniel, the prophets warned us that God would seek vengeances, but my brother Jesus reminded us that there will be salvation for those who choose his way, who turn from the lies and distortions of the Temple leaders who choose to follow Satan rather than God. The followers of Christ are the sons of righteousness spoken of here, and they will be delivered when Jerusalem falls to the Romans."

Daniel smiled and said, "After all these years of writing that, I finally understand what it means."

James closed the scroll and placed a hand on Daniel's shoulder.

"When God wants to reveal his truths, he does so in his time," he said. "Now is the time, and now he has revealed this truth to you. Very soon, you will ascend the Holy Mountain to help make preparations for those who will be saved from the destruction. The same vessel that saved Noah and his family will save us. Until then, keep the keys with you at all times."

Daniel nodded and said, "I promise."

"I am leaving tomorrow for Jerusalem, and I want you to go with me. I believe it is time for you to meet with the Church leaders to begin preparations for the escape."

As James walked away, Daniel felt a pang of sadness. He knew that the Righteous Teacher had continued to anger the Temple leaders and would likely suffer the same fate as his brother, Jesus. He knew he would be called on to take up the mantle, but his love and respect for James had grown tremendously through the years, and he could not imagine life at Qumran without him.

That same day, as he labored over a scroll, Daniel heard a

commotion outside in the compound and walked outside to investigate. A group had gathered around a new arrival, and as he approached them, Daniel could see that it was none other than his childhood friend, Baram.

"Baram! I don't believe my eyes," Daniel said, as he gave his friend a welcome hug. "What are your plans? Will you stay here for a while?"

"No, I am going to Jerusalem to find Leah. But I wanted to see you first, and thank you for coming to see me that day."

"You are tired," Daniel said, "and probably hungry. Come with me and I will show you Qumran, and then we can eat together."

The two men walked through the compound, and Daniel explained life at Qumran.

"We fill the cisterns with water from aqueducts that funnel water from the mountains up there," Daniel said, pointing to the mountains that towered above the plateau where Qumran was located. "We bathe three times a day, and we eat together three times a day in the dining hall. We assemble every morning for prayers of thanksgiving and to read the Holy Scriptures together. When he is not in Jerusalem, the Righteous Teacher presides over the assembly and encourages us with his words."

"How many men are here?"

"We are about 200 strong?"

"How do you feed so many?"

Daniel pointed down the slope to the fields that lay between Qumran and the Dead Sea.

"We farm down there, we have palm groves, and we make things to barter with travelers passing by on the main road."

Baram marveled at the efficient operation there and the contrast between Qumran and his rebel camp.

"We are struggling to survive," he admitted to Daniel as they sat down later to a meal of barley cakes and dates. "We used to rely on some of the local farmers for food, but many have become fearful that they will be discovered by the Romans. Now we depend on what we can steal, and Rami sees nothing wrong with stealing from people who are not our enemies. I can't do it anymore."

"I see," Daniel said.

"I know now that I was blinded by my hatred for the Romans."

Baram spit on the ground and continued: "I still hate them, and I will fight them when they come, but I can no longer stand with Rami and his men. I don't believe that God has his hand on him."

"I am going to Jerusalem tomorrow with the Righteous Teacher. We can travel together."

"Who is this Righteous Teacher you mention?"

"James, the brother of Jesus. He can tell you more about our mission at Qumran and the imminent destruction that will soon befall Jerusalem."

The next day, Daniel, Baram and James made the fourteen-mile trek to Jerusalem, and as they walked together, James answered Baram's many questions. The bond between them grew, as they laughed together at childhood memories before the conversation turned to the tragedy of that fateful night when the Romans came.

"Tell me what happened from your point of view," James said to Baram. "I know it is painful to remember, and even more difficult perhaps to forgive."

"I cannot forgive them. We walked in chains all night, until my mother fell in the street from exhaustion. The Captain beat her in front of us, and we begged him to stop, but that only made him angry again. He spit on us and said he didn't care if we all died."

Baram stared at the ground, and Daniel could see tears forming in his friend's eyes.

"You were just a child, Baram."

Baram wiped away a tear, and forced a smile. "We were both so innocent. My mother... and Leah... I couldn't bear to think about what they were doing to them. So I knew I had to escape, no matter what, at the risk of life. So one day just before dark, as we were all coming in from working all day in the field, I crawled on my belly to the rocks and ran into the mountains and hid for three days. It was cold, and I was hungry when I was found shivering in a cave by Rami's rebels. They took me in and helped me find Leah and free her. I owe them for that."

"But things have changed," Daniel reminded him, "and Rami and his men are not enough to defeat Rome's ruthless legions."

"All I want," Baram said, "is to make sure that my sister will be safe. Can you guarantee me that she will be safe if she follows you?"

Daniel looked at his friend and then to James, who smiled confidently and placed a hand on Baram's shoulder. "Yes, I promise she will be more than safe; she will live among the saints."

After they reached the outskirts of Jerusalem, James left Daniel and Baram to go his family's house. The two men continued through the narrow streets until they reached their old neighborhood and arrived at Azara's house just before sundown. She was excited to see her son and Baram, but Daniel noticed that she had aged considerably since his last visit.

"I don't go out much anymore," she said. "But the good Christians from Nathan's church take care of me. Including your sister, Leah, who brings water from the well."

After a meal and exhausted from their journey, Daniel and Baram rolled out their mats to sleep. As he lay staring at the familiar surroundings from his childhood, Daniel thought how strange it was to be in the same house with Baram after so many years had gone by. He glanced over at his old friend and hoped that he would find the same joy and peace that he had come to know as a Christ-follower.

Daniel and Baram rose early the next day, and after a breakfast of bread and pomegranate, they set out for Leah's house in another district nearby. When she first saw Baram at her door, Leah screamed with delight and threw her arms around him.

"Oh, happy day!" she said as she invited them in to the courtyard, where they lounged on mats, ate bread and drank wine. It was a joyful reunion, and Daniel gave thanks to God for the moment. Throughout the conversation, Leah and Daniel exchanged awkward glances, which eventually became evident to Baram.

"So," he began, "Do you two remember when I pretended to be a Rabbi so I could preside at your marriage in the courtyard?"

Leah blushed at the question, and Daniel frowned at him.

"So what? We were children then; now my beard is long and my time left in this life is growing short."

"Are you saying it's too late to marry?" Baram asked.

Leah heaved a sigh. "Baram! Daniel has chosen a life of dedication to his work at Qumran. The priests there do not marry."

Baram looked at Daniel, who shrugged and nodded that it was true. The three shared an awkward moment until Daniel broke the silence.

"But if I did choose to marry," Daniel said, looking straight at Leah, "I would ask you to be the one."

Leah held his gaze and then broke into tears. "And I would answer yes."

A sudden loud knock at the courtyard door startled them, and Leah sprang up to open it. When she did, Nathan stepped in and it was immediately evident from his pale face and heavy breathing that he had hurried there to bring bad news.

"They are going to kill him!"

"Who?" Leah asked.

Nathan burst into tears, sobbing so much that he couldn't answer. Leah turned to Daniel, who calmly whispered, "James."

He grabbed Nathan's shoulders. "Nathan! Where?"

"The Temple," he managed to say through his tears.

Daniel turned to Baram. "We must hurry."

Nathan offered to stay with Leah, who received sharp instructions from both Baram and Daniel to stay out of sight and be prepared to leave if trouble were to start.

"Let me go with you. I can help," she argued, but it was no use. Both men shook their heads and hurried away.

As Daniel and Baram came to the base of the Temple Mound, they fought their way through crowds hurrying away in fear of the Temple guards and Romans who had ordered them to disperse. They finally reached the base of the Temple walls where men from Nathan's church were gathered around the battered body of James lying on the ground, his clothing soaked in blood and his head surrounded by a dark pool of blood. Daniel knelt at his side, and seeing that the life had gone out of him, began to heave with sorrow.

Baram placed a hand on his shoulder, and Daniel fought to gather his composure.

"Who?" Daniel asked.

One of the men, whose face and arms were bruised, answered, "The Sanhedrin. He was preaching on the Temple steps when they ordered him to stop. Some of the people listening shouted that they wanted to hear more, and that made the High Priest angry. That's when the Temple guards came and carried him to the Tower and threw him down. The fall did not kill him, just as last time, but they surrounded him and beat him with heavy rods. When we begged them to stop, some of them turned on us and beat us back while the others beat him to death."

"You need your wounds tended to," Daniel said.

"We will help him," said a familiar voice from behind him. Baram and Daniel turned to see Leah as she walked up with Nathan at her side.

"I couldn't stop her," Nathan admitted. "We can take him to my house. I assume you will take the body back to Qumran."

"Yes," Daniel said sadly. He closed his eyes and bowed his head for a few moments, praying for strength in the face of losing his leader, mentor and friend. Finally, he stood and spoke to a dozen or so men who were gathered in a voice that resonated with authority. "But we will return to Jerusalem soon, and many times after that, but not on the main road. We will carry James back to Qumran along a secret route, so pay attention to the landmarks and remember the way. When the Romans make their advance on Jerusalem, that path will be the first leg of our escape route. We must be ready to move quickly, so there is much work to be done."

Leah gave both Daniel and her brother hugs and departed with Nathan and the man who had been so badly beaten. Daniel, Baram and the other men gathered up James' body and carried him through the streets to a house that belonged to one of the men. There they wrapped their beloved leader in linens, loaded him onto a cart and made the long trek to Qumran, reaching the compound around midnight. All the men gathered around the cart, and for several hours until it was nearly dawn, they kneeled and prayed and wept over the man who had for so many years served as their Righteous Teacher.

When the sun finally peeked over the distant mountains, Daniel stood and blew the ram's horn. It echoed across the canyons and rock faces and out to the Dead Sea. He raised his arms and praised God, giving thanks for the life of the man who had taken him under his wing and guided him through the seven steps toward becoming High Priest. And then Daniel turned to see that the men in the compound were all looking to him, waiting for him to accept the mantle of leadership.

"The time is at hand," he said. "Today we will mourn our loss, and we will bury the Righteous Teacher. But tomorrow we must return to our preparations for the escape. And with God's hand on us, we will see a great salvation take place that will rival the parting of the Red Sea for Moses."

JERUSALEM, 2008

By the end of their first day in Israel, after soaking in all the sights and sounds of Jerusalem, Dave and his two fellow travelers, Clint and Randall, were exhausted.

"I'm tired and I'm hungry," Dave announced as they pulled into their hotel parking lot.

Randall heaved a long sigh. "I'm too tired to eat."

Clint pulled the car into a parking space, killed the engine and grinned at them. "I'm never too tired to eat."

During dinner, Randall noticed Dave picking at his food and being unusually quiet.

"What's wrong?" Randall asked. "And don't say 'Nothing!'"

Dave laughed. "Okay, I was trying to put some of the pieces of the puzzle together, and to be honest, nothing we saw today was much help."

"What do you mean?" Clint asked, chewing on his steak and slurring his words.

"Don't try to talk and chew," Dave said. "Your mother would not be happy."

"She's not here. But why did you say that? I thought you really enjoyed seeing all of the sites."

"I did enjoy seeing them, and it did help to make the stories come alive. But I'm not sure I gained anything that I didn't already know or believe to be true."

"So what did you expect?" Clint asked. "Some kind of revelation?"

Dave gave the question some thought before answering. "To be perfectly honest, I can't tell you exactly what I'm expecting on this trip. But whatever it was, I didn't get it today."

"Don't worry," Randall said. "Tomorrow is when our journey

begins. All of what you've seen so far is important biblically, but what you will see tomorrow is what really matters – starting with the lecture and tour at the Israel Museum. Get ready for a day of discovery."

"Did I hear the word 'lecture'?" Clint asked. "I'm here to take a break from school, so why am I going to hear a lecture?"

"See, that's the problem," Randall said, pointing his finger at Dave. "You and I care about all of this, but the kids today could care less. It's all about living in the moment."

"What's wrong with living in the moment?" Clint asked. "Can't change the past and can't do anything about the future until you get there, right?"

Randall stared at him, as if searching for the right answer, and finally he had it.

"There is something you can do about the future, I believe. Pray."

"Well I pray that tomorrow will bring us answers," Dave said. "Clint, if you want to skip the lecture, you can wait for us in the museum or outside."

"What's the lecture about?" Clint asked.

"I'll tell you what it's about," Randall said quickly. "The most important discovery in the history of the world: Qumran!"

"Do you really believe that?" Clint asked. "You think Qumran is more important than any of the scientific discoveries that have brought healing and saved lives through the years? Is it more important than the discovery of electricity, or water purification, or…"

"Yes!" Randall said, cutting him off. "Anything you can think of… the astronomer's discovery of the solar system, or the explorer's discovery of the Americas, or gravity, or atoms, or quantum physics."

"Wait a minute," Dave said, laughing at Randall's intensity. "Now you're stepping on my turf. But Qumran is perhaps the most significant discovery of all time, because more than any other discovery it reveals the truth of who we are as humans. Qumran holds the secret to the mysteries of the Adamic lineage."

"The what?" Clint interjected.

"The lineage of Adam, which continues through Noah and his son, Shem, on down to the Maccabeans and then the family of Jesus and James. So many of the pieces of the puzzle that we don't get from the Bible have been revealed in the Dead Sea Scrolls. Now we know that God's plan for his Church fell into place exactly as the prophets and Jesus predicted, and now we know that the Dead Sea Scrolls were hidden away for 2,000 years for a particular purpose – the rest of the story, if you will."

"Dad, are you saying you know the rest of the story?"

"No, but I think that's why we are here, to learn the rest of the story. Whatever happened to the men at Qumran will reveal what happened to the first Christians in Israel who escaped."

An American tourist at the next table, overhearing the conversation, suddenly turned in his chair to face them.

"Excuse me, I couldn't help overhearing you mention Qumran," he said. "That's where they found the Dead Sea Scrolls, isn't it?"

"Yes," Dave answered, "back in the late 1940s and early 1950s. They have been under scrutiny ever since."

"So what's the big deal about Qumran, anyway?" the tourist asked.

"Boy, that's a loaded question," Randall said bluntly. "How much time do you have, my friend?"

"Let me answer that," Dave said. "Essentially, Qumran was a library in the wilderness. It was headquarters for the people of Israel who many biblical scholars believe were most connected to Jesus and his brother James, who both emerged as leaders of the Jewish movement that ultimately became Christianity."

"That's interesting," the tourist said. "I thought the guys at Qumran were just a bunch of religious fanatics who hated the Romans and wanted to rebel against the Empire in God's name."

"No, you're thinking of the Zealots, I believe. They were a sub-group among the Israelites who were bent on rebellion and extricating themselves from Roman domination. The Qumranians, on the other hand, understood that the root of the problem was not defeating the Romans, who they considered to be God's instruments in rooting out the evil that existed amongst the Jewish leadership at the time. In the Scrolls, they referred to themselves and others who became Christians as Sons of Light, and the Herodian Temple leaders, the Sanhedrin, as Sons of Darkness. So they were not preparing to do battle with the Romans – at least not in the conventional sense."

"What do you mean?" the tourist asked.

"Well, it's clear from reading the War Scroll that they were preparing for a struggle, but instead of making swords and armor and training to fight, they believed that by living pure and holy lives, God would provide an army of angels to help them win in the end."

"That's what Eisman said a few months ago," Clint said.

"Yes, but I don't think the 'Heavenly Host' were necessarily angelic beings," Dave continued. "After a little Bible research on that and reading through the War Scroll again, I believe the 'Heavenly Host' were the inspired men who wrote Scripture and taught the truth to the men and women who lived there."

"Interesting," Randall said, "but doesn't the scroll say that the Heavenly Host would 'rain judgment' from the clouds?"

"Yes, but again I don't think that means angelic beings coming down out of the clouds to actually fight humans. Instead, I believe the reference there is to God's judgment raining down on those who had perverted the truth, and that would be actualized through the work of the purified Christians who remained true to the Law of Moses, handed down to him directly from God."

"So what difference does all that make to me, or any of us living two thousand years later?" the tourist asked. "It's just history, right?"

"Another loaded question," Randall muttered.

"There's a lot about that history that matters to us today," Dave said. "Discovering what happened at Qumran, and figuring out where those first Christians escaped to, will lead us to the final answers to questions that have gone unanswered for thousands of years."

"Questions such as?" the tourist asked.

"Well, the first questions that can be answered by looking back at history are basic ones. For example, 'Is there a God, and did he really send a flood but leave a remnant? Was the Law given to Moses by God, and is it providential that so much of our law in America draws from the Law of Moses? Did Moses indeed lead the escape – The Exodus – of God's chosen people out of Egypt and on to the Promised Land? Was Jesus really the long prophesized Messiah sent by God to heal and save and point the way? Is there a heaven and a hell? Just to name a few.

"The Dead Sea Scrolls give us clues to a mystery hidden for two thousand years, and they seem to be pointing us toward a discovery that will answer those questions once and for all. But just as important, that discovery – whatever it is – will answer questions about what's next for mankind... questions like 'Is there an Armageddon around the corner, as so many modern-day prophets predict, or will the planet survive just fine forever?' This discovery will disprove all the false teachings about the last days and those pesky 'end-times' preachers who are making small fortunes selling a false message."

"That all sounds good," the tourist said, scratching his head, "but how do you know you will make that discovery -- whatever it is?"

Dave shrugged his shoulders. "I don't know. Faith, I guess."

The tourist took a final sip of his water and stood to leave. "Well, I hope you are successful in your search for this new discovery, but I hope you don't leave Israel disappointed if you don't find anything. I think you're standing in a long line of people who have been digging for answers for a long, long time."

"Thanks, but don't worry about us," Dave said. "If God wants us here, he will lead us to the answers. All we have to do is start the journey and be alert to the signs along the way."

The tourist nodded and turned to leave, but Dave held up a finger to stop him.

"Can I ask you a question?"

"Sure."

"In today's science-minded society, when more and more people say they don't believe in the divinity of Jesus, or his resurrection from the dead, or that he even existed in history, why do you think so many people still come here to visit the Holy Land? What are they really searching for? Why did you come here?"

The tourist pondered the question before answering. "Just curious, I guess. I grew up in a Christian family and went to church all my life, but I really don't know what I believe anymore. I guess I thought that coming here might help."

"Has it?" Clint asked.

"Not really. At least, not until I tuned in to your conversation. I wasn't planning to visit Qumran, but now I think I will."

"Good," Dave said, "Maybe we will see you there."

After the tourist was gone, Dave turned his chair back to the table.

"Isn't it remarkable how, after all these decades since the Dead Sea Scrolls were discovered, that so many people are unaware of their significance? People come here searching for the truth, but most of them overlook the one destination where the truth might be hidden – Qumran."

Suddenly, Dave felt energized again and realized what Randall had said to be true. Tomorrow would be a great day, a day of discovery.

An hour later, Dave stood at the bathroom sink in his underwear, brushing his teeth when the room phone rang. He quickly rinsed and hurried to answer it.

"Hello?"

"Dave, I've been trying to reach you on your cell phone for the past two hours."

"My cell phone doesn't work over here. So what's going on, Harold? Everything all right?"

"Not really. I think you may be in danger."

"Isn't that why I called you in the first place?" Dave said, but Harold didn't laugh at the quip.

"I've done some digging, and I think I have an ID on the guy that's following you."

"How did you track him down?"

"Let's just say the devil is in the details. His name is Richard Marshall, and he was head of security for a religious organization called End Times Ministries. He was more like Nazi Gestapo than a Christian security chief. Always wore black, and considered himself a bishop, which explains why he wore the priest's collar. It turns out the whole ministry was really just a scam to raise money, and I mean lots of it. They preyed mostly on elderly widows and had entire fortunes willed to them before they were found out. When the heat was turned up on them, all the people involved scattered. All of them were caught, tried and convicted, except for Marshall. He's been on the lam ever since."

"Okay, but why do you think..."

"Hold on, I'm getting to it. Seems that Marshall was actually an obsessive treasure hunter, which wouldn't normally be anything to worry about, except..."

"Except what?"

"The authorities believe he killed some people going after what he thought was a pricey find in northern Africa a few years back. They couldn't pin it on him because he made it look like an accident, but they're pretty sure it was him."

"So what you're saying is, he's crazy."

"What I'm saying is you need to be very careful. This guy is after something that he thinks you either have or are about to have. He's dangerous, and depending on what treasure you're going for, might do anything to get it."

"Okay, anything else?"

"Yes, Marshall paid a visit to Victor Jones right before he died."

"How did you find out about that?"

"Dave, I'm a private investigator. But the short answer is that I was in Dallas on another case, so I visited Victor Jones' wife last week, and she said that a priest had visited Jones the week before he died. She said her husband was real nervous after that, but he wouldn't tell her why. I talked her into letting me dig through Jones' files and phone records and found that he had several conversations with Marshall, although I doubt that he knew Marshall's real identity."

"You think Marshall might have been responsible for Jones' death?"

"Well, maybe not, but maybe he hounded Jones a little too much, or threatened him, and all of that pushed Jones over the edge. We will never know the answer to that, but he's dangerous nonetheless. I would make a few phone calls over there, but none of my old contacts are there anymore. And with the stew about to boil over with Iran and Syria, they have much bigger fish to fry. Anyway, you may want to consider calling off your trip and going back after this guy is dealt with."

"Consider it considered," Dave said. "Thanks for the info, Harold; we'll be careful."

At breakfast the next morning, Dave gave Clint and Randall the news, and the three of them agreed to keep a sharp lookout for any sign of Richard Marshall.

"Wish I had my Glock," Clint said with a mouthful of steak and eggs.

"Are you sure you would use it if the time came?" Randall asked.

"Guarantee it," Clint said without hesitation.

Dave shook his head. "Nobody's going to shoot anybody. And I don't think we have any problem yet anyway. It's just like that scene in Butch Cassidy and the Sundance Kid, where the old Colombian boss hires them as payroll guards and warns them about the payroll bandits. As they set out for the bank with their empty payroll bags, they pull out their guns, poised and ready for any bandits. And the old boss says, 'They're not going to rob you on the way to the bank; they will rob you on the way back." We don't have anything for this kook to want to steal from us."

On the drive to Qumran, with Clint still at the wheel, Dave and Randall reviewed the lecture and their visit to the Israel Museum. As it turned out, Clint had not only attended the lecture, he had sat on the edge of his seat the whole hour and had a couple of questions ready for the lecturer during the Q&A at the conclusion.

"What significance do you attach to the Community Scroll as it relates to the Bible?" Clint asked him.

"Good question," replied the lecturer, a sharply-dressed, middle-aged Jewish man who worked for Israel's Ministry of Tourism."Yes, the Community Scroll was a significant find and was one of the many documents from Cave 1. It provides the best clues about the daily life of the Jewish Christians who lived there. And it does relate to the Bible, especially the Book of Acts, where we learn about their emphasis on communal living -- sharing all things in common, etcetera. There were thirteen copies of the Community Rule scroll, which is more than most of the books of the Bible. And it refers to other groups of Christians in other parts of Palestine, so I think it is a crucial scroll for understanding what the early Christians believed and how they behaved as a group."

"There's a lot more to be learned from the Community Scroll," Randall said, continuing the discussion in the car. Clint was still behind the wheel but genuinely engaged in the conversation. "The Community Scroll was like a charter for the association of churches that were connected with Qumran's leaders, most notably James. They were messianic and certain that God was in control of their destiny. They believed there were two spirits that influenced humankind, angels of light and angels of darkness, resulting in truth and falsehood, light and darkness, righteousness and wrongdoing."

"The lecturer mentioned rankings," Clint said, "I know they're mentioned in the Scroll, but the steps to get there aren't really defined, are they?"

"Clint, you've been busy reading," Dave said. "I've been digging into the ranking system references, and I think there were seven steps. It's more of a hunch than it is something I can prove, but there is mention in the scroll of seven spiritual attributes afforded to those who follow the God of Israel. When I first read those I was reminded of the fruit of the Spirit outlined in Galatians."

Clint held up his hand and rattled them off: "There are nine of them: love, joy, peace, patience, kindness, goodness, gentleness, faithfulness and self-control. I've had those memorized since I was a kid."

"Me too," Dave said. "But after that, I remembered something in 2nd Peter about a list like that. In the first few verses of Chapter One, he writes about all the wonderful things God has given us – grace and peace, knowledge, great and precious promises. But then in verse five he shifts into the individual's responsibilities for becoming all that God wants us to be, writing that we need to be diligent about adding to our faith, virtue. So virtue is the first step. And then he says add to virtue, knowledge. Then add to that temperance, then patience, godliness, brotherly kindness and charity. When he puts it that way, it sounds like steps toward becoming…"

"Pure!" Randall said, finishing the thought. He reached inside his briefcase and pulled out an article. "This is an article I just wrote about the Community Rule. Listen to this:

'The Community Rule scroll prescribed a disciplined lifestyle for members, who were expected to rise through a succession of ranks to become priests, scribes or chief priests. The communities who followed the Scroll's rules typically included a group of ten men who met regularly for meals and study of Scripture and who were responsible for reviewing members who were progressing through the ranks. The foremost priest served as the leader, or Righteous Teacher, and while he was the primary influence about community matters, decisions were made by majority rule. Members shared their collective wealth and sought simple purity in their daily lives in preparation for the time when God would call on them for special service, whatever that may be.

'The first part of the Community Rule scroll outlines the covenant to which members were to commit themselves. The Righteous Teacher was to teach the "Holy Ones" that they must seek God with all their hearts and souls, according to the commandments handed down to Moses. He was also to teach them to love everything God loves and reject everything that God hates.'"

Suddenly Clint slowed the car as it topped a hill and the Dead Sea came into view. They followed the highway that winds its way along the eastern base of the mountains of the Judaean Desert until finally they reached the bluff where the ancient compound of Qumran overlooks the Dead Sea. To Dave's surprise, there were road signs directing them to Qumran, and soon they drove to an area that had all the signs of a tourist stop including a restaurant and gift shop. Clint parked the car, retrieved his video camera, and the three men made their way across the bluff to the site of the Qumran complex, where they walked through the ruins on modern platforms constructed for viewing and protection. Dave read from a brochure, noting the system of aqueducts and cisterns that were located all through the compound.

"Their system of capturing rainwater through the aqueducts was remarkable," he noted. "Truly a great feat of engineering."

Randall looked down the mountainside to the flat area near the sea. "I believe their farm would have been right down there."

Dave shielded his eyes from the sun and peered down the slopes. "What kind of food do you think they grew down there?"

"Dates, from date palm trees. And barley, I think."

"Over there in that corner was the potter's workshop," Randall explained, pointing to areas as he continued. "Not far from there is that long room, the communal dining hall, where they sat at three rows of tables. Archaeologists know that because they found hundreds of cups and plates and bowls there."

"And this is the Scriptorium," Dave said, pointing to another large room..

"Yes, the library in the desert," Randall added. "There would have been tables with inkwells along the walls, where the scribes worked like monks to produce the scrolls. This room was the heart of the movement, if you think about it. This was the clearinghouse for distributing the God's plan for his people, those who would heed the words of Christ and find salvation."

Dave nodded. "The more I learn, the more convinced I am that you are right. By the way, did you notice that inscription at the Israel Museum that said, 'Heralds of Imminent Redemption'? That is who they considered themselves to be, which confirms that they were keenly aware of an imminent destruction. They knew Rome would conquer, but they also had an escape plan for those who were willing to listen and believe."

Clint looked up from his camera and said, "Dad, I think we need more dialog about the escape. How they did it, when they did it, who was in charge, and all that."

"Sure," Dave said, speaking directly into Clint's camera. "Exactly how and when they escaped is a mystery, as is the question of where they went. But we know historically they did, and we also have clues from the Community Scroll, where it says, 'The time to guide them in knowledge and to enlighten them in the wondrous secrets and the truth among the men of the community, to go innocently a man and (his neighbor in all) which is revealed to them. Is the time when the way leads to the wilderness (and) to enlighten them in all which there is to do at the time.'

"So the time was drawing near for the community at Qumran to 'enlighten' the first Christians about a secret way of escape. Jerusalem was sacked in 70 AD, but before that, most scholars believe that Qumran was sacked two years earlier. So the escape would have happened prior to that, likely over a period of months. I believe plans had been laid many years earlier, but I think the death of James in 62 A.D. probably signaled the community that time was growing short. Between that date and 66 A.D. was probably a busy time preparing and planning, and by 68, they were out of there."

"Where did they escape to?" Clint asked.

"We don't know," Randall said, and Clint turned the camera on him. "I believe their first destination might have been Qumran, using the very same secret route they used when they carried the bruised and battered James out of Jerusalem. But I still believe their ultimate destination was somewhere in northern Israel on a mountaintop. And before you ask, no, I don't know which mountain."

Using a map, Randall led them to the site of Qumran's ancient cemetery on the southeastern side of the compound. While Dave and Randall talked, Clint recorded their discussion and panned the area with his camera for 'b-roll' shots.

"It says there were more than a thousand people buried here," Dave said, reading from a brochure.

"Notice that graves were all along these ridges that descend toward the sea. Eisman made a big deal out of the fact that their bodies were intentionally buried on a north-south axis with their faces turned toward the north. They were expecting their salvation to come from the north, and I guess they wanted these souls in the graves to have a good view."

Dave looked northward and pointed to a distant mountain.

"That mountain with the white cap... does anyone know what mountain that is?"

Randall consulted his map and said, "I think that might be Mt. Hermon."

"Oh, really," Dave said. "The same mountain where Jesus was transfigured?"

"Yes, it is," Randall said. "And now that you mention it, Mt. Hermon is at the bottom of the Ararat range but inside the borders of Israel."

The two men exchanged looks, the lights coming on for them both.

"Whoa, I think I captured a moment there," Clint said, moving in closer. "So Dad, what are you thinking? That the Christians escaped to Mt. Hermon?"

"Why not? It makes a lot of sense, the more you think about it. Noah's ark settles down up there somehow, maybe in a canyon or nestled in the rocks, maybe even buried after a couple of thousand years. Noah's son, Shem, becomes the wealthiest man and King of Salem – later known as Jerusalem – and passes on the secret resting place of the ark through the generations."

"Could the Ark really hold up for that long, especially if it was buried?" Clint asked.

"Sure it could. In the biblical description of the Ark's construction, if you recall, it says that it was pitched inside and out, in effect making it an airtight, self-preserving giant capsule. And the secret of its existence was passed right on down to the Maccabees through the same lineage as Jesus Christ."

"Who was also a High Priest after the order of Melchizedek," Randall added. "Jesus came with a radically new message, a warning about corruption in the Temple, and passionate entreaties to all who would listen to follow his way and find salvation from the imminent destruction."

"Imminent redemption," Dave said. "The men at Qumran were heralds of imminent redemption, led by a series of Righteous Teachers, High Priests after the order of Melchizedek. And James succeeded Jesus in that role until he was killed in 62 A.D."

Dave suddenly went quiet and stared at the snow-capped mountain to the north. The sun was creeping lower in the sky, and the reflection from the top of the mountain shot rays of light in every direction -- and for a split second a single beam of intense light in their direction.

"We need to go there," he said. "To Mt. Hermon."

"We can do that," Randall said. "We spend the night in Tiberias and drive there tomorrow. But first, we have to visit another cave."

Randall directed the group to an area at the northernmost point of Qumran and pointed to a cave entrance above them.

"That is Cave 3, where they found the Copper Scroll," Randall said, speaking into the camera microphone as Clint recorded with his Sony video camera. "The Copper Scroll is essentially a treasure map that describes in great detail where a fortune in gold, precious jewels, Temple artifacts, and perhaps even the Tabernacle was located. In his studies of the Copper Scroll and his excavations at Qumran dating back to the 1960s, Victor Jones drew some conclusions that are astonishing, and of course, controversial. Until Jones made a fascinating discovery in this cave, very few people in archaeology or academia gave the Copper Scroll much credence, generally relegating it to Jewish folklore, as opposed to an actual map to real treasure.

But Jones and his team, after years of painstakingly putting all the pieces of the puzzle together, have a very convincing argument that the Copper Scroll is a real map to real treasure, and were able to link that treasure directly to the Temple as part of their find when they excavated here."

Randall paused for effect, and then sat on a rock before beginning again. "Jones' conclusions flew in the face of previous assessments of the Copper Scroll made by mainstream academia and representatives of the Catholic Church. In fact, members of the team that was charged with interpreting the scrolls over the past few decades have said the Copper Scroll was probably a forgery and worthless, adding that to give it any credence at all would only entice treasure hunters, especially those searching for the Ark of the Covenant. Even though they were probably right about the treasure hunters, they were wrong in their assessment, as the evidence compiled by Jones proves. But here's the really mysterious part of Victor Jones' discovery."

Randall paused dramatically before beginning again, and Dave suppressed his laughter. His old friend had warmed up to the camera quite well; maybe too well. But even if his delivery was over the top, Dave surely wasn't one to dim his enthusiasm.

"What Jones and his team did during their excavation basically was to overlay the geography and geology described in the Copper Scroll," Randall explained. "And that process ultimately led them to the discovery of an opening to a descending stairwell which led down to a hidden chamber. But there was no treasure there, even though the chamber is described as having such in the Copper Scroll."

"That chamber is mentioned in II Maccabees 2:5," Dave said. Clint panned his camera over to Dave, who continued the explanation. "That verse says that Jeremiah found a cave-dwelling and placed the Tent and the Ark and the Incense Altar inside and then blocked the entrance. Victor Jones found remnants of the Incense Altar, proving its connection to the Temple, but he found no treasure, leading us to believe that the treasure had been stored there for a while but was then moved. And it is our contention that it was moved at the same time that the men at Qumran led thousands of Christians to an escape somewhere to the north."

Dave looked northward and stared at Mt. Hermon's glistening white cap. Clint stopped recording, and all three men stood gazing northward.

"Tonight we stay in Tiberias, and then it's on to that mountain," Dave said. "Something tells me..."

As they descended the hillsides and made their way back to the parking lot, Dave noticed a familiar black car parked just a couple of spots over from their rental car. He squinted to see who was in the driver's seat but couldn't make out the face through the dark windows. And after a few more steps, he stopped and watched as the driver suddenly backed the car out of its parking space and pulled out onto the highway, disappearing from sight around the first curve.

"I guess neither of you saw that," Dave said, intending it to be a question.

"See what?" Clint asked.

"Never mind."

As Clint drove the car out of the parking area onto the main road, he and Randall returned to an earlier debate about the role of women in the church today. Dave tuned them out and looked through the window at the craggy slopes of the mountains that stretched northward parallel to the Dead Sea. He replayed the events of the escape and tried to imagine hundreds of thousands of Christians making their way along this same route, but in secret.

The debate escalated into an argument, until an exasperated Randall, seated in the back seat, leaned forward and tapped Dave on the shoulder.

"Dave, please tell that son of yours he's lost his marbles."

Dave ignored the comment and changed the subject. "You

know, it just struck me that after James, the Righteous Teacher, was murdered in 62 A.D., there were six more years before Qumran was under siege by the Romans. That would have been the time period when the escape took place. If James succeeded Jesus as the Righteous Teacher and leader of the Christian Church, I wonder who succeeded James. James knew his death was imminent, and there must have been someone in line to take his place."

"I'm sure there was someone," Randall said. "And whoever he was, he had some pretty big shoes to fill.

QUMRAN, 67 CE

An early December sun peeked over the mountains to the north as Daniel raised his shofar toward the sky and pierced the silence with a pure, resounding blast to signify the commencement of Hannukkah, the eight-day Festival of Lights that commemorated the rededication of the Second Temple at the time of the Maccabbean Revolt in the 2nd Century BCE. The blast resonated across the hills and canyons, and the returning echoes served as audible reassurance to Daniel that someone to the north had heard and was waiting to welcome those who would follow him to safety.

The echoes died and all was silent again except for the low whistle of an arid desert wind. Daniel knelt in a prayer of thanksgiving for the new day, and when he raised his head and opened his eyes, he witnessed a rare and fantastic sight. The first snow of winter had created a snowcap on the Holy Mountain to the north, and the early morning sun illuminated it, creating brilliant rays of light that reflected off the white surface and shot across the miles of terrain to illuminate Daniel's face. So brilliant was the reflection that Daniel had to shield his eyes to keep from being blinded.

Before science understood natural light phenomena – such as

the lights of the Aurora Borealis, or the alpenglow, or backscattering – a dazzling display like the one Daniel witnessed was often regarded as a sign from the Almighty. To Daniel, it was a promise. Winter was on its way, and the day of reckoning was drawing ever closer. Much of the Jewish population had grown weary of increasingly heavy taxation from Rome, and a rebellion had gained enough strength to draw the attention of the Roman army. Emperor Nero, who was said to be deranged and burning Christians alive, had ordered the Roman commander, Vespasian, to put down the Jewish rebellion, and word had come that they were already on their way. The coming destruction was imminent, but as he allowed dawn's early light to warm his face, Daniel was at peace, absolutely sure that God's plan of salvation would free the Christians from death, and under his guidance and leadership, reach the Holy Mountain and the place that had been prepared so long ago.

After Daniel made his way down from the hillside to the compound, he found Mishael waiting for him at the bottom. After James' death, when Daniel assumed his leadership role at Qumran, Mishael had become Daniel's most trusted friend and right-hand man.

"He's waiting for you in your room, Daniel," Mishael said, "and I will be managing the field work this morning if you need me."

"Thanks," Daniel said as he made his way to his room, where Baram would be waiting to hear why he had been summoned. Although he had resisted at first, Baram had eventually joined the men at Qumran and took over Daniel's previous responsibilities as a blacksmith. His temper and his hatred for all things Roman had taken a backseat to hard work and supporting Daniel in his new leadership role. But while he clearly admired Daniel and marveled at his wisdom and maturity, he could not bring himself to forgive his sworn enemies – the Romans – as easily as Daniel seemed to have done. For his part, Daniel felt a special bond with Baram, and some of that he was sure had to do with his strong attraction to Leah. Both men found a strength in their relationship that enabled them both to stay true to their convictions and focused on the mission ahead.

"The time has come," Daniel said after he sat down across from Baram in his room. "We have begun the first phase of the evacuation, visiting churches and homes of the Believers in Jerusalem, alerting them to pack secretly and be prepared to move at a moment's notice."

"What can I do to help?" Baram asked.

"The secret route for the escape will pass through Qumran, and after that it will continue through the wilderness to a location far north of here. Because of your travels and your knowledge of the wilderness, I want you to be a scout and guide along the way."

"You are right. I am well-suited for that role. When do we begin?"

"Soon, but first I have something to show you."

The two men set out on the road that led northward away from Qumran until they reached a spot where the road intersected a river, known as the Wadi Nahal HaKippah. They climbed along a ridge until Daniel found the cave and motioned to Baram to follow him inside, where he located two torches and a basin of oil hidden behind a large stone. He handed the torches to Baram, and while he rubbed his firesticks together to create sparks, Baram dipped the torches in the oil. Once the torches were lit, Daniel led the way down a dark passageway until they reached a very large granite stone that appeared to be nestled in a crevice on the floor of the cave.

"Help me move it," Daniel said, and with their backs against the wall, the two men used their legs to roll the stone out of its cradle, exposing a large hole behind it that served as an entryway to a narrow descending stairwell.

"Follow me," Daniel said

At the bottom of the stairwell, they entered a large, spacious chamber, and after he lifted his torch and made his way to the center,

Baram gasped at the sight. All around the chamber were magnificent treasures including gold, silver, precious jewels, and chests full of Temple artifacts and Israel's most precious ancient scrolls, dating back to the time of Moses.

"I don't understand," Baram said. "What is this?"

"Tabernacle treasures rescued many generations ago, after the reign of King Josiah, who tried to abolish the unholy practices of his ancestors and turn the people toward repentance. But their sins were too great, and the prophet Jeremiah warned the people of Jerusalem that they were facing imminent destruction at the hands of the Babylonian army, for the very same reason that we now face another invasion from the Roman army. Jeremiah was chosen to rescue this treasure before the Temple was destroyed, and it has remained hidden here for generations since. But the Romans will be scouring these hills when they return, looking for any remnants of our lineage, so we must move the treasure again."

"But where?" Baram asked.

"North, to a mansion with many rooms that rests atop the Holy Mountain. A secret hiding place for this treasure, but also for his new Church, the Sons of Light."

Baram walked through the spacious chamber, marveling at the massive collection. What he saw next stopped him in his tracks. There in front of him, perched on a raised platform, its gold casing shimmering in the firelight, the Ark of the Covenant. Daniel stood beside him and placed his hand on Baram's shoulder.

"God has chosen me to follow in Jeremiah's footsteps. Those who have believed our warnings and chosen to follow us will be rescued, and they will help us move this treasure to a place that's already been prepared for it, a new Heaven for God's Covenant to dwell. But I will need your help as overseer. As you know from our Scripture studies, there are strict procedures for moving the Ark of the Coventant."

"It will be a difficult task," Baram said, "but I will help. How much time do we have?"

"Vespasian and his army have been called back to Rome. Many in Israel are foolishly interpreting that as a victory for the rebellion, but Jesus warned us not to be deceived. The Romans will return very soon, and they will be stronger. So we must be ready to move at a moment's notice. In the meantime, you will travel north to the Holy Mountain, where you will see your mother at the palace of Agrippa."

"My mother?" Baram asked. "But I can't be seen at his palace. I will be arrested for sure."

"No, it has all been arranged," Daniel said, "and I have been anxious to tell you before now, but it was not time yet. And now it is. Your mother serves in the house of Agrippa, and has developed a friendship with his sister, Bernice, who is herself a Christian. Bernice has revealed to your mother a series of tunnels under the palace that lead to a system of caves and chambers inside the Holy Mountain. Your mother and a handful of slaves tried to escape through the caves but could never find their way out. But what they did discover, at the end of one of those tunnels, was a hidden door. An earthquake had shaken the region two years earlier, and crumbled walls revealed the door. After they dug away the dirt, they found it to be a massive door, large enough for a behemoth to pass through, and pitched so perfectly so many years ago that the intricately carved words on the door were still clearly visible. The huge door was locked shut, far too heavy to penetrate or break down."

Baram waited to hear more, but Daniel hesitated before speaking again.

"Baram, the door has only been revealed by this act of God. James has often spoken of the way that leads to safe haven, and Jesus promised us a safe passage from the coming destruction. Behind this door is a secret that has been hidden since the days of Noah."

Daniel motioned to his friend to follow him across the

chamber.

"There is one more item you need to see," Daniel said as he opened a box used for storing scrolls. He reached in and pulled out a silver scroll, and then handed it to Baram, who examined it closely.

"It looks like a map," he said, "and inscribed on silver."

"Yes, it is a map that will show you the way, the path of our escape that begins at the gate where James was murdered and follows the road to Qumran and then northward to the Holy Mountain. And when you reach the palace, and enter the caves, and find the door, you will also need this."

He removed his necklace that held the two keys given to him by James, and then untied the knot holding one of the keys to remove it. He handed the key to Baram.

"These keys unlock the door to the new Jerusalem. You and I will be the only ones who have a key. Go to Cesaeria Philippi and see your mother. And find the door. Then come back to Qumran and tell me what you have seen."

"Why do you trust me with this?" Baram asked. "I haven't been reunited with you for long, certainly not as long as many others at Qumran."

"It's not just *my* trust that should concern you," Daniel said. "Leah trusts you, and now your mother is trusting in you. Baram, you are not alone in your hatred for the Romans, but it gains nothing to stand against them. They have been successful in their efforts to corrupt the Sanhedrin and all of those who have become nothing more than Jewish Romans. Soon they will destroy Jerusalem, and slaughter its people, and there will be nowhere to hide in all of Israel."

"I know," Baram said, "but the rebellion is growing stronger. Maybe we will soon have enough men willing to fight. Maybe God would have us stand against them, and trust him for the victory."

"I wish it were so myself sometimes," Daniel said. "But Jesus spoke the truth. He was the light and he now shows us the way. And he said that those who follow him will stand with him at the gates of a new home, one where the walkways are lined with gold. We are the keepers of that gold, and now we are part of a story that has been prophesized for generations upon generations. The end is nearly here. The last chapter is about to be written, and I'm asking you to play a role in that chapter. God is counting on me; and now I'm counting on you."

"What happens in the end?" Baram asked.

"Redemption for God's people and the beginning of a new story."

Baram smiled at his friend. "You have become very persuasive in your old age, my friend. I will go and be your scout. And I will return with news of this door and what lies beyond it. But after that, I make no promises."

"One more thing," Daniel said. "If you should encounter the Roman army, and are unable to make it back to Qumran, go to Magdala, near Tiberias and the Sea of Galilee. Go to the synagogue and ask for Mary. She was a trusted follower of Jesus and she will provide shelter until we come through that area on our way to the Holy Mountain. Wait for us there."

"I will remember," Baram said, "but I will be okay. The Romans will never catch me in the wilderness."

The trip from Qumran to Caeseria Philippi was a long one, and by the time Baram reached the palace of Agrippa II, his provisions were depleted and he was physically exhausted. The palace was immaculate, an architectural marvel with intricately carved columns and engraved stonework that seemed to emerge naturally from the huge rock face of Mt. Hermon.

Still worried that the Romans who stood guard around the palace would arrest him, Baram hesitated at first, but finally summoned the courage to approach the entrance. There he was confronted by two soldiers, who demanded to know his name and purpose. When he explained that his mother was in the service of Agrippa's wife, that he had been summoned to the palace by her order, Baram was escorted through the gates of the palace, through a series of hallways and to an area of the palace reserved for slaves and servants.

As Baram walked out into the courtyard where women and children worked at various tasks, he drew the attention of one particular woman, who stopped weaving her basket and rushed to greet him.

"Baram!" she cried, and he turned to see that it was his mother. Suddenly overcome with emotion, Baram burst into tears as he received her into his arms and hugged her as tightly as she hugged him.

"Mother, I can't believe it's you," he said.

She grabbed his face in her hands and said, "God has smiled on us today, and we must give Him thanks and celebrate your arrival. But that can wait. First, you must eat and get some rest."

After a meal unlike any he had ever had before, and after he slept for several hours, Baram joined his mother in the courtyard, where she had assembled all of the slaves and servants of the household to meet him.

"They are all Christians," she explained, "and with the blessing of Agrippa's sister, Bernice. They are hoping that you bring news from the Jerusalem Church."

"Yes," Baram replied. "They are preparing for the Roman army to descend on the City any day now, and preparations are underway for an escape. As you already know, James was murdered by the Sanhedrin mercenaries, and Daniel, my childhood friend and now the High Priest at Qumran, has become his successor and is directing the effort."

"Will they be coming here?" a woman asked.

"Yes, that is why Daniel has sent me here," Baram replied as he held up a silver plate. "Inscribed on this silver piece is a map, cut away from a Silver Scroll. It has been passed down through many generations just for this moment. It will lead the Christians to their redemption, and Daniel has sent me here to follow the map and find the place that has been prepared for us."

"So where does the map say this place is located?" the woman asked.

"At the end of a secret tunnel located somewhere in this mountain is a door," Baram said as he showed them the key. "And this key will open the door."

"There are tunnels behind the palace," Baram's mother, Naomi, said, "We know of their existence, and when we first arrived years ago, we tried to escape through them, but they all lead to nowhere."

"The door has been concealed by rocks, but it is there. All we have to do is follow the map and remove the rocks. And then we open the door with this key."

"And if the key doesn't open the door, what then?" the woman asked.

Baram shook his head. "I don't know. I guess it will mean that it isn't time yet, or this isn't the right place."

"Well, we'll find out soon enough," Naomi said. "But we will have to wait until dark, when most of the guards have retired, so we can go to the tunnels unnoticed. Until then, come with me, Baram. I want to show you something."

Baram followed his mother out of the courtyard and into a wooded area of the palace grounds. They climbed a small hill, following a path that finally led to a small but well-kept house. Naomi tapped on the door and waited, but no one seemed to be home.

"Whose house is this?" Baram asked.

"You will see," she answered, motioning to him to follow her around the side of the house. When they reached the back of the house, they saw an old man fast asleep on a rug under the shade of a small tree.

"He's asleep," Baram said. "Maybe we should come back later."

"Look at him, Baram. Look at his face."

Baram tip-toed to the spot where the man was sleeping and stared down at him. The old man's rugged and battle-scarred body was withered with age, but Baram could see that he was still a large man, who at one time would have been strong. He studied his face until finally he recognized it.

"Mother! Is this who I think it is?"

His mother came to his side and wrapped an arm around his shoulder. "Yes, he was a Captain in the Roman Army in Jerusalem when he came to our house that night. He was a vile and contemptuous murderer, and he had your father killed and sent us all away to become slaves."

"I don't understand. Why is he here? And why do you knock on his door, as if he were a neighbor you have come to call on?"

"His name is Antonius, and he is not the same man we knew then. God has turned him, and now he is one of us, yet another miraculous transformation like the one we witnessed in our brother, Paul. I wanted you to meet him, to see for yourself, and to…"

"To what?!" Baram said, suddenly overcome with anger. "To look him in the face and tell him I don't care that he killed my father? To tell him that it was all right for him to take us all away from our home in the middle of the night in chains? To tell him I suffered for years in the rocks living on rats for food and afraid to show my face in my own home?"

Baram stared down at the man, his anger growing by the second. His heart raced, his face flushed red, and his breathing grew heavy. His mother tried to calm him, but she could see that she had underestimated the deep-seated rage that Baram would experience on seeing Antonius. He turned his back on her, his mind racing and his blood boiling.

"Baram, I'm sorry," she said, but then he wheeled around and shouted at her, the features of his face contorted in anger. His eyes narrowed and he spit on the ground.

"He murdered your husband! My father! He deserves to die!"

Baram made a move toward the old man as if to choke him, but his mother grabbed him and pleaded.

"Baram, please! Don't do anything foolish!"

The old Captain woke to see Baram going for his throat and instinctively attempted to rise from his mat and escape. But it was too late, as Baram had regressed in an instant into the man he was before he came to Qumran, a rebel hiding out in the hills with a band of violent zealots who viciously killed Roman soldiers to steal their horses, weapons and food. He had hated Romans all of his life, and he hated no Roman more than the man in front of him. As if possessed, he choked the old man mercilessly while his mother screamed in his ear and tried in vain to stop him.

Finally, as the last bit of life drained from the old man's body, Baram relaxed his grip and stood over him, staring at the man who had always been his personification of evil, the brutal Roman captain who had haunted his dreams ever since that fateful night. But then the rage subsided, and he became strangely calm. Others from the courtyard had heard the commotion and were hurrying up the path, and his mother's shock and disbelief gave way to motherly instinct.

"Baram, you must go. They will kill you for this."

"They will have to find me first," he said as he started to run through the woods, but his mother grabbed his arm.

"Not that way," she said. "Follow me."

ISRAEL, 2009

After a long drive northward on Israel's Highway 90, the main north-south artery that parallels the Jordan River before it veers northwesterly and winds its way along the western side of the Sea of Galilee, Clint finally pulled into a hotel parking lot in the historic town of Tiberias just as night was falling. All along the way, as Randall snored in the back seat and Harold's warning echoed in his brain, Dave had kept a sharp watch for the black car, but to no avail. And as they walked to the hotel entrance, Dave scoured the parking lot, but again there was no black car and no sign of the man that Harold was sure would be trailing them.

As he was checking in, one of the hotel clerks overheard him giving out his name and walked over with a package.

"Mr. Dave Walker? This came for you by Express Delivery today from the USA."

Dave looked at the return address and saw that the sender was his wife, Rebecca. He thanked the clerk, and after they finished checking in, the men hurried upstairs to see what she had sent. Dave ripped open the package and read a note attached to a ratty shoebox that was taped shut.

"She says, 'Dave, this is the package you were expecting from Victor Jones that never came. The Post Office says it was lost in delivery, but then they found it. They brought it to the house today, so I decided to ship it to you there in Tiberias (you said you would be there today). Let me know you got it – I'm dying to know what's in it… Rebecca.'"

Dave ripped off the tape, opened the lid and pulled out an object wrapped in paper. He unwrapped it and was left holding a key, which was clearly an ancient artifact but remarkably well-preserved.

"Is that it? No explanation?" Randall asked.

Dave looked in the box and found a letter-folded piece of paper.

"It's a letter from Victor, addressed to me," Dave said, as he opened it to read. He glanced over at Clint and Randall, whose eager faces made him laugh.

"What the hell is so funny?" Randall asked.

"You guys! Maybe I should just read the letter by myself first."

"Read the damn letter, Dad!" Clint said.

"Okay, okay… he says… 'Dear Mr. Walker, this key was found on one of my last excavations, in a cave where we had hoped to find the Silver Scroll, which is mentioned in the Copper Scroll and believed to contain directions to the mysterious Temple treasures. I am convinced that the key fits a door that leads to the secret place where that treasure is still hidden today. I regret that I will not be the one to carry the mantle when you find it. And I am sure that when you do, it will be the greatest archaeological find in history. My decades-long search has ended, as my health is failing rapidly. I was never able to find the location, but I have recently learned that one of my contemporaries in Israel may have the answer. I trust you with this key, because I trust your motives. And now you must trust that God will reveal the truth to you. Beware the enemies of that truth. Your friend, Victor Jones."

"That's it?" Randall asked. "That doesn't leave us much to go on."

Dave looked in the box again. "No, there's a business card here, and a note on the back that says, 'On your journey north, stop in Migdal and go to this address. Ask for Seth and show him the key.'"

Dave looked at Clint. "Where's Migdal?"

Clint consulted his iPhone map, while Randall asked to see the letter.

"This is getting real spooky," Randall said. "Serendipitous. We get a package that's been lost in the mail for months, just as we *think* we're getting close to where we *think* we should be going in Israel. I mean the timing is incredible."

"It gets better," Clint said with a grin and pointing to his map. "Migdal is just outside of Tiberias. We can be there in thirty minutes."

Dave looked at his watch. "It's late, so let's get some rest, and we'll strike out early tomorrow morning for Migdal and meet this guy Seth."

At breakfast the next morning in the hotel dining room, Clint was already waiting and obviously excited about something.

"Are you guys ready for some more surprises?" Clint asked as Dave and Randall took their seats.

"No," Randall said, "I need coffee first."

Clint ignored him and said, "I did some more research last night on Migdal. Guess what? The ancient name for Migdal is Magdala, the home of you-know-who."

"Mary Magdalene," Randall said.

"Bingo! And as we speak, the Israel Antiquities Authority is conducting an archaeological dig there, because they believe they have uncovered a synagogue."

"Don't tell me," Dave said. "They date it back to the time of Jesus."

"How did you know?" Clint asked. "That's exactly right. And guess when it was suddenly deserted?"

"68 AD," Randall said.

"Bingo! You guys are good."

"Jesus would have taught in that synagogue," Dave said. "This is a significant discovery."

"Especially for the Israeli Tourist Ministry, who can add another venue to their Holy Land tours," Randall said.

"That too," Dave said, "but I have a feeling we are zeroing in on something spectacular, and I have a feeling this guy Seth will know more about it."

Finding the address proved a difficult task, with Clint and Randall arguing about every turn, followed by a lot of backtracking before they finally found the residence in a modest-income neighborhood. Clint parked the car on the street, and they walked together to the front door. Dave knocked, and a few moments later, a middle-aged Jewish man opened the door and stared at the three men standing on his front stoop. He noticed the box that Dave held in front of him and nodded knowingly. Then he turned and walked back into the house, motioning to them to follow him.

"Hello gentlemen, my name is Seth. I've been expecting you."

He led them to a dining room and motioned to them to find seats around the table.

"I'll be back right back," he said and disappeared into another room. They heard him opening and closing a drawer before making his way back to them. When he got to the table, he dropped a box down in front of Dave.

"I believe you have something to show me?" Seth asked, and Dave removed the key from its box and laid it on the table.

Seth examined it and broke into a broad grin. He opened his box, pulled out a another ancient metal key and held them up side by side.

"I knew it! It's a perfect match," he said as he handed both keys to Dave.

"They must be a thousand years old," Dave said.

"My father says four or five thousand. It's never been carbon tested, though, because he didn't want anyone to know he had it. But that's not all. There's also this."

Seth took another object from the box and laid it beside the key. It was a fragment of a scroll made of silver, and it had the appearance of a map, but without any notations other than a crudely drawn oval at one end of a long line and a rectangle at the other end, with branches of lines that ended nowhere.

"My father believes this plate is a fragment of the so-called silver scroll, which was probably cut out and given to someone who was using it as a map to find the treasure. He was sure that the map leads somewhere to the north, but not beyond the Israeli border, and likely atop a mountain where it has been concealed, in an underground chamber perhaps, for thousands of years. But he could never figure it out."

"Where were the key and map found at the same time?"

"Yes, in a small cave outside of Migdal, which as you probably know, was called Magdala in the First Century when it apparently was hidden there. It was discovered generations ago by a farmer whose family had a farm here in this area. They kept it in a jar for years, until my father, an archaeologist, learned of its existence and bought it from them. My father grew up in Migdal and knew stories about the area that never made the history books or caught the attention of his fellow archaeologists until the discovery of the synagogue."

"So you grew up here too?" Dave asked.

"Yes, but I left years ago and only returned after my father died. This was his house."

"How did he and Victor know each other?"

"My father and Victor met back in the 1960s, but neither one told the other about the map or the keys in their possession until they were both virtually on their death beds. I didn't know about it until my father died and I was given access to his lockbox. He left a note, saying that one day soon, someone would come with another key, and I was to give them his map and key. A few months ago, I got a message that Victor Jones had passed away. So knowing that he was very much like my father, I knew that he wouldn't die without passing on the key to someone. My father and Victor Jones were alike in many ways, and chief among them was their belief that digging around in the past would tell us a whole lot about what to expect in the future. And both men had very good intentions."

"Meaning they weren't treasure hunters." Dave said.

"Exactly," Seth said. "Both men were purely seeking answers to questions that have plagued mankind forever, and they both shared an assumption that finding the location -- or locations -- of the items mentioned in the Copper Scroll would provide very clear and conclusive answers to those questions. But both men were under fire for their findings, and both were constantly hounded by treasure hunters."

"Do you think anyone else knows about this?" Randall asked.

"I don't know if they know specifically about the keys and the map, but I do know that one treasure hunter knows my father was getting close to something."

"How do you know that?" Dave asked.

"Because I received a phone call from him shortly after my father died. He claimed to be a priest working on a history project, and claimed to have known and worked with Victor Jones, but I knew within a few minutes he was a fake."

"How did you know that?"

"Because he mispronounced my last name, and I figured anyone who claimed to have actually known my father would at least know how to pronounce his name. Also, he had a fishy manner about him."

"This is a crazy question," Dave said, "but did you notice him clearing his throat during the conversation?"

"Yes! It was a very annoying habit. So you've talked to him too?"

"Yes, and we now think we know who he is."

"Is he dangerous?"

"Yes, and that's been confirmed by someone we know in law enforcement."

"So what happens now?" Randall asked. "Are you going to follow in your father's footsteps and go looking for the door with us?"

Seth laughed. "No, no, no. I'm an accountant, and I have no professional interest in this at all, other than a raging curiosity. I'm no treasure hunter, and I'm not all that religious. But I do want to honor my father's wishes."

"So where do we start looking?" Clint asked.

Dave studied the map, with Clint, Randall and Seth looking over his shoulder.

"It looks like a road map," Seth said, "but I'm familiar with Israel's geography, and that doesn't look like any road system around here."

"That's because it's not a road system," Dave said, snapping his fingers. "It's a tunnel system. This symbol that looks like an oval is the entrance to the tunnel, and this rectangular box here at the end of this long line is..."

Dave broke into a grin.

"Is a door," Randall said.

"So where are the tunnels?" Seth asked.

"They probably run underneath a mountain," Dave said.

"Yeah, but which mountain?"

Dave looked at him. "We think we know."

Later, as the group said their goodbyes, Dave placed the keys and map in his box, and Seth wished them well as they walked back to their car. Clint drove the short distance to downtown Migdal, to the site of the synagogue excavation. He found a parking spot a couple of blocks away, and after Dave helped him pack his camera gear at the rear of the car, they walked to the site. Along with a few other interested people who had heard of the excavation, they stood behind ropes and watched a team from the Israeli Antiquities Authority hard at work. Clint videotaped the scene, although he was not permitted to go beyond the ropes.

"Fascinating," Randall said. "This is truly a great historical find. No doubt Jesus walked right here many times and taught in this synagogue."

"Just had a thought," Dave said. "Do you realize what this means?"

Clint pushed in tight on Dave's face as he smiled and said, "If this is where Jesus taught, and if those Jews became followers, as

Mary Magdalene was, this was likely the very first Christian church. Ever."

"Wow," Randall said, "You're right."

After circling the site completely, and after Clint felt like he had enough footage, the three men walked back to their car, only to discover that one of the rear windows had been smashed.

"Oh, no, not again!" Clint said.

Dave immediately stiffened and the hair on the back of his neck stood up. He looked up and down the street for anyone or anything suspicious. But whoever had vandalized the car was gone. Randall rushed to the car to survey the damage and see what had been stolen.

"The box is gone! He got the map and the keys, Dave! This is terrible!"

Dave calmly walked to the car and glanced in, as Clint opened the trunk to see if any of his camera gear had been stolen. But it wasn't, and as Dave expected, the only thing missing was the box. He noticed the distress on Randall's face and put his hand on his shoulder.

"Randall, it's okay," he said. "I learned my lesson the last time about leaving anything important in a car. I put the map and the keys in Clint's camera bag when we got out of the car. I should have told you; it would have saved you from this distress."

"No, it's okay," Randall said. "I'm just glad you thought of that."

"From this point on, we have to stay ahead of this guy," Dave said. "Wherever he is right now, he's just figured out that the box he took is full of rocks, and he will very likely double back and follow us again. I'm pretty sure now that he is no longer driving that black car, because I have been keeping my eyes peeled and haven't seen it."

"How did he know about the box, though?" Clint asked.

"He's a pro. Just because we don't see him doesn't mean he doesn't see us. I'll bet he hasn't let us get out of sight since we got here. And he probably saw us leaving Seth's house with the box in hand."

"Like I said, this is getting really spooky," Randall said. "What do we do now?"

"This is indeed getting dangerous," Dave said. "As I see it, we have two options, and I'm open to taking a vote on which one we do."

Randall and Clint both nodded their approval, and Dave pointed south. "We can either high-tail it back to Tel Aviv and catch a plane for home, with the idea of coming back when there's not a maniac following us around." Then, pointing northward, he continued, "Or we can go to that mountain. And keep our eyes peeled and try to find the beginning point of this map."

Randall looked at Clint, who gave a shrug and said, "I'm for going on to the mountain."

Randall shrugged as well, and said, "I don't think I have it in me to come back later. This may be my last chance; and if this is as big as we think it is, I want to be there when we find that door."

Dave grinned at them, and then looked skyward.

"Forgive them, Lord, for they know not what they do."

ISRAEL, 67 AD

After weeks turned into months with no word of Baram's fate, Daniel surmised that his friend had most likely been caught by the Romans or worse. Finally, word came and from an unexpected source – Leah.

"She is outside the gate waiting to see you," said Mishael, who escorted Daniel to Qumran's compound gate and watched as Daniel welcomed her.

"I've come with news of Baram," she said, showing him a folded letter. "An envoy from Caesaria Philippi brought me this letter from my mother, which explains what happened."

"Trouble, I presume," Daniel said.

"Plenty. He killed an old man who had once been a Roman captain."

Daniel stopped and looked at her. She nodded her head.

"Yes, the same Roman captain who came that night to your house."

Daniel closed his eyes and tried to absorb the information. His mind raced with mixed emotions.

"Let's sit," he said, motioning to a large rock that overlooked the Dead Sea below them. After they settled, Leah read him the letter which ended with Baram's escape from the palace into the wilderness.

"So has there been no word from him since his escape?"

"No, but I believe I know where he went."

Daniel looked at her knowingly. "Rami?"

"Yes, unless he was captured by the Romans first."

Daniel placed a hand on her shoulder to console her. "There is another possibility. I told him to go to Magdala if he was in trouble, and find Mary, who knew Jesus so well. She is well-known at the synagogue there, and would provide safe haven for him."

Leah wiped away the tears and forced a smile. "I hope you are right, but I fear the worst."

"Then we shall go to Magdala and find out, if you are willing to risk the journey. There are growing numbers of Roman soldiers to the north, but we can travel the secret route through the wilderness around Tiberias, where I used to play as a boy. Mishael can go with us to help and keep watch. We can be there in two days, if you are willing."

"I am willing."

The next morning, the three struck out along the route that wound its way through the wilderness, a route that Daniel knew well from his childhood. They reached Magdala two days later just as the sun was sinking in the western sky, and made their way through the empty streets of Magdala. Although the weather was warm, all the doors and windows were shut, and as they passed by, some of the inhabitants cracked their doors to see who was walking the streets, but just as quickly they closed and bolted them.

"They have heard that the Romans are near, and they are afraid," Daniel said.

They reached Mary's house, which was also boarded shut, and Daniel knocked softly on the door. No one came for a long while, but finally a window cracked open and a young woman asked, "Who are you?"

"My name is Daniel," he said, "and these are my traveling companions, Leah and Mishael. We have traveled from Qumran to see Mary."

From inside they heard a feeble voice saying, "Let them in, Bethany."

They entered the dark house and while Mishael stayed behind to keep watch through the window, Daniel and Leah followed Bethany to an adjoining room where Mary lay on a mat. She was old and thin, and her face was bruised and scarred.

"You have bruises," Daniel said. "Were the Romans here?"

"No," she said. "They were rebel bandits."

"Was my brother with them?" Leah asked. "His name is Baram."

"We know that he killed a Roman captain at Caesaria Philippi," Daniel explained, "and we know that he fled into the wilderness. We thought he might return to his band of rebels, even though I told him to come here if he needed to find refuge."

Mary looked at Leah and read the fear in her face. She motioned to Bethany and said, "Help me up."

It was a painful process, but Bethany helped her sit with her back propped against the wall. Daniel and Leah sat on the floor with her, and she reached a hand to each of them to hold as she talked.

"I am so glad to see you, Daniel," she said. "I haven't seen you in so long, and I have fond memories of your childhood, living on the farm with my good friends, Raisa and Simeon. They always spoke well of you, and Simeon said you were blessed of God; and that one day God would call on you for a great work. It appears that day has arrived."

Daniel smiled at her. "It is so. But it pains me to see you so badly hurt."

She waved him off. "It doesn't matter. I am old, and they can beat my body until I die, but they can never kill my spirit. It is they who will suffer in the end. Now, listen, my children, and I will tell you what I know."

Mary gave a deep sigh and squeezed Leah's hand. "Your brother did go to the rebel camp, and he told them what had happened, believing that they would welcome him back. He didn't tell them about the key and the map that he had sewn into the pocket of his tunic to conceal them if he was caught by the Romans. What he had not counted on was Rami's anger about Baram leaving the band years earlier. Rami lost his temper and had Baram whipped with lashes in front of the others to make an example of him. As the whip tore away his tunic, the key and the map fell to the ground. Then Rami tortured him, trying to get him to interpret the map and tell him the location of the treasure. But Baram refused, and Rami had him beaten and stoned and left for dead."

"How did Rami know the map would lead to treasure?" Leah asked.

"I told him," Daniel said, interrupting. "Years ago, when I visited Baram at the camp, I told Rami of our plans to escape. And when he asked how we would survive in the wilderness, I told him that our brother, Jesus, has gone before us to prepare a place of refuge, a large mansion in the clouds with passageways lined with gold and other treasures beyond anything he could ever imagine."

Daniel paused as a wave of sadness swept over him.

"Baram was badly beaten, and nearly dead," Mary said. "He crawled away into the darkness and just before dawn, he crawled back unnoticed into their camp, into Rami's tent, stole the key and the map, and stumbled away into the darkness. He didn't think they were following him when he came here. When I learned who he was, and that you, Daniel, had told him to come here, I offered him shelter and tried to heal his wounds. But he was hurt beyond my care, and that night he died in my arms."

Leah began to sob, and Mary squeezed her hand. "I'm sorry, my sister."

"And then the rebels came, I presume," Daniel said.

"Before he died, Baram gave me the key and the map and asked me to hide them in a place where no one could find them. And then I was to show you where they are hidden when you came. Early the next morning, with help from men at our church, we buried Baram in a grave with the other believers. Bethany can show you where, if you want to visit his grave. And then I left the village and walked into the hills near the farm where you grew up, and I hid the key and map in a cave, in a place so remote they will never be found in a thousand years. And when I returned to the house, the rebels were there waiting for me."

"And then they beat you, I suppose, trying to get you to tell them where the key was hidden," Daniel said.

"They beat her until she was unconscious," Bethany said, tearing up as she remembered the moment.

"They are desperate men," Mary said, "with no love in their hearts for anyone who does not conform to their beliefs. Sadly, they believe they can stand against the Romans when they come with their legions to kill and destroy."

Mary smiled at Daniel. "But our brother, Jesus, and James after him, have promised that the path to salvation will be illuminated when that day comes. And you, Daniel, are the one chosen to lead us there."

"You are right," Daniel said. "The day of redemption for those who will follow us is nigh. I only wish my brother, Baram, could be with us."

Daniel put his arm around a tearful Leah to console her.

"Your brother is buried in a grave with the other believers," Mary said, "facing north in anticipation of the redemption that will come from that direction. Bethany can show you the grave, if you want to go there later. In the meantime, we have water for you to bathe and plenty of bread and fish; and both of you need rest."

"I am afraid their is no time for rest," Daniel said. "Misahel and I must push on to the north, to the Holy Mountain behind the palace at Caesaria Philippi, and locate the door. It will be dangerous, so I hope that Leah can stay here with you until I return."

"I will go with you," Leah said. "I want to see my mother."

Daniel nodded. "So be it."

"I will go with you to the cave where the key and map are hidden," Mary said.

"No, that will not be necessary," Daniel said, showing them the duplicate key that he wore around his neck. "I have this key, and the map is etched in my memory. We shall leave the map and key where they are, where they cannot be found in a thousand years."

The journey to Caesaria Philippi was indeed dangerous, as platoons of Roman soldiers and supply wagons constantly traveled the main road that led through northern Israel to Caesaria Philippi. But Daniel followed a hidden trail that paralleled the main thoroughfare, across rocky terrain and sometimes treacherous mountain trails. He and Mishael took turns as lookouts when they stopped to rest or camp at night.

Then, on the last morning of their trek, they rose early, and struck out two hours before sunrise to travel as far as they could under the cover of darkness. Chilled by the morning air, Leah shivered as she adjusted the straps on her napsack and prepared to walk. Daniel noticed and helped to wrap her with her blanket.

"Thank you, Teacher," she said.

Daniel shook his head. "No, to the others I am the Teacher; to you I am Daniel, your friend for life."

With only the light of the moon to illuminate their path, they walked in silence for a while, with Daniel cautiously picking his way through the rocks and boulders along an invisible trail. Then, a half-hour before sunrise, they rounded the last steep mountainside trail and suddenly saw a spectacular sight. While the darkness hid the valley that lay between them and Caesaria Philippi, and while they could not see the slopes of Mt. Hermon, they could see a mysterious spectre of white light, barely shimmering in the pre-dawn light.

"The Holy Mountain," Daniel said, as they paused to stare. Suddenly they were startled by a deep commanding voice coming from the rocks above them.

"Halt!"

They looked up to see the dark, silhouetted figures of a band of rebels, five in all, looking down at them from a rock precipice fifty yards above the trail.

"We travel in peace," Daniel shouted.

"I don't think so," the rebel leader shouted back. "You have something we want."

"Rami," Daniel whispered. "He has found us."

The rebels began to descend quickly, and Mishael shouted, "Daniel, go quickly with Leah. I will stand and fight."

"No," Daniel said, "come with us. Hurry!"

They hurried along the path, which narrowed considerably as it wound around a treacherous cliff. But they could only go so fast, as the path was difficult to see, and a step too far off the path would lead to a fall down the steep mountainside and certain death. Then Mishael stumbled on a rock and fell to the ground, injuring his leg. Daniel and Leah helped him up and they stumbled forward until they reached the other side of the cliff. With Daniel and Leah supporting Mishael, they tried to continue, but Rami and his men were closing fast.

"May God protect us," Leah whispered, as the rebels rounded the last few feet past the cliff and made their way toward them.

Then, as the rising sun peeked over the distant mountains to the east and its rays of light reflected directly off of Mt. Hermon's ice cap, a flash of light with the strength of a thousand thunderbolts shot across the valley and illuminated the entire face of the mountain, as well as the mountains beyond. With their backs to the light, Daniel, Leah and Mishael watched as Rami and his men were immediately immersed in the explosion of light; and though it only lasted a second, it was enough to blind them all. Unable to see, Rami staggered and then stumbled off the path, and the rocks and dirt under his feet gave way, sending him tumbling head first and screaming down the steep mountainside to his death. Then, one by one, unable to see, the other men slowly retreated, feeling their way back along the mountain wall until they were out of sight.

"Your prayer is answered," Daniel said, as he and Leah helped Misahel to his feet again. They watched as the brilliant light subsided, and then Daniel turned to gaze at the ice cap atop Mt. Hermon. He reached for his ram's horn, and facing Mt. Hermon he sounded a familiar call – a song of thanksgiving.

By noon, they reached the palace at Caesaria Philippi, where Leah and Naomi embraced in a bittersweet reunion. Tears of sadness over Baram's death were mixed with tears of joy as daughter and mother were together for the first time in many years.

"Vespasian is advancing with his troops as we speak," Naomi reported later, as they rested in the courtyard and ate bread and fruit, "and they will soon press forward to Jerusalem. No one will be spared."

Daniel showed her the key and said, "God's hand is on us, and his promise of salvation will be kept. Jerusalem will be destroyed, but this key will unlock the door to a new Jerusalem. But we must hurry. Tonight we should enter the tunnels, and find the door. How is your leg, Mishael?"

"It has improved, but I will stand watch tonight when you visit the tunnels."

It was almost midnight when Naomi led Daniel, Leah and Mishael outside the palace walls and around the base of Mt. Hermon to a canyon. She made her way along the canyon wall until they came to a stand of boulders and overgrown shrubs.

"The entrance is behind the rocks up there," Naomi said, pointing up the slope. "This would be a good place for you to stand watch, Mishael."

Mishael found a rock with a good vantage point of the canyon, and the others made their way up the slope until they came to another stand of rocks, behind which was the entrance to a cave, partially concealed by rocks stacked in the opening. After moving enough rocks to enter, they lit torches and made their way quietly along the narrow tunnel, stooping at times to avoid the low ceiling. Although it was gradual and barely noticable, the slope of the tunnel was taking them higher up and into the heart of the mountain.

But then they came to a fork, with one tunnel making a dramatic turn to the left and the other to the right. Without hesitation, recalling the map from memory, Daniel led them into the tunnel to the right, which they followed for another long distance until they came to another fork. This time he chose the left fork and another long tunnel that led to another fork. After hours of walking, Naomi grew short of breath, and the group stopped to let her catch her breath.

"Go ahead without me," she said. "I will wait here for your return."

"We are almost there," Daniel said. "Our destination is at the end of this tunnel."

She nodded but waved him on. "Go, and God be with you and me. I will be fine."

Leaving one torch with Naomi, Daniel held the other out in front as he led Leah by the hand along the long tunnel. But just as he had said, the walk did not take long, as the tunnel came to an abrupt end at a small chamber scattered with rocks and boulders and nothing else. Leah's face registered surprise then disappointment until she looked at Daniel, who to her surprise was smiling.

"Help me roll this."

He motioned to a stone that resembled the stone that was used to hide the chamber in the Cave of the Columns at Qumran. With a concerted push, they easily rolled the stone away from a large hole in the wall. Immediately, they felt a cool, fresh breeze in their faces, and it was tinged with the fragrance of an intoxicating plant blossom.

Daniel closed his eyes and sniffed the air. "The mandrakes send out their fragrance, and at our door is every delicacy, both new and old, that I have stored up for you, my lover."

Daniel looked at Leah and realized that she might not be familiar with the words from the Song of Solomon. Embarrassed, he was about to explain when she saved him.

"God has indeed stored up treasures for his people," she said. "As our brother Paul wrote, we are his Church, his Bride, and we will soon stand at the door. So yes, Daniel, I do believe that is a most appropriate scripture for this moment."

Daniel climbed through the hole and helped Leah into another tunnel that was much more spacious. The walls glowed with a soft blue light that became brighter and more pronounced as they walked along.

"He will light our way," Daniel said, just as the tunnel made a slight bend and then suddenly opened into a cathedral-sized cavern, complete with stalagtites and stalagmites that all glowed with a crystal-blue radiance. The immediate effect on them both was awe and wonder, until Daniel finally pointed to the other side.

"There," he said, "Do you see it? Hidden in the shadows across the cavern."

Leah looked more closely and saw it too. They made their way across the expansive cavern floor, to a spot just in front of a magnificently large wooden door. It stood more than thirty feet high and nearly as wide and framed by a slightly curved wooden wall that disappeared into the earth around it.

"What is it?" Leah asked.

"Perfectly pitched and perfectly preserved gopher wood," Daniel said, rubbing his hand across the face of the door. "He said he would go and prepare a place for us, a mansion with many rooms." He stopped and looked at her. "This is it, Leah."

He searched the surface of the door until he felt metal. He brushed away the dirt and dust until he revealed the ancient lock.

"Here, I found it," he said, as Leah joined him. He took the key from around his neck and positioned it over the lock. He stopped and looked at Leah, who covered her mouth with her hands, holding her breath with mounting anticipation. She gave him an affirmative nod.

It was in that moment that Daniel realized that his life to that point, from the day he first was crippled by the cruel Roman captain, followed by his healing encounter with Jesus, his childhood near Tiberias, his many years at Qumran and advancing through the ranks to the postion of High Priest... all of those years had led him to this one point. Salvation for God's new Church depended on what was behind that door, because there would be no other avenue for escape from the Romans. The prophets had long spoke of their coming, and even those who had doubted before knew that their destruction was imminent.

Daniel looked longingly at Leah. He rejoiced inwardly that she was with him at this moment, when God seemed to be smiling on them both, as if to honor their faithfulness and devotion to him by sacrificing their love for each other.

He inserted the key in the lock and turned it. Immediately, they heard the sounds of a wheel turning and chains rattling and looked up to see that the door was hinged at the bottom and opening from the top.

"Move back!" Daniel said as he and Leah retreated a safe distance and watched as the door was lowered to the ground, creating a natural ramp for entrance into the wooden vessel that had been sealed for a thousand years. They shielded their eyes from a brilliant light that radiated from inside. Then, as their eyes adjusted to the bright light, with bated breath and holding hands, they walked in.

ISRAEL, 2009

After their visit with Seth in Migdal, and the subsequent break-in to their car, Dave decided they should get a room in Tiberias and rest the remainder of the day while their car was replaced. They made plans to get a good night's sleep, and then head out early in the morning long before daybreak to make the drive around the northeastern rim of the Sea of Galilee before heading almost due north toward Mt. Hermon. It was a good plan, but sleep did not come easy for Dave, who lay awake most of the night worrying about the deranged treasure hunter and wondering what lay ahead for them when they finally reached their destination.

Was this just a wild goose chase? Had they come this far only to come up empty-handed when they reached Mt. Hermon? The fact that they had limited knowledge of Mt. Hermon didn't help him answer those questions. What they did know was that Mt. Hermon's high elevation and snow-capped peaks had become the home for a popular ski resort. They had also learned that the borders of Israel, Lebanon and Syria intersected on the mountain, and that a major battle during the Six-Day War of 1967 was fought there.

"I did some research on Mt. Hermon last night," Clint said as he drove out of the hotel parking lot with Dave in the passenger seat and Randall in the back. "Because of its location on the Israeli-Syrian border, and its high elevation, Mt. Hermon is a valuable piece of real estate to both sides. We can expect a pretty heavy military presence up there."

"Wake me when we get there," Randall said, who folded his jacket to form a makeshift pillow for his head. "I didn't sleep so well last night."

"What else did you learn?" Dave asked.

"That the name 'Mt. Hermon' actually means, 'Mountain of the Chief'. How's that for an appropriate name? There's a buffer zone up there between the Syrian and Israeli borders where the UN has a permanent presence, the highest UN-manned position in the world... for whatever that's worth."

"Probably not worth much, but very interesting, particularly if our suspicions are true. Maybe they can send a team out to authenticate our discovery."

Clint studied his father's face. "You really think we're going to find something, don't you?"

"I know it's crazy; we really don't have much to go on. But we've been lucky so far."

"Lucky?"

Dave shrugged. "Okay, it does feel like more than luck; but I'm trying not to build myself up for a big disappointment."

"Right, don't believe it until you put your fingers in the holes in his side."

"To be perfectly honest, Clint, I don't know what's going on. I just know that something is happening here, and I'm not in control anymore. So you're probably right: I just need to relax, let go and have a little more faith."

They drove along in silence for a while. Dave rested his head on the back of his seat and quickly fell asleep.

And then... BANG!

Dave jumped at the sound of a tire blowing out and watched as Clint fought the steering wheel to keep the car from pulling off the road and over the shoulder, which had no guard rail to protect it from careening off the shoulder and down a severely steep slope to certain death several hundred feet below.

But Clint was up to the task and managed to hold the wheel and guide the car safely to a stop, just a few feet from the edge.

"Nice recovery," Dave said, as he sat up and tried to get his bearings. He looked in the back seat and saw that Randall's face was pale and his knuckles white from gripping the car handle.

"You okay back there?"

Randall nodded and said, "I think so. What the hell happened?"

"I guess we had a blowout," Clint said, as they all got out to inspect the tire. "That was close. The car was pulling hard to the right."

Dave got down and inspected the tire more closely, running his hand along the edge until he saw something.

"This wasn't a blowout," he said, standing suddenly and surveying the surrounding area, particularly the rocks and boulders above them. "Somebody shot the tire."

"Are you sure?" Randall asked.

Dave frowned at him. "Don't know why I would make something like that up. We need to call the police."

"The phones don't work out here," Clint said. "He probably knew that, and has been waiting here for us."

"But how did he know we were going to be driving here at this moment?" Randall asked. "Has he been camped here all night waiting for us?"

"No, I think I know the answer," Clint said. "While you guys were asleep, about thirty minutes ago, a car passed me on a long stretch of road coming out of Tiberias. In the dark, I couldn't see who it was, but I'm guessing he followed us out of the hotel parking lot."

"He could have killed us if we had gone over the side of this mountain," Randall said. "He's a lunatic."

"Yeah, but not stupid," Dave said. "He knows we have a map, so he figures he doesn't need us anymore. Which means we are in serious danger. Let's see if there's a spare so we can get the car back on the road."

"Too late," Clint said, as they all turned to see a car speeding in their direction so fast that all three men froze for a moment, uncertain where or how to run to safety. The car hugged the curve and came at them on a path that would crash into their car and take all three of them with it over the edge.

"Help us, Jesus," Randall whispered, but loud enough for all to hear.

And then a miraclulous act of nature occurred, just as it had two thousand years earlier. The sun reflected off of the ice cap of Mt. Hermon, creating a dazzling flash of light like none that Dave and the others had ever seen before. It illuminated the entire face of the mountain as it had when Rami and his band of rebels met their fate. With their backs to to the blinding flash, the three men watched in dumbstruck horror as the blinded driver of the car slammed on his brakes and tried unsuccessfully to stop the car before it careened off the roadbed and over the shoulder of the road. The three men raced to the edge and watched as the car plunged down the mountainside, tumbling end over end multiple times before smashing into the rocks and boulders on the canyon bottom far below.

"I believe your prayer was answered," Dave said, as he turned and gazed at Mt. Hermon's ice cap. The mountain's white peaks were still illuminated by the morning sun, but now it was just a warm glow that was growing dimmer.

"That was..." Clint said, searching for the right word.

"A miracle," Randall said. "And I don't really believe in

miracles."

Dave let go a deep sigh and said, "Neither did I until we came on this trip. Let's change the tire and get going. We'll have to report this to the authorities."

An hour later, they arrived at the base of Mt. Hermon, where they located an Israeli Army outpost and reported the incident. After filling out forms and answering questions, they were allowed to go. As they left the building, however, one of the soldiers who had been in the room listening to their story approached them in the parking lot.

"Excuse me," he said with a thick Israeli accent, "but I couldn't help overhearing. I believe I might have some useful information for you. Can we go somewhere quiet to talk?"

He led them to a small restaurant where they sat in a booth together. After introductions, the soldier gave them his personal history, explaining that he had grown up in the Golan Heights area and was serving his mandatory two years in the Army.

"But my real love is archaeology," he said. "And I plan to work in the field after my tour of duty is up. But even now, during off hours, I explore this area. Just last week, I made a discovery not too far from the ruins of Agrippa II's palace."

Dave held up his hand. "Wait, don't tell me. Tunnels."

The soldier was surprised. "How did you know? I haven't told anyone about them."

Dave laughed, and Clint and Randall joined him.

"I'm sorry," Dave said. "I can't explain how I know, and we are laughing because it seems that everywhere we go on this search brings us into contact with someone who knows exactly what we need to do next."

"So you think I am an angel?" the soldier asked with a grin.

The smile left Dave's face. "Yes, actually, I believe that is exactly who you are."

"Well, I don't feel much like an angel, but as it turns out, my name is Gabe, short for Gabriel."

An hour later, after the group toured the ruins of Agrippa
II's palace, they sat together on a boulder and waited for Gabe, who
promised to meet them at the top of the hour after he was relieved of
duty. They munched on sandwiches and Clint "rolled camera" while
Dave and Randall gave a video update.

"This is Agrippa II's palace," Dave began, "and you can see
the massive rock face behind us where Jesus told Peter that he would
one day build his church on this rock. We believe that this rock, this
mountain in fact, is the location where a hundred thousand or more
Christians escaped to after the Romans destroyed Jerusalem. If our
theory is correct, not only was their new home located here, it was also
the home of the treasures from the Temple."

Dave stopped when he noticed Gabe walking toward them, and
Clint loaded his camera back into the bag and prepared for the walk
around the base of Mt. Hermon. Gabe helped them carry their gear as
he led them to the canyon and up the slope to the hidden entrance to an
ancient cave.

"Hold on," Clint said after they entered the small, dark cave.
"I'll turn on my camera light to illuminate the path."

Dave held up the map in front of the light to study it. "Looks
like we go until we come to a fork, and then we continue on down this
one."

They walked together quietly, bending low to avoid the low
ceiling, and following the map when they came to another fork or side
tunnel. After a while, dirty and exhausted, they paused to rest, and
Randall's breathing grew heavy.

"I'm not sure I can go any farther," he said. "You guys go
ahead, and I'll wait here."

Reluctantly, Dave agreed, and he and Clint and Gabe continued
until they came to the end of the tunnel and the same small chamber
with scattered rocks and boulders that Daniel found two thousand

years earlier.

"There's nothing here," Clint said.

"No, there is plenty here," Gabe said, "if you look at this with the eye of an archaelogist."

"Meaning what?" Clint asked.

"Look at that large rock over there. Can you tell why it is out of place with the other rocks?"

Clint examined the rock. "Yeah, its shape doesn't look natural. It's too rounded, as if it were made to..." He pushed the rock and it moved a few inches but then settled back to its original position. Dave and Gave saw what he was doing, and all three men put their shoulders to the rock and it easily rolled aside, exposing a large hole and the entrance to another tunnel.

"Do you feel that?" Dave asked, licking his finger and holding it up to indicate a breeze.

They entered the hole and stepped into another tunnel, the wider one with the blue aura along the walls, the same one that led Daniel two thousand years earlier to the enormous cavern, with its stalagtites and stalagmites that glowed with a blue light that illuminated the room.

"This is amazing," Clint said. "Is this Heaven?"

"No, but I believe we are getting close," Dave said. "Look!"

They looked to see where he was pointing and followed him to a shadowy area of the cavern, where they walked up to what appeared to be a massive wooden wall. Gabe pulled a brush from his pouch and whisked away dirt and dust until he came to a crack in the wood. He followed the crack until it was out of reach above him.

"What is it?" Clint asked.

"I can't say for sure," Gabe answered.

Dave stood back from the wall and said, "It's a door. Look for a lock."

Gabe handed brushes from his pouch to both of them, and they all set to work brushing away the dust, until they were able to see the outline of the door. And then Gabe found it.

"The lock! I found it!"

Dave hurried to see. He reached in his coat pocket and pulled out the key. He held in position for a few moments. He looked at Gabe, then Clint.

"Are you ready?"

Clint smiled. "I'm ready."

Dave nodded, inserted the key, and turned it in the lock. The lock clicked open, and with help from Clint and Gabe, he swung open the door and were dazzled by a brilliant light that emanated from within.

"What is it?" Clint asked.

"The New Jerusalem," Dave replied.

Then... they walked inside.

EPILOG
MT. HERMON, ISRAEL, 68 AD

For a moment, standing together just inside the huge door constructed from perfectly preserved gopher wood, and bathed in brilliant light that engulfed them, Daniel and Leah felt as if they had been transported into another world. The light felt warm and penetrating, reminding Daniel of that moment on the mountain so many years ago, when Jesus touched him with a healing energy that consumed his frail body, freeing him from lingering pain and his aggravating limp.

"I can't see," Leah said.

Daniel squeezed her hand a little and said, "Don't be afraid; He is here with us."

Then, ever so slowly, as their eyes adjusted, they recognized the source of the light a short distance away, a form that became more distinguishable as a man in white linens, walking slowly toward them. Leah stood trembling as Daniel suddenly fell to his knees and bowed his head. Through the brilliant light, he had recognized the man whose radiant body had taken on the characteristics of both man and God. Then Leah recognized him too, and fell to her knees as well.

"Messiah," Daniel whispered, the word resonating inside the cavernous environment that was slowly coming into view. They each felt a hand touching them on the shoulder, and a warm energy permeated their bodies.

"Rise and greet me," Jesus said, as he helped them to their feet. "Welcome to the home of my Father's redemption for his people, the same vessel that saved his remnant from the Great Flood."

"Noah," Daniel said. With his eyes having fully adjusted, he and Leah could see from the curved contours of the walls that they were indeed standing inside a huge, cavernous boat filled with stairways leading to multiple stories and literally hundreds of rooms.

"My Father and I have prepared this sanctuary from the Romans for you and all those who have believed me. The end of the age is here, and Jerusalem's days are over. This is the New Jerusalem, and all who have heard my words and follow me are welcome to come in."

Jesus turned to Daniel and said, "You have proven yourself a true and faithful servant, patient and diligent in your preparations for this moment. You will receive your reward soon. But first, you must return to Jerusalem, gather my Church and bring them to this sanctuary, along with the books and treasures of the Temple."

"As you say, I will do," Daniel said.

ISRAEL, 70 AD

The legions of Roman soldiers who descended on Jerusalem in 70 A.D. showed no mercy. It was a massacre and destruction of epic proportions, just as Jesus had prophesied. Literally millions were slaughtered, as ruthless soldiers went door-to-door pillaging, murdering and eliminating all avenues for escape. All avenues, that is, except one. History tells us that more than a hundred thousand Jewish Christians did escape from Jerusalem, but exactly how has long been a matter of conjecture. So far, no written account exists of what happened to the first Christian Church after 70 AD. How could that many people possibly slip past the advancing Roman army? Where did they go? What happened to them?

If those Christians who escaped did in fact constitute the first Christian Church, the answers to those questions have huge implications for Christians today, and they may fly in the face of traditional orthodoxy. For two thousand years, what happened to those earliest Christians remained a mystery, but the discovery and intensive studies of the Dead Sea Scrolls in the mid-20th Century gave new life to the quest to solve it. From all over the world, people descended on Qumran, and they continue to do so today. Some come with better intentions than others, but they all come seeking answers. And no one wanted answers more than Dave Walker.

ISRAEL 2009 A.D.

Dave had come full circle in his search for the truth, and now he was on an airplane back home, seated between Randall and Clint. After years of research, battles with academia, bashed windshields, near-death encounters with a greedy villain, his long journey finally ended at Mt. Hermon, at the end of a long, dark tunnel and through a door that led to the secret that had remained hidden for thousands of years.

He moved his seat to the reclining position and rested his eyes. He was tired, but a smile lingered on his face. For the first time in many years, a dark cloud in his life had lifted. *The truth shall set you free.* Those words from Jesus were never more appropriate in his life than at that moment. The truth that he and his companions had witnessed with their own eyes he was certain would not only set them free, but in time would set the entire Christian world free.

"How do you think this will go down at the Vatican?" Randall asked, leaning close to Dave's ear and whispering.

Dave pondered the question. "What we saw behind that door changes everything. Sure, there will be shakeups as the news breaks and people see it for themselves, but the truth is the truth, no matter how you slice it."

Clint, who had been working quietly on his laptop, leaned in and said, "Hey Dad, I finished editing that last piece that we shot at Caesaria Philippi. You want to watch it?"

"Sure."

Clint handed Dave the laptop and helped him adjust the headphones. For the next few minutes, Dave watched the video from the day before. After their discovery deep in the bowels of Mt. Hermon, Dave had stood in front of the cave entrance and explained on camera what had transpired. He summarized his journey to that point, and finished by saying that each discovery led to another, until they finally arrived at Mt. Hermon.

"Now the picture is complete," Dave said, speaking directly into the camera. "Over the past few years, the pieces of the puzzle came together, and now we know the whole story. Over a hundred thousand Christians escaped Jerusalem and made their way to Mt. Hermon by way of a secret trail known only to the men at Qumran, which Jesus had referred to when he said that he was 'the way, the truth and the light'. Only a handful of men at Qumran knew about the trail and the destination including of course James, the Righteous Teacher and brother of Jesus. Before he was murdered in Jerusalem, James passed on the secret to his successor, and we now know who that successor was, because he recorded his story and left it for us to read inside the Ark. His name was Daniel, a high priest at Qumran, and it was he who finally led those earliest Christians to this spot."

Dave paused a moment and wiped away a tear.

"Sorry," he said, still speaking to the camera. "As you might imagine, this experience has left me – all of us, actually – feeling a bit emotional. And now... sitting here in this place... knowing that Jesus spoke to his disciples here... promising them that this would be the foundation, the rock, on which his Church would be built... well, it's just overwhelming. For so many years, we have dreamed of this day."

Dave pointed to the cave entrance. "Today, with the help of a map, we found this tunnel, and we made our way through a system of tunnels that led us eventually to a huge chamber. At the far end of the chamber we found a great door made of gopher wood, which had been perfectly preserved since the days of Noah thousands of years ago. When we opened the door, we were immediately dazzled by a mysterious brilliant light, and as we entered I could feel the warmth from the light, and I felt rejuvenated, as if God was filling me with His Holy Spirit. After we became adjusted to the light, we found ancient records from the men and women who made this their home after Jerusalem fell including this Silver Scroll."

Dave unrolled the scroll and read, "Behold, the tabernacle of God is with men, and he will dwell with them, and they shall be his people, and God himself shall be with them, and be their God."

Dave paused long enough for the words to sink in, then continued. "I cannot tell you how marvelous the Ark is inside. It is truly an architectural wonder, with multiple stories and hundreds of rooms, just as Jesus had described it. And then, in one rather large area of the Ark we found the storehouse, which was filled with all the treasures from the Temple including artifacts, gold, silver, and of course the Tabernacle, the Ark of the Covenant. We touched nothing, and we left everything as is so the rest of the world will be able to witness what we've seen, and at long last know and believe the truth."

Dave opened his Bible and found a scripture. "I want to read you a passage from Matthew, Chapter 24, Verse 22: 'And except those days should be shortened, there should be no flesh be saved: but for the elect's sake, those days shall be shortened.' It can now be said quite clearly that Jesus was victorious over death and was waiting for Daniel to lead his Church to the New Jerusalem. He had returned in power, destroyed his enemies, and married his bride, while Jerusalem was in ashes and all who had followed the Herodian Temple leaders perished at the hands of the Roman army.

"The records we found inside also indicate that after a while, Jesus opened the doors to the Ark again, and all of the Elect were sent out into the world to spread his gospel message to the world. And after they were gone, he closed the door and sealed it for two thousand years... until this very day. What happens now, I'm not sure. But I am sure that the evidence is clear that Jesus did save his people, and all who believe him have been vindicated. And all who denied him will be powerless, as their credibility will disappear with this discovery."

Dave smiled at the camera. "In other words, Jesus is still victorious!"

As the video ended, Dave handed the laptop back to Clint and rested his eyes again. He wondered what would happen next, even if he was no longer worried about it. The experience had left him trusting God one hundred percent, and whatever happened, he knew that God was in control. He tried to imagine what those 144,000 Christians experienced while they were in the Ark for so long, probably months or years. How could they have survived so long in that environment, unless.. and then it hit him.

"Superluminal light!" he said out loud, causing both Clint and Randall to look at him for more. "John Stewart Bell. He described superluminal light as coming from no place and no time. That suggests that all nature is directed from no place, no time. In other words, eternity! Where God is, because God is not subject to time or space. The brilliant light we saw inside that Ark, that made us feel so warm and safe, was superluminal light."

Randall grinned at him. "I think you're right for once. Remember when Peter said that one day is with the Lord is as a thousand years, and a thousand years as one day. I think you figured it out. Those Christians were living in the presence of God, the glorified Jesus, and time stood still for them while they were in that Ark."

"So what happens now?" Clint asked. "Where do we go from here?"

"I'm not sure, but I am sure that God will lead the way. He has brightened our pathway for these many years, and I'm sure we are part of a plan to bring this new revelation to the world. Maybe we should write a book, put the story out there on the internet. Make a movie. Create an organization that will broadcast the good news to the world."

"I like that idea," Clint said. "We'll need a name."

Dave was silent for a moment, then he smiled.

"I already know the name. Light of the Way."

THE END

Acknowledgements

We would like to acknowledge each person and every organization who contributed to *Qumran, Heralds of Imminent Redemption*. Each bring to the table special talents, insights and information that added depth and historical accuracy to this story. Of course, we believe Divine guidance brought each one to us, and so the Lord Jesus is due all praise.

Elder Norman Randall of the Primitive Baptist Church, who taught us and inspired us to tell this story. His knowledge of the Bible and the Jewish faith proved extremely helpful as we toured Israel together.

Dr. Robert Eisenman, whose books and teachings enabled us to grasp the Qumran and Dead Sea Scrolls connection to first century Christianity.

Pastor David Curtis of the Virginia Berean Bible Church, for sharing his scholarly Bible understanding. Helping us to understand Bible prophecy and events of 70 AD.

Karen Hutto, whose comments, notes and edits to our manuscript were invaluable. She has supported this effort from its genesis.

Bill Deignan invested many hours with us in strategy meetings, and has produced our top-quality videos and internet content.

Bill Wages traveled to Arizona to shoot and produce our book trailer.

Jim Barfield of the Copper Scroll Project unselfishly shared his time and information regarding the Dead Sea Scrolls.

The late Vendyl Jones, for sharing details of his lifetime search for The Ark of the Covenant.

Dr Bill Lightfoot of Brenau College, Gainesville, Georgia, who got us started on the right path with his recommendations.

Gus Whalen of Featherbone Communiversity, for his guidance and encouragement.

The Israel Museum, Jerusalem, Israel, whose excellent display of the Dead Sea Scrolls and details about Qumran were enlightening.

The Qumran National Park, Qumran, Israel, the most fascinating place to discover secrets and mysteries of first century Christianity.

Mt. Hermon Ski Resort, for their kind assistance and lifting us to the top of Mt Hermon and safely back down.

The Franciscans, who operate the first century village of Capernaum, Israel.

The Churches at the Mount of Beattitudes, on which it is believed that Jesus preached the Sermon on the Mount.

The Palace of Agrippa II, Hermon Stream Nature Reserve and Archaeological Park, Banias, Golan Heights, Israel, where Peter made his confession and Jesus declared he would build his church.

The Israel Ministry of Tourism and the Cincinnati Museum's Center for the Dead Sea Scrolls, who sponsored the Dead Sea Scrolls exhibit in Cincinnati.

The Hebrew Union College – Jewish Institute of Religion, for their work to save, protect and understand the Dead Sea Scrolls.

All the many organizations who help distribute information through their websites and publications regarding first century history, religion, and life in Israel.

Light of the Way

Research Library and Suggested Reading

1. *Holy Bible*

2. *The Dead Sea Scrolls* — Wise, Abegg, & Cook

3. *The Mysteries of Qumran* — Samuel I. Thomas

4. *The Dead Sea Scrolls and the Bible* — Pfeiffer

5. *Beyond Creation Science* — Martin & Vaughn

6. *The Dead Sea Scrolls Today (2nd Ed.)* — James C. VanderKam

7. *The Archaeology of Qumran and the Dead Sea Scrolls* — Jodi Magness

8. *The Dead Sea Scrolls and The First Christians* — Robert Eisenman

9. *Beyond the Essene Hypothesis* — Gabriele Boccaccini

10. *The Dead Sea Scrolls Translated* — Garcia Martinez

11. *Dead Sea Scrolls Uncovered* — Robert Eisenman & Michael Wise

12. *James the Brother of Jesus* — Robert Eisenman

13. *Jesus at Qumran* — Robert Feather

14. *The Dead sea Scrolls Deception* — Michael Baigent and Richard Leigh

15. *The Old Testament Pseudepigrapha Volume 1, Apocalyptic Literature & Testaments* — James H. Charlesworth

16. *Jesus and the Dead Sea Scrolls* — James H. Charlesworth

17. *The Dead Sea Scrolls Today (1st Ed.)* — James C. VanderKam

18. *The New Testament Code* — Robert Eisenman

19. *The Dancing WU LI Masters* — Gary Zukav

20. *Light from the Sky* — Freeman

DVD Collection

The Secrets of the Dead Sea Scrolls — The Orion Foundation
Treasures of the Copper Scroll — Lightcatcher Productions
Lost Treasures of the Copper Scrolls — A&E Networks
Time Machine: The Search for John the Baptist — A&E Networks